Dancing with Granny

A Hap Maryland novel

By Tom Blackburn

This paperback edition of Dancing With Granny, A Hap Maryland Novel, is Copyright © 2016 by Thomas R. Blackburn. All rights, including the right to reproduce this book or any portion of it in any form, material or electronic, are reserved to Tom Blackburn Books of Washington, DC.
ISBN 978-0-9826576-4-5

Tom Blackburn   ℬ   Books

DANCING WITH GRANNY

Prologue

The summer had been a dream of life on the road. The kid and the very experienced woman were more like sisters than daughter and mother. Both sexy; one leggy and fresh, the other athletic and knowing, dancing from town to town across the broad and believing Midwest, grifting a living as resurrection angels for a traveling evangelist. Coming down the aisle in hooker clothes and getting dunked and saved night after night, from Shullsburg, Wisconsin to Dickeyville, from Toolesville, Iowa down through Missouri, slipping into Knob Noster and Diggins, glimpses of slick bodies in wet angel robes sliding into the narrowed eyes of farmers, and scandalizing their wives.

But now the Old Reverend was gone and the weather was chilly, sliding always north toward November. Instead of sunshine and laughter about the hick name of the next town full of marks, there were cold winds and tears and morning sickness. The last of the easy money went for a one-way ticket on Trailways.

They stood in a place called Lonnie's Convenient and Transmission on Missouri 266, a couple of miles west of Springfield. There was snuff and oil filters, and Little Debbie snacks made of cornstarch and foam. The kid scowled at these, and turned away. She looked to the guy behind the counter like thirteen or fourteen; skinny, pissed-off, the way a kid that age always is; and dressed light for the weather. Straggly pale curls.

"Don't be stubborn," her mother said. "You don't eat, you

won't make it past goddamn Indiana, for shit sake. Take something, I'll pay for it." She dropped her voice a little, not much. "You're eating for two now, you little whore."

The counterman – Lonnie himself, or a successor in the business, or dependent – raised an eyebrow and looked west up 266, where it curved behind a limestone bluff. He was sixtyish, lean, badly shaven, and stricken by some disease that made it hard for him to straighten his back or discipline his hands to make change. The oaks outside were the color of dried blood, tossing under the wind. The girl turned her back on the counter to stare at the sun rising into the far deck of cloud.

The counterman saw a flash in the west, reflection from a flat windshield. "On time, pretty much," he said, wanting to cheer folks up. "Third time this month."

The mother smiled. "And today just the seventeenth. Good sign, don't you think? Come on, honey, it's your new life." The girl looked a dismayed appeal that her mother missed, being focused on the bus that was slowing, easing off the pavement onto the dust and gravel. A paper cup tumbled ahead of it, fleeing the west wind. The bus blew off some air pressure, and the door opened.

"Here's your ticket, through to Fayetteville. You get to St. Louis, you change for Charlotte. Charlotte, change for Fayetteville. Think you can keep that straight for three days?"

The girl shrugged and sighed, "Fuck you, Mommy." The appeal and the dismay were gone, covered by sulk.

"That's my girl. You'll thank me when you get some sense. Here's the twenty bucks you should of charged that bastard to knock you up. Your new dad is a cop named Wetmore Parsonage. You can call him Daddy or Wet, but if you laugh about that, he'll slap you silly. He'll be in Fayetteville to meet the bus." Anyways, she thought, soon as I call. She kissed the sullen girl on the forehead and ran to her car.

She left Lonnie's parking lot fast, almost clipping the bus driver headed for the Men's. Her tail lights, bright in the dawn gloaming, shrank westerly to the bypass. The girl looked out at the bus, retched a little, and opened the door. The counterman stumbled after her and stuffed a Moon Pie into her coat.

1.

We could start this like a '20's farce, with a ringing telephone on an empty stage.

A maid enters and picks it up. "Good afternoon, the Maryland residence." And right away, you know where you are.

But Suellen (who was nobody's maid, anyhow) had gone into town for the day. I was a little surprised to hear the phone, really. It had kept pretty quiet since Suellen's project - what she called her Strumpet's Seminar - hit the news.

Not the Gabbro *Intelligencer* or WGAB - "All Country, All the Time" - of course. If our media had one principle, it was that Gabbro, North Carolina was a crime-free zone, right down to prostitution and parking. (And yes, I know, prostitution is both a legal crime in most places, and almost everywhere a nasty form of violent slavery. Just, not so in some little places like Gabbro, North Carolina, where it was something more like a cottage industry that gave a few smart, handsome, and - OK, a little lazy - ladies a living where there was no other ready source, and some lonesome men a sad, forgivable illusion of companionship.)

But the Raleigh *News and Observer* had got wind of it, and filled a white space inside their "Life Styles" section with a headline, "Hooker Unrest in the Cotton Patch" and a thumbnail photo of Suellen with Gabbro's two prostitutes, and three from the neighboring town of Bozlee, around our kitchen table. They were planning a job action, and that's what had caught the editor's fancy, limning a country town's mustachioed pillars going without their fun because the prostitutes were on strike for better working conditions. Little they knew. It was passing truckers, not hypocrite city fathers -

Hell. If I don't get that phone, I'll never finish this.

"Hap Maryland speaking."

Brief silence. A telemarketer, then. I was ready to slam it down when a country kind of voice said she'd been hoping to speak to Miss Ransom.

"Suellen is not available just now. Can I take a message?" Figuring another client for the Strumpet's Seminar, emboldened by the jolly-looking picture in the *N&O*.

"Well, if you could please have her to call Miss Darlene Feely at (417) 555 - 5100. May I ask when you expect her?"

Darlene Feely, sure, I bet. "I'll do that, Darlene. I expect her back around dinnertime. Is this about ... Are you a ... are you interested in the job action?"

"I beg your pardon?"

Survival instinct kicked in. "May I tell her what your call was in connection? With?"

"I am secretary to Mr. Amos Verry, Esquire, of Morris, Gerard, and Verry in Springfield, Missouri. I cannot be more specific than that. If you would kindly see to it that Miss Ransom gets my message? It is important, but not urgent. Thank you."

"I will do that, Ma'am." Just as soon as I get her attention away from hooker uplift.

Suellen Ransom was raised by a hooker for a life as a hooker, and escaped it by the sheerest of luck. I think she felt a moral obligation to reach back and give a hand to girls who hadn't.

Oh, well, there are a few unfair things about that. For one, Trudi Ransom, Suellen's mother, wasn't exactly a prostitute in the full frontal sense. No, she was a woman without other advantages, who used her looks and what tools came to hand to make her way and raise her daughter in a mean and horny world. From time to time, intercourse was one of those tools, and she would use it freely when she could to obtain advantages, cash, or other good and valuable considerations.

For another, Trudi, by Suellen's testimony, did what she could for as long as she could to keep Suellen from having to do the same. Though when the time came that she could think of no easy and pleasant alternative, she was ready enough to serve up Suellen steaming on Venus' half-shell, rather than starve. And finally, Suellen escaped the life she was headed for almost entirely by her own intelligence and determination. She was helped a great deal by her foster father, a Fayetteville part-time cop, who inherited her from Trudi abandoned and pregnant. Wet Parsonage gave her a home, applied the flat of his hand to her fanny once or twice when she needed it, and otherwise stayed out of her way.

Suellen, the upshot of this nature and nurture, was a tough twenty-something, and a cum laude chemistry graduate from Gabbro College who was deciding when or whether to take up a fellowship at Chapel Hill to become a doctor of the philosophy of chemistry, such as that might be. And she was a lesbian feminist with a social conscience. It was this last that she'd brought to the service of Gabbro's ladies of the afternoon. Suellen happened to be in the bar of the Holiday Inn and Truck Stop out on the bypass one July late afternoon when Sheriff Tucker Pardee got a little rough, hustling DeLoris Potter out. DeLoris being Gabbro's leading, and senior in terms of service, trollop. Tucker rued the incident, as I know because he told me.

"Shoot, Hap, I hadn't got hardly no sleep the last five-six days, what between night duty and then the baby. DeLoris was kinda slow about movin on from the bar, which I flat had to clean up cause the Chamber was meetin there in ten minutes. I hustled her along, I gotta admit, and she caught a heel in the doormat, which is one of them kind with little holes in it just the size of a lady's shoe heel. Hell, a hooker's, more so. Anyways, she got hung up and started to fall. She yanked on me, and I lost my balance. I expect it looked a little like police brutality, from a certain angle."

From the angle, he meant, of a quick-eyed photographer that the least you could say of her, she was no Gabbro girl, even if she did live there. Suellen got a good shot of DeLoris sprawled knee and elbow on the welcome mat with her little black skirt hiked up around her rump, and Tucker lurching over her in a way that you figured, at least, a Rodney King incident right here in Gabbro.

Tucker had never been completely reconciled to some of Suellen's ways, and had made no secret of it with her. So more to irritate Tucker than anything, Suellen had gone on from there, sitting DeLoris down in the bar as her particular guest, buying her a pink lady and interviewing her about how many times this kind of thing happened to working girls like her. DeLoris, at first at a loss what Suellen's angle was, loosened up under sympathetic questioning and a second pink lady and said, yeah, it was kind of tough, when a girl had just come out to the Holiday because it was a good sort of place to meet nice fellas, and once in a while get asked for a date.

"A date?"

"Sure." DeLoris took in Suellen's minimalist chest, leather wristbands and streaked buzz cut, and figured she might have to spell it out a little.

"I like fellas, see. And they like me. They like a good time, what it is."

"Who doesn't? Do they pay you a fair price?"

Pay? Of course not. What did Suellen take DeLoris for? Truckers have a lonesome and boring job, and a lot of them, they like to look at a friendly face after staring at four, five hundred miles of concrete. DeLoris was more than glad to be that face, when her other option was to clerk the 7-11. She let them pick up the tab for drinks and a meal, maybe, because it made them feel like civilized men, and not some goddamn gypsies. And if they wanted to give her something nice because they had a good time, enjoyed her company, got a break from the road, well, what was wrong with that?

"Not a damn thing," Suellen nodded. "Fact is, though, you're a hooker, aren't you? Listen, I was one myself, and my mom before me, and proud of it. The thing is, though, it's dangerous work, and tough to keep your dignity and sense of self, all that. I'm not knocking you for it, long as you can do it on your own terms. Do people appreciate you for the service you provide? Does Tucker Pardee?"

DeLoris snorted, maybe a little doubtful about Suellen's claim to hooker credentials, and maybe a little unsure about what "own terms" might mean. "Appreciate? That what that looked like to you?"

Suellen had gone on from there to talk to one or two of DeLoris's colleagues and then a few truckers - I think she lost the leather and put on a skirt for it - long enough to find out, and get it confirmed, that Gabbro County was known from Florida to Cleveland as an oasis. It was one of the few spots left to get laid cheap and clean, with girls that were too innocent to ask themselves what they were getting for the same thing at South of the Border or Myrtle Beach.

Of course, it wasn't like oats or pork bellies, where you get the high, low, and trend on the WGAB farm report every morning. The fact is, when prostitution is an entrepreneurial cottage industry not regulated by mob pimps - which blessedly was the case in Gabbro County - there is no real Market in it at all, the way people mean when they talk about the Invisible Hand and letting the Market prevail. Gabbro's harlots didn't talk to Charlotte's strumpets or Fayetteville's hookers, so it was devil take the hindmost. The truckers knew this, and swore each other to reticence when they talked price with the girls. I do not dare think what wiles Suellen used to open them up.

"Shit, Hap," she said to me the next morning over breakfast. She was wearing boxer shorts and a tank top that presented a vee of sweat front and back, letting me know that she'd done her workout already, some time before I came out at 6:30. "Those girls are getting screwed twice. They need a goddamn agent."

"You?"

"Oh, no," she said. "I can't get bogged down in that kind of stuff. Just, it kills me to see somebody as dumb as DeLoris Potter risking her life and pissing it away fifty bucks a trick, which barely pays her rent. It never occurred to her those guys'd pay anyhow two-three times that, which seems to be the market along I-95. And that's for girls that are so used up and drugged out, it's a miracle a trucker can even get - "

She broke off, and waved her toast at a fly. "Anyways, no. Her age and looks, she could make a good living at it for a while, save some money for whatever comes next. I'm gonna get her and whoever else she wants to bring along together, and give them some advice about hygiene and managing assets, and that's the seminar."

She poured herself some coffee and aimed the pot my way. "You wont your coffee jacked up?"

She glanced at me, and put down the coffee. "Shit, I'm sorry, Hap." Her voice was gentle.

I sat back and looked at the ceiling, and then smiled at

Suellen. "That's OK. You know what, I'm almost, almost over it. You go ahead and ... "

Damn, damn, damn. Sure I was almost over it. So why was it so hard to talk, all of a sudden? What it was, Suellen sounded so much like my late and horribly missed wife Lee, when she said "You want ..." whatever, anything, in the Gabbro County voice she'd picked up by living here. Lee was forever asking if I wonted my coffee jacked up. I cleared my throat savagely, gritted my jaw, and told Suellen she could go ahead and talk any way she wanted. What I really wonted, was my life jacked up. Or given shape, or brought to a close. Without Lee, it had become a leisurely helter-skelter of coming and going, doing and neglect, with no more purpose or content than one of the fitful dust devils that moseyed up the road outside our house, tarried, and dispersed. Suellen scraped her chair and came to stand behind me, cradling my head and giving me a dutch rub. Her belly was hard as a post.

"I miss her too, Hap. You're such a good guy, shit, you don't deserve this kind of grief." The knuckles slowed, to my relief. "Well, that sounds flippant, doesn't it? I meant literal, grief type grief."

"I know. Thanks."

I ran a hand through my thin and rumpled hair. Grief. Another good word done to death by hip talk that made it into something no worse than bother. Until you experience the real thing. Suellen started clattering breakfast stuff into the sink. "You ever thought of hooking up with somebody?"

I patted her butt. "I've enjoyed being hooked up with you,

up to now. Otherwise, no thanks. It's my turn on the dishes."

Suellen turned and looked me in the eye. "Hap, I meant actually getting laid. It's been more than a year."

That was one of the good things about Suellen Ransom. She always said exactly what she meant.

2.

There were a lot of good things about Suellen, more than I could do justice to without droning on like the geezer I was becoming. She liked a lot of the same things I did, such as sitting without talking for long times, maybe sucking on a beer or a glass of tea while the cicadas sang the sun into the woods across Lake St. Luke. She was funny, when I was in a mood for funny, and unobtrusive when I wasn't. She pitched in and did her share of work and more, so that the lawn was neat and the garden throve for the first time since Lee was alive. She didn't take anything about life or about me so seriously that it threatened to wreck our oddly balanced little household. And - bless her butchy little heart - she was no sex threat.

She was, though she didn't act it, unlucky in love, too. She had set up a semi-lesbian household with my daughter Bethany, first in Chapel Hill and later in a wing of our house in Gabbro, after Bethany suffered the rape that produced my grandchild Lee Morgan. Suellen still lived here after Bethany got sold on heterosexuality by an ex-SEAL named Baley, married him, and moved out. She stayed partly because she was crushed by Bethany's defection and had nowhere else in particular to go; And I didn't have the heart to boot her. It took our good Gabbro folk a while to figure out that I wasn't just a dirty old man cohabiting with a much younger woman - though that was the literal truth - and another while to get over why that wasn't a scandal. Namely, that my housemate and I were on separate planets in sexual matters. And if hers was as much Mars as Venus, mine was Pluto.

Oh, I used to be a big fan of sex. We all are, right? When Lee was alive - and well before I found out, post mortem, that she'd been stepping out on me, with a popinjay who had been a childhood boyfriend of hers - well, it was a world apart, full of dusk and color and joy. But without love, it is a terrible sell. One time, six months or a year after Lee died, I got restless and went up to Chapel Hill, to an educational consultants' retreat. Partly because that's what I do for money, and partly to see if there were any presentable middle-aged women there who were also in the market. It might have been a way to get laid with some dignity; but there weren't. The unattached women were thirtyish, and had a wonderful knack of letting their line of sight sweep right over my shadow without catching on anything worth pausing over. I came home feeling both obvious and invisible.

The whole thing - for that matter, my erotic life from the age of twelve up - was just Maryland family genes trying to use Hap Maryland to produce more Maryland genes by holding out this savory little shiver that seems so wonderful while you're working up to it. Like we used to hold out dog biscuits, to get our late mutt Covington into the bathtub against her principles. Or like it's some joker that a couple of times a week all your life says Knock, Knock. And every time, you say, Who's There, and every time it's the same stupid joke. That's the part the irritates the life out of me, how we go through it over and over, just in case it didn't take, that first thousand, or ten thousand, or million times. And of course, in my marriage to Lee Morgan, there had been that extra punch line when the first wave of chuckles died away: However gorgeous our sex life was, it wasn't quite enough for her.

Well.

Suellen had her sociosexual life in Fayetteville and Chapel Hill. On the rare occasions when the whirl passed through Gabbro, I was introduced to house guests of similar bent; and a rum troop they were, fawnlike men and bearlike women of reversible vices, with once in a while a thoroughly corporate lady in a pantsuit. I shyly greeted and hosted them in a background sort of way, and otherwise did not interact.

Though I used the word "butchy" about Suellen just now, it was not obvious that she was of that, or of the opposite persuasion, within the jungle of gender. She seemed to constitute a sex of her own: smart, sinewy, a little feline; liked or lusted after, it was clear, by most of the men and every woman jack of her circle. Heck, I liked her a lot myself. Living with a smart and pleasant woman who is in tiptop physical condition, but with whom sex is out of the question, is a relaxing sort of thing. Try it some time if you doubt me. So it was a bit of a surprise when Suellen took an interest in my nonexistent sex life.

"Don't you think I'm a little past that?" I asked her.

"What I think isn't the question. Are you?"

"I expect so. I haven't thought of it, but if I did, I guess I'd have to say it's kind of a relief. Talking to me about getting laid is kind of like somebody talking to Jesus about setting up a 401k. It's the last thing on my mind. Your strumpet project got you worrying about it?"

She backed off, a little stiffly. "Nope, nope. Sorry. Not my business."

"Aw, c'mon, Suellen. It's sweet of you, really. But I'll tell you right now, as far as I'm concerned, sex is over with. You need a eunuch to look after your clientele, give me a buzz."

"I hear you, Saint Augustine. I heard you twice."

"What I tell you three times is true. I'm not in - "

"But I'll tell you something that I know from hard experience: Guys don't turn off. Maybe ever, but not at your age for sure. Last I knew, when Lee was still around, you were plenty capable."

"On a completely different subject, I hope, you had a phone call yesterday. Here, wait a second...."

I handed her the note from Miss Darlene Feely.

"She a hooker?"

"Just what I barely stopped myself from asking her. We have to wish her a happy marriage to somebody named Outfit. But not to her boss, I think. She is a secretary for a lawyer named Amos Verry."

"I saw that. How do you know he's -- oh, the "esquire," jeez. Where's 417?"

"Um..." The name of Mr. Verry's town sat behind a veil of geezerly forgetfulness and laughed at me. I shrugged in irritation. "She told me, but it slips my mind. Somewhere in the Midwest.

You could look it up."

She did, running her finger down the list at the front of the skinny Gabbro phone book. When she hit it, she got quiet and pale.

"Springfield, Missouri."

"That was it. You know somebody there?"

"It's the last place I saw Mom."

"Mm. Nothing I can say to that will keep you from calling him, will it?"

"Nope. Should it?"

I thought that over. Why didn't I want her to mess with stuff that might have to do with her mother? "I can't say what I'm thinking without sounding callous. So I guess I'm being callous, but here it is. If this has to do with your Mom, she's gone, and nothing you can do will bring her back."

"What makes you think I want to? We don't even know what this guy is, what he wants. Maybe she left me something."

"Yeah. Maybe he's selling time-shares on Lake of the Ozarks. How about calling up Wet, get his take on it?" Figuring Wet Parsonage, who had even less use than I did for Suellen's late mommy, would back me up.

"I'm not gonna drag Wet in on this. I didn't drag you, for that matter."

I sipped coffee. "No, you didn't. I apologize for mucking into your business."

"Cut it out." She ran a hand through her hair. "You have every right, or anyhow, I hereby invite you into my business." She clicked her thumb rings and drummed on the table. "I hate to call Wet this early in the day. He isn't sleeping right."

"Wet keeps funny hours. You can bounce out of bed with clear eyes and all, because you're a third his age, and you didn't stay up all night on a stakeout."

She was right, though. Wet Parsonage was still the best cop in the sheriff's office over in Cumberland County. But his hold on the establishment was so shaky that his card read, "County of Cumberland, Office of the Sheriff / Wetmore Parsonage, Off Duty." He was one of those high-scoring incorruptibles who make the regular joes look bad, and gets all the crappy assignments as punishment. The last time he'd been down to visit, we both thought he looked tired, shaky, and gray.

"What the hell," I said. "I don't know why I'm fighting you. Here."

I tossed her the phone, and she beeped out the 417 number. Let it just be a small clue about Suellen, that she didn't turn her back or wander out of earshot during the conversation that followed.

"This is Suellen Ransom, returning Mr. Verry's call." Very short pause. "This is Suellen Ransom."

She listened a bit, and then leaned back in her chair.

"Yes, I could, but I'd have to know who I'm talking to, and what's up .... Yes, I know your name, Mr. Verry, your secretary left it with my - with the person who took the message. What can you tell me that would convince me that Mom was your client? She - excuse me, but she hated lawyers."

He talked softly for a long time. This time, what he said made her lean forward and bow her head over the table. The trouble with a buzz cut is that you can't drop hair over your face to hide tears. I decided it was time to scram, but Suellen grabbed me as I walked toward the door, and pulled me back, pointing at my chair. I sat, while the phone continued its mournful woffle, wuffle sounds against her ear and she blew her nose and scowled.

I was glumly sure that she was getting gory details about her mother's death, which - from what Wet Parsonage told me - resulted from a botched poker scam complicated by a sex triangle, and involved multiple knife wounds in a crappy gin mill outside Branson, Missouri, during the afternoon lull. It was videotaped by a lucky tourist. All in all, it was about as messy, painful, and humiliating as they come. When Suellen had heard enough, she sighed and sat up, squeegeeing her cheeks with the back of her wrist.

"All right, Mr. Verry. Her maiden name was Gernreich. She married my father, Corporal Eddie Ransom, in Heidelberg, Germany, in 1980. The bar where she worked in Fayetteville, North Carolina, was called Randy's Grill. At that time, we lived at the Executive Mobile Court on I-95. I last saw her in November of 1993 in a Trailways station outside of Springfield, Missouri."

There was another clump of woffle, and Suellen blew her nose on a napkin and said, "Off-duty, Cumberland County Sheriff's Office."

Mr. Verry's voice became a great deal quieter, and tailed off into the falling tones that signal the end of a conversation.

Suellen gave him our address and told him thanks, she'd look for it in the mail, at which the phone got alarmed. I could actually distinguish the words "or Federal Express."

"Fine. Whatever." Suellen beeped off the phone, and looked at me a little shakily. "What makes you so damn smart?"

"Dumb luck. What makes you ask that?"

"He's sending me a box of Mom's stuff. I already wish to hell I'd never called the guy."

Well, that all happened on a Tuesday. On Friday afternoon, I had an appointment in town with Forde Morgan, the editor of the Gabbro *Intelligencer* and a distant uncle of my late wife's. Forde and the *Intelligencer* hadn't done much about Lee's death except to report it with a sketchy obituary, and he'd been getting grief (in the dilute sense) from the faculty of Gabbro College ever since. Lee had been a faculty member of Gabbro back when it was damn-near-bankrupt Gabbro State College, and had led a faculty buyout and a turnaround that made it one of the top liberal arts colleges in the state.

Now one of the national magazines had run a "Bargains of Higher Education" story that spotlighted Gabbro, and Forde was ready to run a good-sized feature. He wanted some "personal glimpses" from me. I dreaded it, but Forde owed me a fee for some consulting work I'd done for the *Intelligencer* over a year ago, and I'd made paying it a condition for talking about Lee. To my dismay, he took me up on it, and a check came in the mail the same week. Now I was stuck with the interview, because my finances weren't such that I could give it back. I stoked up on Valium and walked into town, not daring to drive under that influence.

Even that was a mistake; the shortest way into town is a path that runs around Lake St. Luke. That path, I walked the morning after Lee and I first made love. It had hardly changed; the same trees, the same birdsong, the same bugs. Well, OK, distant descendants, but in Gabbro County, even bugs keep track of ancestry. I found that I knew the path well enough to stay on it while swimming in tears. Tranquil tears, thanks to the Valium; probably the least satisfactory kind.

The interview with Forde went by in a numb haze. I do remember thinking that he was a pretty good interviewer, following up chance remarks to see if they might lead to an "angle," building them into the picture when he thought they did, but never getting distracted from what he was doing. From my drugged perspective, it felt like I could see the structure of his story developing, a kind of invisible pyramid on the desk between us, to which Forde added block after careful block until it came to a point on top. It was aesthetic, it was classical, and if I didn't want to, I didn't have to visit the tomb at its heart.

Forde leaned back and followed my gaze to the top of the pyramid. "I reckon that'll do it, Hap. You know why I haven't done this before."

"Guess not," I guessed. "I haven't missed it."

He blew his nose. "Couldn't bear the thought, any more than you. Let's talk about something else."

Getting up and walking out of there seemed like more

trouble than it was worth. And anyhow, to go where?

"Such as?"

He crinkled slantwise at me. "Hap, everbody in town's been dying to ask you, and I guess I get to be the point man. What's it like, sharing a house with a lesbian troublemaker?"

"A bowl of cherries. This going to be another feature story?"

"Hell, a course not. Not a word of what you say on that subject will ever see print. I'm just being a nosy asshole, and you're welcome to agree with me."

"You're a nosy asshole. On the other hand, I know damn well whatever I say to you, you won't have to print, because that's not how news travels in this town. I wouldn't mind getting some basic facts out into the gossip mill, if they'd take the place of whatever people are making up. You want to ask me a little bit more focused question?"

"Sure. You sleeping with her?"

I snorted. "Not hardly. You can do better than that."

"Sure can. But if you'd said yes, the conversation woulda been over with. Oh, let's see. Where's she from? What's she like? She got any plans? Who are these amazin folks she turns up with, down at the Terminal from time to time? Is it true she's some kind of science genius?"

"Whoa. Let me work backward. She's plenty bright, and I don't think Gabbro College even began to find out how bright. She's thinking about going to Chapel Hill for a PhD. That's Latin or Greek or something, for "teacher of the love of learning" and I guess that's what's holding her back, since I don't know that she has any ambition that way. The people you see her with are her friends from Chapel Hill and Fayetteville, and I guess wherever else you find that sort of oddball folks. I don't know whether she sleeps with them or not. When they stay with us, they sleep in Bethie's old room, and I don't eavesdrop. Some of them are clever and entertaining, and I guess all of them are human beings like you and me, Forde.

"Same goes for Suellen herself; she's just a bright human being who came through a ghastly childhood somehow, with a brain and a good heart. She's amazingly pleasant to me. Without getting physical, damn it, so put that eyebrow back down. She keeps herself in rock-solid shape with exercises and running, it makes me tired to look at her sometimes. She's from Fayetteville, in the sense that that's where she was born. She came here from the Midwest, where her goddamn grifting whore of a mother ...." I blushed and tossed a hand. Seemed like the Valium was wearing off.

Forde's eyebrow went back up. "You were acquainted with the mother, I take it."

"I knew her, yes," I said, with perfect accuracy. "Didn't have much use for her."

"So I detect. That how Suellen got into this hooker's union business?"

I sighed. "That where this was heading? Maybe so, I guess. Maybe she just had enough vision and imagination to see what nobody else wanted to, which is that Gabbro, North Carolina is known among truckers coast to coast as about the cheapest place to get laid in the contiguous states. Hell, probably Alaska and Hawaii too. She just figured, why should our hookers be at the bottom of the pole? It probably draws an undesirable element."

Forde shrugged. "To the bypass, anyhow. Couple fellas on the Chamber passed on a complaint from the truck stop. This job action from the ladies has hit some of the businesses pretty hard. Trucks seemed to be rolling on through more these days. Diesel sales are off four percent, and that's the difference between making it and not, some of them. Wanted to know if they was some solution to it, that'd put things back to normal."

I grinned. The Valium was definitely wearing off, or else my pride in Suellen's cause had managed to punch its way to my glee center. "Condom machines too, I bet. Well, gosh, Forde. Why doesn't the *Intelligencer* run a story? 'Prostitution slump threatens diesel sales.' That'd sell some papers for you."

"Faye'd kill me. Or worse yet, she'd quit, and then who'd do all the work around here? Heh. Reminds me of the one about the fella runnin for mayor, sez he stands for Constitution, Institutions, and Pros - perity."

"I haven't heard that one since the seventh grade. Why don't you tell your buddies in the chamber to tell the truck stop they could work hand in hand with the girls out there, run some Happy Hour specials, and give the ladies a cut. That way, the girls could afford to keep giving their little discount, and the truckers'd at least be getting something extra to make up for paying a decent fee for their fun."

Forde crumpled a page from his notebook and threw it in the wastebasket. "I can't believe we're seriously discussing this." He slumped into a scowl, and shrugged. "Not a bad idea, though. I'll pass it on, see if it flies. You oughta go into the consultant business. You want a cut, if this works?"

"And take it out of the mouths of the working poor? No way."

We finished a little after five, and I walked the long way home, by way of the public library, rather than run the memory gauntlet again. When I got home, a gleaming maroon Nighthawk motorcycle stood in the driveway, and I heard a string of yaps and grunts coming from the back yard. As I came around the corner of the house, I heard a savage "Yah!" and Suellen lurched past me off balance, and landed hard on her shoulder. She rolled and jumped up, glaring at me with crazed eyes.

" 'Kout, Hap," she grunted. "Be done in a couple minutes here."

She was wearing a bikini bottom. Her opponent stood similarly dressed - which was a little more seemly in his case - in a square of trampled grass that was delineated with duct tape. Both of them were slick with sweat and something else, something musky-smelling that made the sweat stand up in beads. Suellen bore a number of strawberry marks on her back and knees, and a new one was blossoming on the shoulder that had just met the grass, competing with the rose tattoo that twined thornily from a position somewhere within the bikini, over her collarbone to her shoulder blade.

She crouched and approached the trampled area warily, head-feinting to get him moving. The other acknowledged these with minor movements of his hands and feet, never seeming to commit or lose poise. Suellen head-faked right, lifted her right foot, and then planted it again, lashing out with her left leg to land a solid kick on her opponent's ribs. Take that, stranger, I thought. Way to go, Suellen.

He grunted, grabbed her ankle before she could get it back, and pulled her past him, slapping her twice in the belly as she went by. She grabbed for his neck, but he parried it with a forearm, and got a wrist. He threw himself backward, his foot socketed into her belly just above the bikini, and she lifted off like bag of mail to land three feet beyond the ring on her back. Her breath whooshed out and she lay writhing and gasping, a couple of handprints on her gut and her face the color of raspberries. The thug that was doing this to my friend yanked her back into the square of tape and placed a bare foot on her throat.

"Hey," I said, and meant it.

The guy looked over his shoulder at me with a reptilian eye, and started to twist his foot slightly. He was a head shorter than me, shorter than Suellen in fact, and his body looked like one of Suellen's woven bracelets; as lean as leather, hard, merciless. Devoid of marks, except for the play of light over muscles so well-defined that his skin seemed painted directly on them.

I considered backing mildly into the house and reappearing with the Glock I keep on the back closet shelf. But I wasn't sure I could move without his crushing Suellen's larynx. As he turned back toward Suellen with a mildly contemptuous smile, she slapped his foot off her neck, slammed herself over onto hands and knees, and stood up between his legs.

He jumped back, but she'd anticipated it, and angled her body accordingly. He Oofed as the small of her back crunched into his groin. His arm slammed a chokehold around her neck, but for a tiny instant, both of his feet were off the ground. While she had him like that, Suellen grabbed the wrist at her throat, spun, and flipped him a good six feet through the air onto the gravel drive.

It was the master's turn to crash and gasp, and while he was doing that, Suellen went to her knees at the edge of the ring, threw her arms out to the side, and bowed until her forehead touched the grass.

"Oh," he said. "All right, then."

Suellen turned on the hose and stood under it, clearly exhausted. But her sparring partner gave her a peck on the cheek, introduced himself by way of a casual handshake that about made sausage of my fingers, hopped on his Nighthawk, and roared off. Counting I guess on the wind of his passage to clean him up.

"What the hell do you call that?" I asked.

"Some Korean thing or other, that means 'Land Hard.' I never can keep it straight. It's got one of those R's that sound like a N. You get points for throws, provided the guy lands outside the tape. But you only win when your opponent either passes out, or touches the ground with his forehead."

"Or dies. Evidently your buddy Nigel is a master at it."

"Neville. He's Gray, which is about second or third from the top."

"Holy shit. So there are people in the world who could make mincemeat out of him?"

"Road kill. He never should have let me slam him like that."

"That was probably my doing. I said something that distracted him."

"There you go, see. A Brown would have paid no attention to you." She turned off the hose. She was still panting, drawing heavy summer air into a torso slimmer than Neville's, but less sinewy only in very minor, girl-related ways. The water skittered over the rose tattoo like a crowd of transparent ladybugs.

"Still, Neville's pretty good. Not quite good enough to do just that, of course. He repairs motorcycles for money, which he wouldn't have to if he'd concentrate a little more. The whole thing is not to lose your edge."

"Uh huh. And the oil is to make it harder?"

"Gives it more of a challenge, yeah."

"And going topless?"

"Well, shoot. With the oil, one of the few things you can grab is clothes. If I'd worn a top, he'd of had such a big advantage, I'd never have a chance."

"Not that it might distract him, or anything."

She snorted and looked down at her modest charms. "Me? Anyways, not him. A Green or Yellow, probably they'd get distracted, lose their edge."

"I bet. Well, do Hard Landers ever kick back with a beer afterwards, or is that too edge-degrading?"

She headed for the house to get some clothes on, I hoped. "Watch me."

So I pulled out a couple of Urquells, and when I'd got about a quarter of mine under control, she showed up, toweling her hair. She was wearing flip-flops and a pair of boxer shorts. Period, again. The adamantine definition of her muscles had relaxed a little, and she wasn't breathing hard. The oil was gone, but the strawberry marks were smeared with something pale green.

"Um..."

"You mind? I tried a shirt, but a couple of these places are too sore to have anything on them at all."

"What the hell. Your mom was like that when I first met her, though I must say... never mind. Anyhow, who's going to check?"

There was a roar and a crunch of gravel behind me, and a brown truck the size of a summer cottage rolled around the corner of the house. "Scuse me," said the guy in the brown uniform, whom I knew to be a regular at the Terminal Café. "UPS. Miz Ransom?"

Suellen draped herself with the towel, which was too small for the job, so she had to clamp it under her arms. She kept her eyes locked on his while she signed his little electronic doodad, so he couldn't admire the tattoo. When he'd backed out the driveway - taking out a camellia because now there was no reason not to peek - she sighed, and took the beer.

"Sorry."

"Pooh, don't be. Thanks for not strutting just to tease him. As it was, you made his day. Plus, anyway, I inoculated us this afternoon by telling Forde Morgan the Real Deal on Suellen Ransom, which will be circulated in more authoritative circles than that guy has access to. Is this the famous box from Missouri?"

She rolled it around in her hands and shook it. It rattled. "I reckon. What's the real deal?"

"You're a regular human being just like anybody else."

"You said that? Some friend you are."

"I figured a little truth might distract him from the rest of it."

"The rest of what?"

"I forget."

She went back to toweling her hair, so I watched the sun go down.

Before that was accomplished, Suellen's tummy growled, and I promised to order a pizza, if she would promise to either finish dressing or stay out of sight.

"Ya," she said. "Those pizza guys got a lot of clout in this town."

While I was ordering, Suellen put the box the kitchen table and got a carving knife out of a drawer. She stood a long time then in a slant of yellow sunlight and looked at it, the knife glinting half-forgotten at her side. At last, reluctantly, she slipped the blade under the tape and sliced it open.

3.

1. One beanie baby (Doodle the Rooster).

2. One certificate from Fayetteville General Hospital, attesting to the in-wedlock birth of Suellen Gertrud Ransom, WF, 7#3Oz, 20", adorned with an inky footprint of the newborn and signed by Charles Otis Bannerman MD.

3. A bundle - held by a rubber band that broke as soon as Suellen touched it - of report cards up to fourth grade at the James B. Hunt Elementary School, County of Cumberland, North Carolina. One of them states that Suellen is doing remarkable for a youngster with no stable family life to speak of.

4. One short, curvy-stemmed pipe. The bowl contains a crusty black substance that would surely have interested a drug-sniffing dog, if one had been nearby.

5. One pocket diary for the year 1992, of which the first half or more was used by someone whose nearsighted tiny writing shows a certain force, for example in the passage, *"Grounded for watching MTV instead of working on stupid English. Mom is a tierant with a heart of stone, nor the least understanding of child care."*

Not that I peeked into it then, with Suellen standing right there.

6. One jack of clubs, crumpled and smeared with something dark that makes him one-eyed. On the back, a poodle

and a scottie playing strip poker.

7. One brass key, fastened to a champagne cork by a waxed red string.

8. One laminated newspaper photo of Trudi Ransom and little Suellen waving small American flags during a Fourth of July parade at Fort Bragg. Trudi looks about as I remembered her - lithe, cynical, eyes anywhere but on the camera, a smile that said, Ja, look at me, the good Yankee. I had once seen Suellen at the age she showed in the picture, but had forgotten the Shirley Temple dimples, the blonde curls, the pink horn-rim glasses and the deciduous front tooth.

9. A miscellany of small objects, coins, paper clips, and ball pens, enclosed in an envelope from the firm of Morris, Gerard, and Verry of Springfield, Missouri.

"You were a little cutie, weren't you?"

"You can't think how many guys a certain age wanted to put me in movies."

"Yeah, I could. What do you think the key's for?"

She flipped a hand. "Damn'f I know. This was one of those dorky little mysteries you read like comic books, it'd fit a bus locker where we'd find the lost will, or something."

"Will?" I let the slam at my reading pass. I like Travis McGee stories; Suellen would sometimes, when I was well into one of the sacred canon - my current re-read was The Dreadful Lemon Sky - flop into a chair next to me with something technical and uplifting, turning a page once every ten minutes with a superior sniff. But I noticed that a page or two of Rushbrooke's <u>Statistical</u> <u>Mechanics</u> put her into dreamland about as fast as a whole chapter of MacDonald did me.

"You know. Or whatever clue."

"Did your mother have a will?"

"I forgot to ask. You'd think he'd of told me if there was one, don't you?"

"Maybe. Maybe the will was, give this box to my daughter. Maybe this is the whole estate."

"Estate." Suellen snorted and bounced the rooster in her hand. "I pestered the life outa her for a goddamn beanie baby. She had this one all along, whyn't she give it to me? Damn it all." Her eyes were bright with tears now, and she slammed it down on the table. "What the hell was she waiting for, you think?"

I tossed a hand. "Most people, I include myself, can't believe the right moment is there when it comes by. And after that, it's too late. Can I see that?"

She looked reluctant. "What, this? Why?"

"Sometimes those things are valuable, depending on how old they are."

She opened the little tag. "Date of birth, 3-8-96," she read. "Well, that's stupid. I wasn't even living with her by then."

"Mm. So at least she wasn't holding it out on you. Look, Suellen, does the rest of this stuff look right to you?"

"Right how?"

"Well... authentic. Do you remember it?"

"The report cards and the diary, sure. The rest of it, pretty much. The hash pipe ... mm, well. I think it belonged to my so-called father. It's us in that stupid picture. I remember that, all right. It's the last Veterans' Day parade before he got killed. We never went to one after that. I guess that's my birth certificate, or why not? What's on your mind?"

"Nothing, as usual. Just, the beanie baby bothers me. It's out of line with the rest of the stuff." I was desperate to take her attention off the bloody jack of clubs.

"Ya, somebody's trying to scam us with phony memorabilia from a dead hooker. Excuse me, I think supper's here."

Headlights swept the front windows, and a door slammed in the drive. But then so did another one and another, followed by the woosh-thunk of a van door. It sounded like more than one set of footsteps on the walk, and pizzas don't get delivered by giggling bunches of women.

Suellen whapped her forehead. "Ach, shit fire, the whores! They're meeting here tonight. I'm sorry, Hap, I forgot. Look, let 'em in, will you, while I call the pizza place and up the order? Also put on some more clothes. Thanks a ton, sweetie."

Bing, bong.

I opened the door on a little crowd of prematronly women, fronted by DeLoris Potter, dressed down for politics in sweats and a ponytail. They were all wearing stuff that would have been fine for a Band Booster's Club meeting, except for one, standing a little apart, who'd apparently come straight from work in a skirt that barely covered her butt, a see-through peasant blouse, and blonde beehive hair the size of a rum hangover.

"Um," I said. "Come in, please. Suellen's - "

"C'mon in," Suellen yelled from the kitchen. "Don't mind him, it's customer appreciation night. Anybody want Sicilian?"

DeLoris Potter yelped that she did, and gave me a big old purse-mouth air kiss as she sashayed out to the kitchen, looking around like a tourist at the White House.

The beehive sauntered in last. She looked tired, and pushing forty. As soon as she was inside, she took off the hairdo - revealing close-pinned dark hair that was a better match for her eyebrows - and put it on the hall table with her little clutch purse. The wig, on the other hand, was a good match for the wall paint, which I recall Lee having chosen after much waffling between "Sunrise" and "Candleglo." I forget which one the hooker's hair now matched. "Candleglo," surely.

Her face was lined and a little weary, like she'd passed a brief youth in a coalmine hollow, and come to Gabbro - Lord! - in search of opportunity and bustle. With her pinned-flat hair and dark eyes, she'd have looked more at home in a cotton housedress, in a black-and-white WPA photo, than in a committee of fancy ladies. Though plain, she was not. There was a cleverness in her face that was not in the others'. Lines about the eyes that spoke of time in the sun, or possibly of habitual merriment; a one-sided stretch to her mouth. Even the upcurve of her nose gave a little relief to the somberness.

As for the rest of the guests, well; you'd never mistake them for starlets or nuns. There were five of them - seven, with Suellen and Candleglo - which is plenty to chase a tougher guy than me. I checked the front walk for stragglers, shut the door, grinned uncertainly at the assemblage, and retired in dignity with growling tummy, to commune with McGee. Travis had just got another desperate woman to agree to give him half what he could recover of what had been stolen from her, and The Busted Flush had been bombed to flinders, partly atomizing her. I figured it would hold me until I could get at the leftover pizza.

It was a little hard to focus on fiction, with the yells and giggles and sudden silences from the kitchen. Three or four voices, one of them DeLoris's, seemed to dominate the proceedings. There was more than one crisis point, to judge by the wax and wane of solidarity. At one of them, something made of glass broke, occasioning a sudden silence and some tears.

The parliament of whores broke up at ten or so, by which time I wasn't hungry any more. Suellen turned me down on another beer, so I took one into the garden by myself. I was halfway down it when she appeared, holding a repulsive-looking clump of stuff on a paper napkin.

"They're gonna do a parade down Church Street Saturday, and the Tri-County chapter of NOW's counterpicketing. I think it's gonna be a hell of a sight. We saved the goozly stuff from the middle for you. Want it?"

"That was sweet. OK, I guess."

She handed it over - the half-handful of cheese, pepperoni and garlic that sits at the middle of the pizza box when a group of people who have taken slices have all been too mannerly to scoop it up with their fingers.

"Yum." I swigged it down with beer and wiped my hands on my shorts.

"Don't get all cleaned up yet. There was a slice of Sicilian veggie left. Want that?"

"Seeing to it the old man eats right?"

"That's it. Want it, or no?"

"Sure."

While she was in the house, I heard the phone ring, so I took another slug of Urquell and went back to watching the moon, looking for meaning in its careless pattern of blobs and glints. There is an exact combination of lunar phase and booziness where The Sea of Tranquility looks like Lee's profile. I was seeing if I was going to hit it right this month - and thus rip my heart out again - when Suellen reappeared without my slice of pizza.

"That was Cumberland General. Wet's in there, and giving me as next of kin. I gotta go up there right now."

"What? Somebody shot him, or what?"

"They didn't say, just he's in 'serious condition.' When I asked what from, sucker said she couldn't give out that kind of information. I gotta go."

"Wait, I'll come with you."

At Cumberland General, it was a major achievement for Suellen to get in to see Wet, and out of the question for me. I settled in a kin-dumping area dominated by an unkillable TV that, pushing midnight, was re-blasting daytime programs at a hundred decibels. I took it as an intellectual challenge to concentrate on the relatively deep fare of <u>People</u> magazine. After a maddening hour, Suellen came out looking a bit relieved. Her lips were moving, but damned if I could hear over the sound track.

"...Beanie ulcer," she concluded.

Judge Judy bammed her gavel. ***"You will shut up when I'm talking,"***

"What?"

"Your honor - "

"Shut up, I said. You had your turn to waste the time of this court, and now it's mine."

I fled with Suellen into the sullen, bug-bickering night. "Jesus, how does anybody stand that without going mad? What?"

"They say he's got a bleeding ulcer. He's on IV's for a while, and then clear liquids. He has to watch his diet, and stay off anything that irritates his stomach. He lost a lot of blood, they think."

"Jeez. Can I get in to see him?"

"Just go, I'll take you where they've got him. This place is so disorganized, nobody'll know the difference. Look like you're supposed to be in there."

I looked purposeful and serious, striding past a couple of orderlies swabbing fluids off the triage area, and going through a door that said, "Staff Only." When we turned a corner by an abandoned nurse's station and ducked into Wet's room, I just looked serious, and I didn't have to fake it. He had a tube in his arm, and another up his nose. There were probably others, but I didn't make a survey. I was too shaken by his face. It was more gray even than it had been on his last visit. Sickness had drawn him down to a rumpled bag of cells, lacking all form. His eyes were half-closed, sunken, and focused nowhere. The grooves and wrinkles that defined his normal expression of skeptical amusement were muddy trenches in which dog-weary whiskers slumped, waiting for the razor. I stopped a stride past the door, choking on a greeting that died in my throat.

Wet rolled a yellow eye at me, and went back to his examination of the middle distance. "Christ, hotshot," he wheezed. "I can't stand a cheerful hypocrite. You think I look like hell, just say so."

"You always look like hell, Wet. When you look good, I'll know the mortician's been at you."

He snorted. "I can't wait to get where I can stand up straight, so I can put you here in my place. What was that little jingle... 'As you are now, that's how I was ...' Somethin somethin."

"As I am now, so you must be," Suellen finished it for him. "You got my permission, Pops."

"Yeah. That was all I needed, I'd be outa here." He held out a weary hand and took Suellen's. "Thanks for comin up, though, honey." Wet's voice broke a little on that.

Suellen got flushed and tearful. "Forget it. We were on the way to Chapel Hill anyways."

"Yeah? One in the morning?"

Suellen looked stubborn and didn't say anything. Wet let it go with a little squeeze of her hand. "You gonna get off your butt and take up that fellowship?"

"I ... maybe. Depends."

"Yeah." Wet looked up at her. It looked as if rolling his eyes back gave him a bad headache. "What's botherin you, baby?"

"Nothing."

He mustered the energy to glare at her. "You remember what I done the last time you lied to me, you little hellion?"

Suellen got pink again. "I'm not... All right. I'm worried about you, Wet. You look... well. Kind of sick."

The glare softened for about two seconds, and came back.

Suellen tossed a hand. "All right, God damn it. I got a bunch of crap in the mail from Mom today. From her lawyer. It ... some of it was kind of sorrowful."

Wet looked pained. "Yeah? She died when, back in '96, and he just gets around ta sending it now?"

"He says he didn't know how to locate me. Like, Mom never gave him your address." She narrowed her eyes at him. "Or did she?"

Wet looked away and breathed a couple of times. He couldn't do it without rattling. "I'm losin my marbles. Use to be, I coulda thought up a story to distract you. OK, she did. This ain't one a them death's head confessions, but I admit I got a couple inquiries which I done my best to respond appropriately to."

"Yeah? What'd you say, I ran away from home, sent you a card from ... " She waved her arm. "Pago Pago, somewheres? That what you told him? Shit, Wet, thanks a lot."

"He'd a never believed Pago. I told him you'd got married and moved to Fort Wayne with a dentist named Prober." Wet's eyes closed and he started to gasp. After a time we realized he was laughing.

"You believe there actually is such a guy? I like to shit when that Miz Feely called back and said they was lucky this Prober didn't sue them for alienation of affection, after the real Miz Prober picked up the phone and had God's own time persuading them she wasn't you; an' then the time they had convincing her Prober din't have another missus stashed away somewheres." Wet wheezed a couple of times, and sighed. The long speech had tired him. "Well, I done my best. How'n hell'd he find you?"

Suellen looked sulky. "He had a bot programmed to look for my name. It hit on the story in the News and Observer." She bit her lip and grinned at him. "Don't tell me. So you told them this dentist divorced me last year, and I never told you. I'm sure's hell glad you taught me not to lie."

"That mighta worked. I told him you run off with a oil rigger, and I got a card from Mammoth Cave right after his first call. OK, so, you real glad he found you?"

Suellen was silent at that, and stayed so after we left Wet half-sleeping. Silent as we slipped out through the dozing triage area, chewing her thumbnail and staring in silence down the tunnel of mist and nightbugs back to Gabbro. As we rounded the lonesome corner of Church Street to head out home, she spoke at last.

"I could deal with all the rest, or let it go. It's that bloody jack of clubs."

I sighed. "I know."

4.

Wet Parsonage phoned the next morning. It woke me from a dream that seemed intensely interesting in retrospect, though I could recall no single idea or image from it. I let the phone ring, hoping Suellen would be finished with her workout, and get it without my getting involved. It was bound to be for her anyhow. But it rang and rang, and when the answering machine kicked in, it stopped, and started up again a few seconds later. I groaned and fumbled Lee's old Princess phone off the nightstand.

"Yeah." I tried to see my alarm. 6:08, Jesus. I'd made it to bed a little more than three hours ago.

"Listen, hotshot. I want you ta run down what that no-good slut sent Suellen."

"You want a list? I'll try, Wet. You know what the hell time it is?"

"Better than you do, my friend. Start talkin."

"Jesus. I don't know." I yawned and tried to take the phone under the sheet with me. "A beanie baby. A playing card. A bunch of miscellaneous crap like paper clips and pencils. A bunch of old..." I think I dozed off for four seconds. "...Old school stuff. Is this important?"

"Very." Wet started to say something else, and then started coughing. By the time he'd recovered, I'd hauled myself out of bed, into a pair of shorts, and down to the kitchen. The box was still on the side counter where the prostitutes' meeting had relegated it. There was no sign that Suellen had passed that way since she patted my shoulder and stumbled off to bed when we got home at 2:30 this morning. In the dusky kitchen, it looked like the same bunch of yard-sale leavings it had been the night before.

The place reeked of stale smoke and the kind of scent I guess off-duty prostitutes use, and full ashtrays. I dumped those, opened a window, and walked into the yard with the phone.

"Wet?"

"Yeah." His voice was a sick cricket.

"I've got the box, but I'm taking it outdoors. Suellen's still asleep, and I don't want to make a lot of conversation. Hold on just a second." I took the phone and the box around to the side of the house that faces east.

We were late enough in the summer that the sun was still below the horizon. A cricket and a katydid reminisced in the wet grass. Faintly, the square of duct tape still showed where you could Land Hard without losing points. The silver fire of Venus burned in a dark bay between decks of cloud, bright enough to cast my shadow on the wall of the house. My house, bathed in Venuslight. It seemed an omen for change; like a voyage, or getting laid. I prayed to stay where I was.

"OK, I'm looking. What was it you were after?"

"Just tell me what's there."

"Well, all right, Mister Holmes. A bunch of grade-school report cards, a key, a jack of clubs smeared with what looks like blood, and if it is, it's Trudi's. I'm thinking of making that disappear, it's really tough on Suellen. A hash pipe; a laminated photo of Trudi and Suellen waving little flags. An envelope full of pencils and desk crap. A beanie baby and a birth certificate."

"That's all?"

"Some shredded newspaper, but not enough that the thing didn't rattle when we got it."

"Crap. Where's the newspaper from?"

"Crap, yourself. It's shredded. You want me to search through it for the masthead excelsior? I'll call you back in a week."

"I ain't got a week. That's the kind of dumb-ass question I get from Cumberland jackass County deputies all the time. Like it's too much trouble?"

"I guess not, if I knew why I was doing it. That something you forget to tell them, too? Look, the box was sent by UPS from Springfield, Missouri. I'd bet a bundle it's the Springfield Wazoo Whatever, wouldn't you think?"

Wet sighed, and it turned into a cough. "Probly. But if it ain't, see..."

He let it trail off as if he didn't want to insult me by spelling it out.

"All right," I said. "If it ain't, either it wasn't sent from Springfield, or Mr. Verry had access to an out-of-town newpaper. Unheard of for a Midwestern lawyer, of course."

"We're not doing cerebral navigation here, Maryland. Just see what you can find out. If it's the Springfield paper, maybe it's from the guy's own hand. If it's, I dunno, Chicago or Cleveland, OK, maybe he gets those papers, or maybe somebody there's faking it, or took something out. There's something missing."

"Missing?" I looked again in the box. "By gosh, you're right, Wet. There was a kid diary there last night, and now it's gone. I expect Suellen took it out to look through for old time's sake."

"Find out, but that wasn't it. There's no videotape?"

"Nope. Never was. We're not talking about the famous death tape, are we? What kind of jerk would send a tape of somebody's murder to their kid?"

"Somebody that thought the kid oughta have it. Somebody that promised the kid's mom to send her everything."

"Trudi wouldn't have known about the tape, I think we can safely say."

"No, but she coulda used language that would force this Verry to send the tape anyways. Lawyers are funny that way. They cover their butts."

I snorted doubtfully. "Suellen didn't say anything about a tape after she talked to Verry, though."

"Yeah? She give any indication she knew there was bad stuff in it?"

"Yes. Maybe." I glanced back at the kitchen door. "I'll ask her when she wakes up."

"Do that, hotshot. Call me if it's anything ... No. Just call me. I do not want Suellen lookin at that tape, you hear me?"

I told him we had no issues there. Who would want to see a video of their mother's murder? I padded back to the silent kitchen to make coffee, and took a cup of it along with the Intelligencer out to the metal glider on the screen porch. Forde Morgan had an editorial column that, with the help of a swarm of suggestive dots, hinted idly about the drop-off in diesel sales out on the bypass ... and certain stories in the Raleigh papers ... and how there'd been a spike in aspirin sales at the By-Rite <u>and</u> Wampler's Pharmacy, though a slump in other necessities, dot dot, wink wink.

I guess Forde figured it might be fun for his readers to connect the dots. I turned the page. While I was reading the real estate section to see what was selling for how much, and so what I might hope to realize by selling this house, the sun began to filter through the morning glory on the screens, bringing a sultry breeze, a smell of cut grass, and a growing conviction that I could learn all I needed if I got a little more comfortable on the glider and draped the *Intelligencer* over my face.

The phone on my belly woke me to the sweaty carping of flies and midmorning traffic, and carried a troubled contralto.

"Dr. Maryland?"

"This is Hap Maryland."

"I understand you consult on educational matters."

"Yes? Among other things."

"Educational Consultant" sounds grand enough, unless you're in the biz yourself and you realize it's puffspeak for a guy who can't hold an administrative job, and doesn't want to teach. What I did was, I would do little jobs for people that they could perfectly well have done for themselves, but were too rich, lazy, or dumb; such as, visiting college campuses to get ground truth on their student-recruitment claims, or settling intradepartmental squabbles that neither side trusted any insider to adjudicate; or untangling the finances of a department, or once in a while a whole college, that had got themselves in a jam through wooly-headedness. I use the childish and patronizing tricks of motivational speakers to motivate fossilized or research-fixated faculties to take seriously their duty gladly to learn and gladly teach; and when their finances permit, I soak them plenty for the privilege. Otherwise, I charge according to ability to pay, which had not been a strong feature of my recent clients. If I didn't line up a good one soon, I was going to have to switch brands of beer.

The contralto broke a convenient thoughtful silence by asking, "How much do you know about sex?"

I couldn't help it. I snorted. "Know? All there is to know, which is damn near nothing."

"Good." She sounded as if she'd just checked something off on a clipboard, the instructions to which said, Skip to Section II.

"Why is that good?"

"May I come to your office? I have a proposition to lay before you."

There are qualities of silence. Mine may have been ironic. Sardonic, even. I give myself no private-eye airs.

"Oh, shoot. I mean, I need help, and I think you will find the, the situation of interest. Of financial interest."

Oh, well, then. "I operate out of my home. To be perfectly frank, out of my screen porch, which is where I am right now. Are you in Gabbro?"

"I'm calling from Greensboro."

My reputation must have spread like kudzu. Greensboro is a good hundred miles of back roads from Gabbro.

"I see. Well, take NC 73 off of I-40 - "

"I know where you live. It will take me the better part of two hours. Would, oh, three o'clock be all right?"

"Today?" Duh.

"Please. It is a matter of some urgency."

Urgent, but not important, I hoped. "I can fit you in. Ms...?"

"Paula Vanek. I am in the Department of Women's Issues at Tri-Cities Tech."

Uh oh. "All right, Ms - Dr. Vanek. I'll see you at three."

"Will there be other clients there? I would prefer that our meeting be private and confidential."

"Then let's make it 2:30; can you get here by then? I just received a cancellation, and that will give us time to finish up before my next appointment."

I liked the way she kind of took that seriously, still somehow packing a bubble of amusement into her reply.

"Very kind of you. Two thirty, then."

Paula Vanek sported grey-streaked red hair done back in a ponytail, green eyes, an orange tank top, and bib overalls that truncated abruptly in tight shorts. Long, freckled legs connected those to feet that she had dressed in pom-pom socks and Tevas. She carried one of those zippered vinyl pouches they hand out at scholarly meetings to carry treatises in. Hers said "IXth Congress, GAFS, Prague, 1999." She looked familiar, but I couldn't put my finger on where I might have seen her before.

"Gafs?"

It took her a couple of seconds to see what I was asking. "Oh, that. The Global Association of Female Scholars. A bunch of damn scribbling women, I expect my dean would say, if he dared. We give each other support on women's issues in academic settings, world-wide."

"Like trying to learn CPR without uncovering your face?" Something a Middle East stringer had talked about in the Raleigh paper.

"Like just trying to go to school, in those countries. Generally, men are flippant about us, but the problems are real."

I nodded, accepting the rebuke. "I don't doubt. I have some experience of that sort of thing - " I held up a hand. "Not from the victim's point of view, of course. My late wife was troubled by it as a professor, and did what she could - "

"Your late wife was a saint. That is one of the reasons I have come to you."

Well, maybe not exactly a saint, quite yet. The college of cardinals kept stumbling over that teeny extramarital action she couldn't seem to break off, until a brain tumor broke everything off. Two years after her heroic death, grief and anger still couldn't agree on equitable shares in what was left of my heart. I wasn't going to ask Paula Vanek where she got her opinion.

"What's the pitch, Dr. Vanek?"

She unzipped the satchel and pulled out a sheaf of papers and a pack of Gauloises. "Do you mind if I smoke?"

I shrugged and waved a hand at the screens. "Many of my clients do. It's why we meet out here."

She nodded, and pulled a lighter out of a pocket in the bib. "Stupid, self-destructive habit."

With the glow of the lighter on her face, I saw who she was, and leaned back to see if I could figure out her game.

"You need to know up front," she said, leaning toward me earnestly and picking a flake of tobacco off her tongue. "I don't have a lot of money. If you try to help me and fail, I will have a tough time to pay you even your expenses."

I grunted noncommittally, and she sighed, and blew a reek of French smoke at the morning glories. "But if you succeed, I am prepared to share what I realize with you, fifty-fifty. I believe that is the usual arrangement."

I had to laugh at that. Yes, it was the arrangement Travis McGee usually got. "Goodness. I think you want a fellow down in Fort Lauderdale. You can't have gotten more than a glimpse at what I was reading last night. Would you be more comfortable without the wig and the contacts?"

She nodded, and I could see her ticking off another box on her interview form.

"Pretty good, though a really sharp operator would have waited longer, and used his advantage." She yanked the wig off by its ponytail, and shook her head to free up the cap of hair that had been pinned close to her head last night. In the morning light, and fluffed out, it was not as dark as it had looked last night. More the color of a good strong IPA, and it showed a few grey hairs itself. The green contacts stayed in. Or maybe the brown ones of last night were the fakes.

When she was reconstituted, she leaned back and gave me a tilted look. "What was it?"

"Um," I said, not being sure. "I guess something around your mouth. If you'll excuse a personal remark, it looks a little more fun-loving than you sound today. I noticed it last night."

She exercised some of the fun lines. "Not bad, given the competition."

I couldn't ask, without sounding ungallant, if she meant the other hookers or the see-through blouse. "Thanks. What's a professor of Women's Issues doing at a prostitutes' strike meeting?"

"Are you asking from the standpoint of morality, or class? Prostitution is my field of study."

"I see. And your costume was intended as a disguise? As protective coloration?"

"No. I didn't have time to change."

I leaned back in the glider. "I assumed that. Particularly when I thought you were... well, one of the girls."

"I am."

I pulled out a notepad of my own, and put on my best consultant's poker face. Which actually pretty good; I had restorative surgery on my face after a bad burn, and it's not hard for me to be inexpressive.

"You are a prostitute as well as a professor, then." I made

notes on the pad.

"You find that amusing? Titillating?"

"Do I look titillated?"

She gave it some time. I thought about trying not to look titillated, but doubted I could improve what was on my face already. "You look a little amused, in a dyspeptic way. I am particularly interested in the men who patronize prostitutes." She gave me a challenging look, and added, "As customers," tartly enough.

I raised an eyebrow, and kept my mouth shut.

She tapped ashes from her Gauloise with an air of impatient regret. "There is not a single reliable study of johns, and they are the mainspring of the whole transaction. The so-called classic study is based on police interviews. Cops, interviewing johns!"

"OK. And your studies produce reliable data because..."

She nodded. "Because they don't know they are being studied."

I tried to picture that. "How do you manage it? Hidden cameras? Mickies?"

"Hidden cameras, sometimes, depending on what I'm looking for. Why would I need drugs?"

"So they'd forget that they didn't get what they came for, and got interviewed instead of laid."

"The interview takes place first, and - if I flatter myself - is subtle enough that not one in a dozen catches on. At most, they think they've met a prostitute who pretends, in a particularly skillful way, to care about them. They admire my act, as one of them called it."

I nodded. "Even so...Well, doesn't the word get out?"

"I think you're beginning to ask about matters that go beyond what you need to know." She shrugged, and pulled a half-smile across the fun-loving mouth.

"What kind of anthropologist would I be, and how long I could stay in the field, if I disappointed my informants? I'd be lucky to survive a dozen encounters. I will say that I am very particular about hygiene, and the transaction does not proceed until I get complete cooperation from my subject on that."

I could imagine. After the interview and the drinks, she would know what would persuade the john to get scrubbed up and fitted with a condom, and never lose motivation. Not that it would be that tough, I supposed. She was at an un-ageing age between 35 and 45, and pertly handsome. Behind the sophistication, the earnestness, the laugh lines, there was a darker weariness that would draw a certain kind of man - or a certain part of all men - into itself; the fall harder to resist the longer it lasted.

"Don't you get guys who like the experience so much they want to give you repeat business? Isn't that a classic of prostitute literature? It must be a nuisance."

She smiled, a little self-deprecatingly. "The Blue Angel situation. It's rare, at least when I'm the angel; but it happens. I have a followup protocol that I can use with men like that, and learn something about the subclass. And I see to it that they don't particularly want a third visit."

Protocol, subclass. I flipped a page over. "You mentioned survival just now. This isn't exactly a safe line of inquiry, I'd think."

"I am very careful. My interview is based on sound personality inventories, and if anything at all gives me concern, I have a dozen convincing mechanisms for breaking it off. I have done so only twice in six years, neither time with any bad consequence."

"OK. But otherwise, you follow through with the trans- ... uh, forgive me, but with intercourse for money. And your Dean is giving you grief about this research. For some reason."

She tapped her cigarette hard. "The little puke. I came up for tenure this spring, and my department backed me a hundred percent. So did the outside reviews. I have twice as many publications and twice as many advisees as the rest of the department put together. Some snot of a Congressional aide ran across where I acknowledged NIMH support for some of my work, and got it into the Congressional Record that NIMH was funding prostitution in North Carolina, right at the time their appropriation was in mark-up. Barry got a call from Jesse Helms, and he put the word down to the dean. Instead of sticking up for academic freedom, the little puke overruled the unanimous departmental recommendation for tenure."

"And Barry is..?"

"_Doctor_ Stanley Barry. The Academic Vice-Provost, and a man with very clean hands. He never wields the actual knife if he can find a willing toad. Which was our little puke of a Dean."

"I get it. And it was up or out?"

"Of course. I appealed the denial of tenure, of course, but it looks bad. I start my terminal year next month. There will be a hearing on my appeal some time around then. I need somebody to appear there with me, and say things that would sound better not coming from me. Also, of course, I could use any bright ideas you might have."

She ground out her cigarette, and blew the last smoke down-breeze toward the driveway, where I could see Suellen walking in from her afternoon workout, pale and sweat-soaked. Keep your shirt on, Suellen.

"So here's the pitch," Paula Vanek said. "As of June 30 next year, I'm out of a job. I am looking, of course, but academic jobs in my area are very scarce. Needless to say, or I wouldn't be at that cow college. I'm nearly desperate. If you can figure something out where I keep my appointment at Tri-Cities Tech after this year, I am prepared..." She broke off with a sigh, ran a hand through her mop of hair, and ironed the fun lines out of her mouth. "I will split next year's salary increase with you, fifty-fifty, from July 1 on."

"Aw, look, Dr. Vanek. First of all, Travis McGee is fiction. Half of your raise would be way, way too much, and anyhow ... "

Anyhow, I hate academic squabbles. The parties to them are invariably smart, polite, correct, and mean as dirt. They tend to be negative-sum struggles in which the losers lose more than the winners gain, partly because the winners rarely cared all that much about the substance of the quarrel, and the losers never accept having lost, keeping up a brushfire of guerilla backstabbing for semester after semester, over curricular doctrine that both sides have lost interest in anyhow. And in fact, the stakes are almost always trivial except for tenure squabbles, in which the human importance of the outcome does nothing to ennoble the squabblers. A tax audit or a good, hateful divorce is hopscotch by comparison.

And besides, who said Jesse Helms is wrong on every issue just because he's Jesse Helms? Did I want to go to the barricades for a professor's right to moonlight as a prostitute, and write scholarly papers about it? How about a prostitute's right to daylight as a professor, and get extra tricks out of that?

I turned back to her, and she held up a hand. "You forget I have a second income. And in any case, half of something is better than nothing. I think that's what Travis's chickies always say."

"Yes, they do. And I'm glad it was you, calling them that, rather than I, in the company of a professor of Women's Issues. But the rest of what I was going to say is, No. You should be talking to the AAUP, or a lawyer."

"I'll take those in reverse order. All the lawyers I talked to know not the first goddamn thing about academic freedom, and started talking about the legality of prostitution itself. It's a misdemeanor, sure, but so are a lot of things that nobody worries about. The AAUP has turned into a snotty version of the Teamsters Union. They work through local chapters, and ours is negotiating a perks package for faculty spouses. The Dean is supporting it, which will change if they do anything for me. Don't think I didn't thrash around on this for months before I called you up. Hi, Suellen."

Suellen sagged onto the porch in a bubble of airy, lemony chickie sweat. Some guys apparently find the smell irresistible, loaded as it probably is with pheromones and stuff. "Hey, Paula," she grunted. "Wha'd he say?"

Paula started stuffing things back into her zipper pouch. "He said No."

"Told you. Listen, Hap, Paula's very, very righteous on this, and she's getting screwed."

"So she's been telling me. But I am very reluctant to get into a tenure ... an issue around a tenure decision. I've done three or four, and every time, that's the last job I get from that place. And besides, ... "

Suellen held up a hand and started peeling off her shirt. "Don't make up your mind yet, Hap. Sleep on it, get back to her. You might change your mind. Please." She paused in the striptease with the shirt halfway up the stem of the rose tattoo. Her abs and obliques were back to killer level, shining with sweat.

"Trust me on this," she said. "Paula's a real asset, and she really needs the kind of help you can give her. Just tell me you'll think about it for a day. Read a couple of her papers." Her elbows started rising. A rosebud made an appearance.

"OK, OK." I jumped up and headed for the door. "I'm thinking. Leave a reprint, and call me tomorrow morning, Dr. Vanek. Best of luck."

I meant the last to be a warning that I wasn't going to be bogarted into something I didn't want to do, by a brace of brazen femmes. A hooker and a lesbian stripper, by God. As I headed upstairs to get a shower before Suellen could use up all the hot water, I heard them laughing. Suellen had known I'd get flustered when she took her shirt off, damn it.

5.

"I eschew and denounce the hegemony of phallocentric discourse to read and speak from the position of the clitoris. This is a position - "

Suellen snorted milk out of her nose and folded onto the back step. "From..." she gasped. Her eyes bugged in merry disbelief. "From <u>where</u>? She reads and talks with her <u>clitoris</u>?" She giggled helplessly. "White woman speak with fucked tongue."

Bethany stamped a foot and pivoted away with her hand over baby Lee's outboard ear, and pressed the other to a breast. "Really, Suellen."

Suellen mastered herself and looked, if this is possible, hilariously repentant. "Aw," she said. "I apologize to Snookie. And you. Maybe not to your expert there. Go on."

Bethany hoisted baby Lee a little higher on her hip and turned a page. Lee - a gorgeous little thing who bore the name and many of the genes of my late wife, the beloved deceiver - looked solemnly at her Auntie Suellen and gummed noncommittally on an arrowroot biscuit, waiting I guess to see what mommy would say about it.

"From the <u>position</u> of the clitoris. *A <u>position</u>,*" Bethany read, with steely emphasis, *"which has in the past been carelessly construed to reframe Derrida's employment of "the hymen," a term which he uses to indicate textual operations that give entrance into the hole, the Derridean absence -"*

Suellen exploded again, stomping and clutching her ribs. "Oh, my God. Oh, that's too...What if she got twat ... hee, hee ... twat-strain from reading under the covers?" Bethany lowered the book and glared, waiting for Suellen to pull herself together.

It took a while. "Haw, shoot," she managed at last, wiping her eyes and grinning. "You're making all that up, right, Beffie? About the Derridean hole? They don't give PhD's for that? Hell, I'm wasting my time with quantum mechanics."

"You may well be," Bethany said. "But hundreds of very smart people take this - " shaking The Clamor of the Clitoris: Reconstructing Prostituted Womyn at Suellen - "very seriously indeed."

No need to ask Bethany - the stepdaughter I'd eased into this life from the position of my late wife's Derridean absence - whether she took it seriously. She was the dreamy theorist of the two of them, blowing iridescent palaces of belief where Suellen would buy, grudgingly, into what the laws of thermodynamics and the dictates of experience forced upon her. When Bethany read about the Strumpets' Seminar in the News and Observer - not being so close to me or Suellen as she once had been - she'd brought over some reading on prostitution she'd found on a Web bibliography, and that she thought might help things along.

"C'mon, Suellen," I said, trying to be helpful. "If you sort of translated into ordinary language, there might be something to it."

"Ya, right, I'm sorry, Beffie," Suellen said. "You're sweet to take the trouble. I'll read 'em, I promise."

If it kills me, seemed like. But I think Suellen really wanted not to lose Bethany; and maybe it was mutual, because Bethany grinned a little and pulled another book out of Lee's diaper bag.

"This'n's supposed to be a little more down to earth. So to speak." She held it up. Right away I had hopes for it; a catchy single title, no colons, no subtitles. Here was somebody, on evidence, who was willing to make a decision about important things. Johns, Jades, and Johnsons was twice as fat as Clamor of the Clitoris, and adorned with the colophon of a trade publisher to boot. Not to mention a familiar author: Paula Vanek.

Suellen brightened and grabbed it. "Hot damn," she said. "Saves me a trip to Chapel Hill to find it. You had this all along, you little vixen?"

"Got it from Amazon," Bethany said. "I had to keep it and the other'n in the box, and bring 'em over right away. I think Plummer would of been OK, but if his Uncle Chavis'd seen them, we'd have heck to pay."

Suellen gave her a quick kiss and a noogie, sandwiching Lee between them and smushing arrowroot slime across her shirt. "See this, Hap? Required reading, if you're going to take her case."

"All I needed to know," I said, and went into the kitchen to clean up breakfast. I could see the pitch coming a mile away, and after considering it overnight, I still hadn't made up my mind - meaning, I still hadn't thought up a good excuse - for turning Paula Vanek down in her quest for justice. Other than, I guess, that I had no great sympathy for someone who could be a scholar about men who boff women who do it for pay, but dumb as a brick about

Southern academic politics.

Nor, on the other hand, had I a plausible excuse to give my hungry bank account for turning down any paying job, even if I screwed her down - excuse me; *persuaded* her to offer something more realistic than half of the salary increase I would be seeking to restore to her. Neither of those was the sticking point, though.

No, the bad, bad rub of it was this: as I left Paula and Suellen on the screen porch and fled to the shower yesterday, I noticed - I couldn't help noticing - that for all her age-appropriate facial lines, the fanny Paula Vanek had chosen to stuff into those bib hotpants was tight and handsome. The kind of butt you'd expect, maybe, on a fifteen-year-old flouncing around the mall, or a ballet student. Not a fortyish academic. It had to be her major stock in trade, out there trolling for interviews. I caught myself remembering it twice during my shower, and sucking in my middle-aged gut when I stood towel-wrapped at the sink to shave and brush my teeth.

And cursed myself for a fathead.

*

"It has been generations since men could be lighthearted about patronizing a whore, if that was ever really so. Since the pill and the sexual liberation of single women, prostitutes have served primarily as the loser's resort, the purchased receptacle for the frustrations of awkward, furtive, or otherwise isolated men who lack the minimal confidence it takes to establish a fulfilling sexual relationship with a woman. This book is an introduction to that

population."

"Don't tell the truck drivers that," I said. "Still, though, it's a nice change from the reconstructed clitoris. Is that P - is that Vanek's book?"

Suellen nodded. "Uh huh. Sucker's jammed with numbers and graphs. She's got a whole section of interviews, and a floppy in the back with spreadsheets - heh, new use for that term - on economics, shoot, demographics, state-by-state price structures. Thing's a goddamn opus. Listen to this."

Suellen hoisted a hip onto the counter and gave me more:

The median price of a single-intercourse encounter with a street prostitute varies by more than three-fold between Portland, Oregon and Portland, Maine. But that ratio is within 5% of the ratio of median single-family home prices in the two cities. Indeed, this parallelism holds true over every market area for which data were available, and for every class of sexual worker, with a family of linear regressions (v. Fig. 4.15) that is almost eerie."

Suellen held *Fig. 4.15* up for me to *v*. "Tell me the size of some joker's mortgage, and I'll tell you what he's paying to get laid, within 5%, holy shit."

" 'A single-intercourse encounter?' That's telling it like it is."

"She couldn't hardly call it a 'fuck,' could she, in a hard-core scholarly text? What's a house cost in Gabbro?"

"Median?" I ran some of the house prices I'd seen in the Intelligencer through my head. "I guess forty, fifty thousand."

"God, that's pathetic. Still, though.... yeah, look here! Look where Gabbro would plot. Shit, we're way off the curve, even for street hookers, let alone escorts and call girls, which I don't hardly think you can find here anyways. Just plain whores oughta be knocking down twice what they do, though, look."

I looked. Suellen had pencilled in a point for Gabbro's housing and prostitution markets. I was staggered at the paltriness our Y coordinate. "No wonder truckers like it here. Think we ought to take that to the Chamber of Commerce?"

"Ya, half those bozos never got as far as graphs in school. No, Hap, what you oughta do is, you ought to take her case."

"Paula's? Because Gabbro County prostitutes are getting, uh, short-changed?"

"Huh uh. Because she told me the name of the Dean that's screwing her."

I sighed, not wanting to talk about it. "Not literally, of course? That'd be too easy."

"I wouldn't be all that surprised." Suellen came over and put a hand on my shoulder, turning me to look at her. "Hap, this 'little puke' that she calls him? It's Tim Summerton."

I dropped the sponge into the cooling scum of dishwater. "That's all I needed to hear. No way, huh uh, Suellen, and I mean it."

Tim Summerton, I guess I must say here, was that stealthy beau of my late wife's. He'd been a young math instructor at Gabbro College who had dated Lee off and on before we were married. He'd been so perfectly manly and sporting about Lee having chosen me instead of him for marriage that I should have known right then, there was a joker in the deck. After Lee died, he left Gabbro for other academic pastures, and I thankfully lost track of him. Hell, everybody has old flames if they're breathing at all; but with Tim and Lee, it didn't stop there, and that's all I'm going to say about it.

Well. Except, I guess, to say that further contact with Tim Summerton was so far down the list of things I meant to do before I died, that I intended to die before I got to it.

"So," Suellen shrugged. "OK. I get it. Painful subject, blah blah. Just, I guess I'm surprised you could pass up a chance like this."

"A chance? Watch me." I pulled the strainer up to empty the sink, and had to stand there and hold it to keep it from sealing off again. While the tepid suds drained past my fingers, I thought of Wet's morning call.

"You know, Wet called up first thing this morning."

Suellen's face clouded. "How'd he sound?"

"Not great. I'm worried as hell about him. He wanted to know about the box of stuff. There was no videotape, right? That tape the tourist supposedly shot of your mother ..."

"No way. I'd have seen something like that."

"Good. How about that little diary? Did you take it to bed with you, or something?"

Suellen picked up the box. "No, it's right..." She rustled around in it. "Did you take it out?"

"Nope. It's not there. I told Wet about it, and he thought there might be something - I don't know. Important, in it. Significant."

"I doubt it, truly. But it's gone, anyhow. Come on, Hap. You got to've taken it out, or just put it down somewhere. The whores came right as we were looking at it, and I never thought about it again until just now."

"I went off to read <u>The Dreadful Lemon Sky</u>. I was sitting in the garden with just a beer and no diary when the hospital called. Did you show it around the circle of discussants last night?"

"Nope. Damn, I bet one of them clouted it, though. I figure out who it was, I'll toss her butt from here to Fayetteville." She shrugged. "Not that it meant anything. I got along fine without it for years. Anything else missing?"

"You mean, like the silver candlesticks? I don't think so."

She stretched, and levered her shirt up a hand's width. "Speaking of Fayetteville, though, I think I'll go back and see how Wet's doing. Wanta come?"

"Thanks, I guess not. I promised Bethany I'd stay with Lee this afternoon. Anyhow, Wet might like some time with you to himself."

"Don't be lugubrious. He'll be OK."

"Of course. Call me at Bethany's if you won't be home for supper."

After Bethany came home to end the babysitting stint, she launched into a discussion whether she ought to go ahead and - as she had not yet done - add her husband Plummer Baley's family name to her own and Lee's. None of the motivations I had on that question were things I could readily discuss with Bethany, viz:

For change: Anything that would change that baby's name from Lee Morgan - for Bethany had been unwed Bethany Morgan when the rape occurred that started little Lee off in life, and Bethany had grittily purged all trace of the vile father from the event - would be a welcome relief to me. Not just because of the rape, but because "Lee Morgan" was also, of course, my late and ambivalently mourned wife.

And besides, I thought the world of Plummer Baley, the wonderful lad Bethany had married, about one second before little Lee's birth. I admired Plummer for doing that, and for any number of other reasons, and so did everyone who knew him. I would consider it an honor to have my grandchild bear his name.

Against: To anyone else in Gabbro County, the name of Baley was synonymous with gumptionlessness, poverty, dull wits, and a cheap laugh.

There was some basis in reality for this perception: a succession of Baley men who were about the most gormless to be found anywhere, and a crew of women who seemed to get plainer and meaner with every generation. What Aggie jokes are to Texans, Baley jokes are to Gabbro Countians - those with the IQ themselves to remember jokes.

That Plummer Baley - a preacher of wit and power, a successful contractor, and a former Navy SEAL - was a shining exception to the rule would not protect little Lee from a lot of snideness and cruelty in grade school. But you can hardly tell your daughter you would name the kid anything but her beloved husband's name, to avoid her beloved mother's. I copped a plea.

"Gosh, Beffie," I weaseled, "I can see good arguments both ways. Seems to me, you and Plummer need to make that decision on the basis of what will feel right to you, down through the years."

"I'd like to hear the argument against."

"Well, gosh ..." I tried to look like I was thinking about the memory of sainted Grandma.

"It's 'Baley,' isn't it?"

I affected incomprehension. "Of course not, I just - "

At that uncomfortable point, Plummer himself got home from supervising the installation of a gigantic and elaborate rood screen in Saint Ann's Catholic Church. She kissed him and drew herself up to stand by him like a Valkyrie.

"Well, Plummer and me are showing people a Baley family with smarts and gumption, dammit," she said. "And Lee is gonna do the same."

I turned up a hand. "Then I think you just answered your own question."

She cocked her head, and beamed at Plummer. "I guess I did. Daddy, you're some hot consultant."

"If people are going to think for themselves, there's not much left for a consultant to do."

I suppose I could print that on my business cards, if I found independent wealth and got bored with the business. I went from Bethany's to the courthouse, where the County Clerk's office wanted somebody to tell them that five years of flawless electronic records-keeping meant that they could retire their old, one-of-a-kind hydraulic rotating file. So I told them that; though not without a pang for the old Rube Goldberg contraption that had served them for fifty years after its invention by a local backyard mechanic.

"Gosh, I guess you're right, Doc," the clerk said, when I pointed out that they were spending more every year on repairs, upkeep, and the outsize post-bound books that required special typewriters, than it would cost to upgrade all the computers in the Courthouse. "Still, it sure seems like the end of a era."

Seeing a chance to sell more easy work, I offered to surf around on the Web to see if there wasn't a museum of dead-end inventions - I put it more diplomatically, of course - that would be willing to remove the contraption and put it to pasture before an admiring public. And a contractor, such as Plummer Baley for example, who could suggest and construct useful space where the thing had been.

"He one a them Baleys?" the clerk snickered. "Can't be. I hear he's pretty good."

"Try and hold both those thoughts in your mind at once. They're both true."

He made an effort, and achieved it. "I'll be," he swore.

"Uh huh. That'll be $250 for the consultation. No charge for the referral."

It was Suellen who was surfing when I got home. She had her laptop open on the kitchen table, and her face over the screen was tearful, drained and devastated.

"What is it?" I asked. "Wet?"

She seemed paralyzed by what she was seeing; her head barely swiveled the negative. "No. Mother of all shit," she breathed. "Look at this. Wait a second."

She clicked on something, and turned the screen around so I could watch.

It was a little hard to get a bead on it at first. For one thing, it wasn't a great laptop; the screen was dim and washy, and what it showed was chaotic. Music came from the little speakers, starting up in the middle of a bad cover of "Stand By Your Man." The scene was overstuffed with a shifting crew of actors, and the action dragged and jerked because of the low-quality video.

I still hadn't gotten oriented to what was going on - something involving a floozy-looking woman at a table with a crew of male lowlifes in a bar or roadhouse somewhere - when a tinny scream drowned the tinny music. One of the lowlifes lurched up from the table and launched himself at one of the women. A knife semaphored jerkily three or four times, and the woman heaved convulsively, throwing off the attacker, who kept yelling obscenities over her screams. Suellen, at my side now, tapped a key and the action stopped.

"Know her?"

"No," I said, and was suddenly afraid. "C'mon, Suellen. It can't be..."

Suellen executed an alt-shift-F-something, and the mouse drew a box around the woman's face. Zoom, zoom, and now the blurred face, splashed with blood, almost filled the screen. Suellen rattled another F key, and a couple of frames jerked forward while the face collapsed, tilted, and came into focus. Recognition sent a shock wave from my belly to the back of my throat.

"Oh, my God, no. Not on the Web, Jesus."

"Yeah," Suellen managed. Her voice was bloodless and draggy, dying from multiple stab wounds. "Yeah. Right there on the dubya dubya dubya. That's my Mom."

She turned and stumbled out the kitchen door.

6.

The newspaper that was shredded in Trudi's box of mementoes was the St. Louis Post-Dispatch. I deduced that not from any sliver of it that said so, but by finding a fragment of its trademark Weatherbird cartoon from the front page, and remembering having seen it as a kid in Iowa. I checked on the Web version, and even found the date when the Weatherbird had uttered the fragment of wisdom on the scrap I held. July 10, of the current year, which was consistent with its being used as packing material for a box we received on August 4th. And so what?

Wet Parsonage agreed. "So nothin. Nice work, though, hotshot. Now, where'n God's name did she find a movie of Trudi gettin done, on the internet?"

"A porn site, that evidently got hold of the tourist's videotape. Alt-dot-sex-slash-snuff something something. Offered him a hundred bucks for it, probably. You can see some breast in it, earlier on."

"I lived too long. Why'd she even go lookin for it?"

"She's not real clear on that. I think it was Paula Vanek who suggested it."

"Who?"

I sighed, in a hand-washing way. "This Professor of Women's Issues from Greensboro, that Suellen's got friendly with.

She's a sex expert with a lot of firsthand, nuts-and-bolts experience."

"Christ. Why'nt I marry her off to a truck mechanic when she turned 15, like she wanted?"

"She'd be right back where she is now, but with three kids. Count your blessings."

"I got too many ta count already, and they keep multiplyin. Thanks for the detective work, though. Make a cop outa you yet."

"Preserve me."

Wet made some feeble joke about how well-preserved I already was, yawned, and signed off. I hung up, maybe not quite as worried about him as I'd been. His voice sounded a little stronger, and he didn't cough once, the whole conversation.

Suellen came back in toward sunset, from wherever she'd gone after she showed me Trudi's death. She was mucky, red-faced and scratched. I think she must have just walked out the kitchen door and kept on in a straight line across fences and fields until she hit some lonesome arm of Indian Girl Swamp, and made a 180 when she could wade no farther into the brambles and duckweed. I heard the shower running, and under it her voice, hardly recognizable in lamentation.

She came out at dusk, grey-faced and blue-lipped. Our water comes from the coastal aquifer, winter rains from the Smokies groping toward the sea under a thousand feet of sand. It is the same 43 degrees winter and summer, and when that's all you run, it can damn near stop your heart. I folded her into myself. She seemed as hard and chilled as root vegetables.

"Mom," she said, and her teeth rattled. "My crazy Mom."

I gave her rosehip tea and a blanket, and sat up with her until she dozed off. I went to bed on the screen-porch glider when I started to fall out of the chair. In the night, I woke once to hear her soft footstep behind me in the hallway, and once a faint rattle from the kitchen.

She woke me in the morning, seeming recovered. Deep vees of sweat front and back showed me she'd been up long enough to do a heavy workout. But her eyes were shadowed over hard facial grooves.

"I gotta go out there," she said. "Can you lend me some money?"

"Sure," I said, without thinking it through. "Where, Branson? For what? They surely got the guy."

"You know that for a fact?"

"Well,... well, no. I guess I just never thought - "

"No," she exploded. "Me neither, no, God, *I* sure never thought. I never bothered my head, did I? Even after I heard she was killed, I didn't let it be really real. It wasn't something that really...like, took place , some afternoon when I was sixteen. Dating army brats and hanging out at Cross Creek Mall. What do you expect I was doing while that happened? Sneaking perfume at Belk's? While that knife was cutting her up like a rack of ribs? And at that instant when she knew this was it, she was dead, you think maybe she looked across the room and saw the dork with the camera, twiddling his focus, and she was thinking, oh, don't, don't let Suellen see me like this? Was that the very last thing she thought? And what was I doing right exactly then? Frenching some zitface redneck and thinking wait'll I tell Annie! Agh!"

"Hold it," I said. "Suellen, don't - "

She raised a hand, both arms, like someone who has stepped on a mine. "Oh, don't worry, Hap. I'm not gonna 'beat myself up,' which I could see you were gonna say that, so don't bother."

She started to pound on her knee, and the porch floor boomed with the impacts. "But I'm gonna beat somebody up, you bet. I'm going out there, and I'm going to find out who killed her, and what happened to him, and if they didn't catch him, I will. And if they did, I'm going to find out why he did it."

"Please, Suellen. Whoa. Are you sure that's something you want to know? Suppose they did catch the guy, and they let you interview him, and it turns out she ..." I turned up a hand.

"Go on," she said. "Don't spare me."

"You know her better than I do. You loved her and you know some admirable things about her. Heck, I was friends with her once, and I admired a lot of things about how she operated. But you know the kinds of ... well, subterfuges and deals and situations she got into, that often as not involved some kind of scam or cheat, or whatever."

"Ya, she never got a PhD or tenure anywhere, did she? She cut corners a lot, because she had to, to take care of me."

I ran a hand through my thinning supply of hair. "Look. You go out there, and you find out this, what looks like a poker game, that it was some kind of racket, or ripoff. Maybe Trudi's not even a big player in it, maybe she's just bait. But one of the rube victims catches on, and loses his cool, and assaults - well, he kills her, and now he's serving twenty to thirty for aggravated manslaughter or something, or he's out on parole. Either way, you figure some way to confront the guy, you're as resourceful about that kind of thing as your mother ever was. And maybe he's this clueless loser, the kind of guy that gets ripped off a lot. Legal costs have bankrupted him, and his kids never come to visit him, and his wife's getting a divorce. Then what? Assault him, throw him around like a gunny sack, land him hard, and end up in jail yourself? For what?"

She nodded. "So I'll know. So I can climb out of the shitswamp of no-mind ignorance I've been wallowing around in. Even if that business you just invented - nice going on that, by the way - even if it's something like that, at least I'll know and understand, instead of mooning around like a goddamn debutante."

She held my shoulders and squared around before me, wanting me to understand. Maybe even wanting me to approve. "She took care of me the best she knew how. And I took care of her too, you don't know. She'd be ready to do the stupidest things, and I'd have to hold her back. And in the end it was me that did the really stupid thing, and got pregnant. Sometimes I've hated her for shipping me off to Wet then, but the main thing was, it meant I wasn't there to keep her from doing crazy stuff."

Her eyes started to fill, and she scrubbed them savagely

with her shirt tail. "So I owe her just that one thing, Hap. Knowing. For all the things she did for me, and spared me from, and humiliated herself and kept her chin up and busted her butt to give me." She flipped a hand and snorted, or sobbed.

"For the beanie baby, OK?"

7.

Suellen left for Branson the next week, riding an '83 Harley she borrowed from Neville. I'd come up with a grubstake for her by selling the almost-unused Saturn that Lee had bought to drive herself to educational meetings around the state. It had a little over three thousand miles on it. I very much imagine that she also used it for out-of-town trysts with Tim Summerton. The only thing that didn't depress me about the business was the laugh Suellen got from my suggestion that she drive the Saturn out to Missouri. It was certainly her first since she found the death video.

"Excuse me? A *Saturn*? I look like a real estate lady to you?"

"Excuse me. It was good enough for Lee."

She whapped herself on the head. "I'm sorry, Hap. I didn't used to be so snotty and self-centered. Did I? I begged Lee not to get that thing. Every little prom queen buys one soon as she gets her first real job all by herself. All Lee could see was, they treat you nice when you buy it. Yeah, and laugh their butts off afterwards, because you never tried to screw the price down, and it's gonna fall apart in three years. I notice you never drive it, either. It's just gonna sit there and you're still paying good money on it."

I had to grin at that; I'd told Lee the same thing about Saturns myself. "OK. I didn't used to be so stuffy. Tell you what, you take it into town and sell it for me, and we'll do the Travis McGee thing. You can keep half of what you recover, beyond what she financed."

I cleaned out the Saturn, including a glove compartment full of Lee's stuff that made it very hard going. A lot of it, of course, was obsolete registration cards and warranties, school stuff, and unidentifiable phone numbers scribbled on scraps of newspaper. Some were things that only Lee would have had, and they were painful to see. A few were things that a woman who was carrying on extramaritally might well have. By the time I dug down to the bottom and found a couple of Tim Summerton's business cards, I was a sobbing wreck. I dumped all of it in the trash except Tim's cards. I don't know why I kept them. Maybe thinking I'd brandish one at Lee the next time I dreamed of her. Maybe that would chase her out of my heart at last.

Suellen drove the damn thing out to the dealers' row on the bypass and shopped it back and forth until she'd jacked the price a good 20% over book. In a lot of ways, Suellen was still her mother's daughter. She took the dealer's check to the bank before he could change his mind, and turned it into a handsome stack of $20 bills, which we divided at the kitchen table, one-for-you-and-one-for-me. I came up with a bit more when the County Clerk's check came. And off she went.

I got phone calls from Knoxville, Paducah, and Springfield and, eventually, postcards from Nashville and Big Spring, Missouri ("846 million gallons of cold water gush daily from this popular tourist attraction. Swim! Fish! Hike!"). Her message was, STILL KEEPING COOL. I CALLED WET LAST NIGHT AND HE SOUNDS A LITTLE BETTER, OUT OF HOSP. TUES.

PAULA SAYS HI. Because, oh yes, she'd recruited Paula Vanek as a traveling buddy and relief hog-driver. She told me Paula was strung out over her looming tenure appeal, and needed a vacation. If that was supposed to make me feel bad, it didn't. I figured Paula probably saw it as a chance for gathering data. I pitied the truck driver that tried to hit on that pair.

In the last phone call, from a Springfield motel, Suellen said Amos Verry was being a jerk, and had broken two appointments through Darlene Feely, but that Feely swore she would see to it that he kept the next, which was scheduled for the next morning. I told her to dress soberly and not to take bullshit, but not to come across as fixated on her mother's death. I was missing Suellen - maybe I was addicted to sweat pheromones - so I tried to sound upbeat and busy.

In fact, I was now totally out of paying employment. I did an alarmingly easy net-worth calculation and survey of assets, and figured that, as a household of one, I could hold out for a couple of months, if I bought cheaper beer or none at all - which wasn't all that different - and ate frugally. I put ads for business in the *Chronicle of Higher Education* and the Charlotte and Raleigh papers. When waiting for the phone to ring or the *Intelligencer* to come got good and boring, I phoned Bethany and asked if I could come over and use her DSL line for a little Internet research.

"Oh! Daddy, thank God. I'm about to go out of my mind here. I need to get in to St. Ann's to help Plummer, and I can't take Lee there, the power tools scare the dickens out of her. I was just reaching for the phone to ask if I could drop her off with you.

How soon can you be here?"

"Depends on traffic. Forty seconds, maybe a minute. Change her pants while you're waiting."

The electronic path to the video clip of Trudi Ransom's death was a lot less sunny and firm than Suellen's plunge into the sludge and duckweed of Indian Girl Swamp. I went past stuff it would never have occurred to me anyone would conceive of, let alone think to "share" it. The URL turned out to be annexed to an S&M bulletin board where not just Trudi's degradation but those of many women were on show and no doubt gawked and reveled in by every well-wired misogynist on the planet.

With a faster line and a better monitor, a little of the jerkiness ironed out of it, but there was a limit to how much the end-use hardware could improve it. By trying this and that, I found I could replicate Suellen's tricks of stopping the action and blowing up subframes. I went back to the beginning and tried to see what occasioned the attack on Trudi.

It was a card game, all right, and money flowed pretty freely back and forth across the table. Once I knew which one was Trudi, she was unmistakeable, decked in an ultralow-cut peasant blouse, her hair done up in the same towering do she'd always used for business. At one point, early in the hand that ended in death, she developed an itch on the side of her nose. I stopped then, and stepped through, frame by frame, to see who seemed to respond to the signal, if that's what it was. But, frustratingly, the camera panned around the room for a while, evidently guided by a tourist who was trying to capture the Branson Experience in all its color and excitement. By the time he panned back to the card game, Trudi had no more than seconds to live.

I also isolated and blew up the face of the knifesman. He was never more than sideways on, so I never saw his face in a memorable way. Still, I couldn't imagine that the guy wasn't in prison. He was pretty ordinary-looking, maybe a little sallow, if I could trust the color rendition. Smooth skin, black hair that hung in a comma over his forehead. You had the feeling he didn't need to shave much. And when he had his big moment, of course, his back was to the camera, and he emerged from a confused ruck of people, so it was only by his shirt that I was sure he was the one I'd been watching all along.

Finally, all other ideas exhausted, I let it play through Trudi's death, with no stop-action or closeups. I got those in nightmare replays that night. In the worst of them, she was seducing me, as she once did when I thought Lee would never marry me. We wore black Ninja suits, and when I pulled her to me, she was already a skeleton. My knife grated on her breastbone.

The tourist with the camera had been shaken at first - to judge by the lurch and swing of the camera, and its dizzy examination of the ceiling - before settling in to get as much of Trudi's agony on tape, or chip, as possible. The cameraman had stayed with her, crowding forward to follow her slump to the cluttered floor, forsaking all other sights such as what happened to the killer; whether he was nabbed on the spot and wrestled into submission, or walked out untouched.

When the stream ran out, and the action froze for the last time on Trudi Ransom's slack and bloody face, I killed the link and shut down the computer with shaking fingers. I went to check on snoozing Lee then, and stood over her cradle, breathing baby powder and the ammoniacal twang from the diaper pail in the corner, until I could stand up straight on this earth and hear the bugs again.

Well, I wished Suellen luck in her quest. That she might quickly find the truth about Trudi's death, and that it would be merciful to her. How rarely one's wishes have the remotest relevance to what is actually about to happen. Had you noticed?

It was while Suellen and Paula Vanek were waiting to see Amos Verry that a brace of ladies came a-knocking on my door again. Turned out that - and who could blame her - Suellen had forgotten to tell the Strumpet Seminar she'd be gone, and that they would have to work out the details of their protest march without her.

"Shit fahr," said one of them, a ponytailed and buxom lass from Bozlee. "We wonted her take on a couple issues that come up."

"Oh," I said. And, what the hell. "Maybe I could help."

"Oh, I truly, truly think not," the other interjected with a little laugh. "The last thing - well, no offense, but this is not exactly something a male could conceivably help with." She was a pudgy lass with chunky ankles and Birkenstocks, and I have to admit I had trouble picturing her in Paula's miniskirt and see-through. But then, sex is a many-splendored thing, and who says there's no market for a lay that starts with the clunk of sensible shoes?

"Sorry," I said. "And since all the women that used to be here are gone, I guess that's - "

"Aw, for shit sake, Louise, get off it. Look, you see anything wrong with this?"

The ponytail held up a sketch of a sign, or maybe a bumper sticker. *"I'm a whore and I vote,"* it read.

"Why," I said. "Why, uh, no, I guess not. You have a lot of representation in Congress."

"See," the chunky one squawked. "The Phallic Hegemony on the hoof. His contempt for congresspersons and for sex-industry workers is undifferentiated."

"Ya, right, Lou," the other shrugged - and my ears pricked up at the "Ya" like an old dog who misses his master - "See, the issue here is, what can we call ourselves? I got no beef with hooker, whore, or prostitute. Tart, even. Just, I kind of think 'whore' works good on a sign, though, see, like this one. Can you see *I'm a sex-industry worker and I vote?* I mean, c'mon. Just for starts, it'd hafta be in about six-point type."

"Short words are often the strongest," I nodded. "How about, *'I'm a tart and I vote?* That's punchy."

She chewed a knuckle thoughtfully. "I dunno. Sounds like pastry, all of a sudden."

"Uh huh. Well, *'whore'* seems OK to me, then. It's a perfectly respectable word with a very long pedigree. Could they get you on any kind of - I don't know, public indecency rap for parading it on a sign?"

"That's the issue. DeLoris, she's worried about it. I think, hey, cops think that, they can walk a mile in my moccasins, you know?"

Louise bristled. "*Whore* is a term of male domination and contempt. I will not march under it. Not that I am one, in the first place, but - "

I held up a hand. "Hold it. You're not a, uh, a prostitute?"

"Of course not. What do you take me for?"

I couldn't help myself. I am a bad fellow. "Really? I would have sworn ..." I let it tail off. Louise rose and took it, and about a yard of line.

"That's a goddamn insult, you bastard," she roared. "I'll bloody see you in court, you think you can insult me - " She stopped, too late. The pony-tail turned to her slowly.

"Find that insulting, do you, Lou?"

Louise did her best. "Of course not. Only in the mouth of a phallic prick - "

The pony-tail waved it off. "Why'nt you excuse us for a minute, Lou? I'll see you in the car."

When the door slammed, she turned to me with a crooked little smile. "You done that on purpose."

"I... Well. Yes."

She held out a slim and muscular hand. "My name's Carrie Connelly. I'm a whore, and I don't give a rat's heinie who knows it or what they think about it. How'm I gonna make enough to retire, I don't get the word out?"

I shook her hand, wondering how I knew the name. "Glad to meet you, Carrie. If I can help in any way, from the male point of ... Well. From the standpoint ... oh, shit. From, you know, a gentleman's perspective, why, let me know."

She grinned, and looked suddenly like anybody's baby sitter. "You may lay to that, Mr. Maryland. I owe you one."

She turned toward the door, so I didn't ask, One what. But the grin did ring a bell.

"Wait. Did you run off to South Carolina and marry, what, a quarterback or something, a few years ago?"

Carrie Connelly sighed. "That make the papers, here in Gabbro?" She sketched a headline with squared-off fingers. "The Cheerleader's Big Mistake?"

"Nope. Some folks thought you were dead. I'm glad to see you're not."

"Not yet. Not that Biff din't do his best every time he got sauced, which was right often after he flunked out."

I nodded. Her nose, which was mostly cute and straight, bore a little dent that marriage to a Biff might have put there.

"My late wife," I said, with a little back-tip of the head, "was married to one of those, you know, wife-beaters, before me. She said you could tell Jaycees from white trash because they never bruise you where it'll show."

"Uh huh, well, Biff never made Jaycees. Thanks again, sir."

I opened the door for her, not wanting her to go. "You're very welcome, Carrie. 'Bye."

Forde Morgan's obituarial appreciation of Lee came out in the *Intelligencer* the next day. I read it with my eyes slightly averted. There were no surprises and no mentions of Tim Summerton. The quotes from me were things I could imagine saying, even if I didn't remember saying them. I called Forde to thank him for his general tastefulness and light touch.

"Hardest part a this job, Hap. Speak nothin of the dead if not good. With Lee, that was pretty easy. Some folks, of course, it's a challenge to fill a couple inches with good points."

"Yeah. What do you know about Branson, Missouri, Forde?"

"Branson? Wife drug me out there a couple years ago. Hick version of Nashville, if you can imagine that. Or Vegas, without the gambling. What brought that up?"

"Aw, Suellen's gone out there, on some kind of quest about - well, her mother got killed out there."

"Sorry to hear it."

"Yeah. It was a while ago, and off the record, … well, we discussed her before, you and I. It was not a devastating loss for the rest of us. You wrote one of your obits on Trudi Ransom, you'd be telling lies after the name and date. She got killed in a bar brawl, and Suellen feels guilty, or something, that she didn't... I don't know. React more to it at the time. Make sure the guy that did it gets punished, I guess. Find out what it was about."

Forde grunted skeptically. "Bar brawl don't sound like Branson. One thing they got goin for them is, they keep it clean. America this and Jesus that. Bunch a twenty-somethings, tryna break into country music, waitin tables, keepin their faces polished. You'd die of overeating before anybody'd say boo to you. Well, I expect they attract their share of lowdowns like any other place they's a lot of money circulating."

"I don't know a whole lot about it, and I must say, I don't care to know more than I do."

"Uh huh. Len... Wait a second...Len Saffel."

"Sorry?"

"Saffel. S-a-f-f-e-l. Features editor for the Springfield-Branson <u>Beacon</u>. You really wanta know anything about anybody in that corner of the country, Len knows it. Last I knew, anyhow. He mighta ate himself to death on rootbeer malts by now."

I rang off, as the Brits say, with no intention of consulting any Len Saffel, and strolled downtown to see how the March of the Underpaid Prostitutes was shaping up.

It was timed to coincide with a Jaycee car raffle that brought all the Gabbro folk with nothing better to do onto the streets, along with Tucker Pardee to maintain order. Gabbro County's half-dozen marchers were joined by some others from even smaller and more put-upon markets, for a total of maybe fifteen. Laid end to end, they wouldn't have reached across Church Street and back.

I have long since outgrown the myth of the Whore With the Heart of Gold - cured of it by no other than Trudi Ransom. But on this August day, they were full of spirit and pride, and it wasn't at all hard to see them certainly as people with hearts like anyone else. More attractive, for that matter, and a lot more hopeful. Carrie Connelly twirled a baton and did cheerleader routines all the way from First Baptist to the Chamber of Commerce.

The others formed themselves into a "J" for Justice, like a marching band, and then the ringed-cross female symbol; though sometimes it was more just a crookedy line of women. Carrie joined them, and dropped out to sign an autograph for a little boy, and rejoined, and finally just panted fetchingly and waved her sign, which was pink on black and about eight feet high. DeLoris Potter marched in a leopardskin double-knit pantsuit under the banner of Sexual Congress-People for Fair Pay. She'd gotten somebody in the Gabbro College chemistry department to inflate some helium balloons that it took me a minute to realize were condoms. They made a nice addition to her banner.

When the tail of the parade caught up, in front of the Chamber, a soap box and a miked podium appeared from somewhere, and Carrie Connelly made a short, punchy speech about fair pay for a fair night's work. Somebody from the Gabbro College chapter of The Feminist Alliance got up and talked at earnest length about Sybils and ur-prostitutes, glazing whatever eyes were not focused on Carrie.

The show was picketed ("Go And Sin No More") – but at least not stoned – by some Baptists who'd gotten wind of what was up. The dunkers were counter-picketed by The Feminist Alliance, which in turn had to deal with some hisses - on the grounds that prostitution is phallist female slavery - from the Research Triangle

Chapter of NOW. All in all, counting Jaycees, I bet a hundred people got their consciousness raised or otherwise altered out there. In our town, that's a good day's work.

I didn't spot Louise the chunky-legged un-hooker in any of the groups. But I know there was at least one Fayetteville reporter there, a stringer with connections to the national press. Carrie and her sign made a *USA Today* I picked up later in the Fayetteville airport. I heard she got a flood of business and two offers of marriage out of it.

When everything seemed to be running down, Tucker and I took the core group of planners out to the Holiday Inn and Truck Stop for beer and pizza. I don't know what made me think I had any business doing that, except that Tucker didn't have room for all of them in the county cruiser, and I pretty much felt like Suellen's deputy in her absence. I had no one waiting for me at home, anyhow.

The marchers, already as high as red-tailed hawks, ordered pitchers of eponymous pink ladies and fell to whooping and tee-heeing and comparing notes about which Baptist client they'd spotted in the picket line. Then they turned to seeing if they could embarrass Tucker and me, and succeeded pretty well. I don't think I laughed as much or as hard in the last three years as I did that evening. I left at midnight rumpled, crimson with lipstick, grinning if unlaid. Catching myself running a narrative for Paula Vanek about the whole scene. Remembering she was in the Midwest. And blistering myself for the small twinge of disappointment.

But when I got back to the house, there was a message from

her on the answering machine, asking me to call immediately.

"Suellen's gone," the little tape squawked. "She's just goddamn gone."

8.

You can fly from Fayetteville to the Springfield-Branson airport in two jumps, going through Memphis on Northwest. You can do it at a day's notice, if you're willing to sink half the payoff from selling your wife's car into a short notice, open-return ticket. I did both those things; my conversation with Paula was that worrying.

Before I left, I called Paula and learned that Suellen had started calling Amos Verry, of Morris, Gerard and Verry, when they were a day out of Springfield, trying to set up a time when she could get filled in on the essential details of Trudi's death: date, venue, perpetrator's fate. Maybe wheedle a letter of introduction to the law enforcement and prosecutorial side of it. I already knew he'd broken the first couple of appointments. He broke one more, then called Suellen back, apologetic as could be, and asked her to meet him for lunch in a little diner by the courthouse.

He called the motel room again at one o'clock, caught Paula by luck as she walked in the door from lunch, and asked to talk to Suellen. Paula was savvy enough not to tell a stranger where Suellen was or whom she was meeting, which led to some confused sparring until he said that he was Amos Verry, damn it. That he'd waited at the diner for an hour, and Suellen had stood him up. Suellen never called or came back to the motel, and when she'd been missing for 24 hours, Paula called me, five minutes after I'd gone to root for the whores' march.

It was on the Memphis to Springfield leg, stuffed into a window seat, while I was entertaining a hope that I would arrive in Springfield to find Suellen retrieved, Paula Vanek sheepish about hauling me out here expensively for nothing, that I heard a muffled sob from the guy wedged next to me in the middle seat.

What you do on these occasions, of course, is, you find something really interesting as much in the other direction as possible, and hope the guy isn't about to blow in some way. I was by the window, but the view was limited, a cloud deck probably two miles below us and a vault of dark-blue sky above. I scanned it, ears cocked to my right while the guy blew his nose, joggled my shoulder digging out another tissue, and uttered a sigh profound enough to blow salty tear breath across all three seats.

I risked a glance and found the guy staring at the skyscape. He swiveled his flowing eyes to me and shook his head.

"Sorry," he said. "M'dog died last week."

I thought of the late Covington, in her improvised backyard grave for the last year. "Sorry to hear it. Dogs have a way of getting under our skin, don't they?"

He shook his head. "Daisy was a great pup, jus' the best I ever knew. But they're temporary patterns, like the rest of us." He held up a book, "Zen, Dissipative Structures, and Human Existence" by somebody named, I think, Radko Brkczec. I may have missed a consonant or two.

The guy blew his nose. "Therapist gimme this to help with

the grief. What this guy points out is, any living thing is just sort of a pattern. A dance, like, of molecules and dust. Organized by DNA, all that, into something we think is a solid thing. A friend, a d-d.... a dog. Ourselves in the mirror. OK, we change, but only real slowly. Think we're pretty much the same, year in and year out. What we don't see is that molecules and stuff's going in and coming out all the time, fitting in to the pattern. Or, he says, it's like we were like this enormous marching band, spelling out something big an' complicated. A whole person, a whole life, maybe. But, see, twirlers and drummers an' - I dunno, tuba players, are always running in and outa the pattern, except we don't see that. What we think is the real living thing, it's just the pattern. Just the dance." He gritted his teeth. "The dog is a dog pattern, the guy is a guy pattern."

I thought of the Wet Parsonage pattern, slowly bleeding marchers, down to a skeleton crew of disheartened clarinets slogging toward the end zone. My fellow traveler stuffed the hankie into his coat pocket and held up his hand.

"Looks pretty solid, don't it? But it's just part of the marching band. Half-time only lasts so long, and then the whole thing comes apart." He twiddled his fingers in the space before him. "Anybody remembers us, they're just patterns, too." He shook his head, heavily. "I'm still working on the next step, which s'posably happens when you see the Nothing behind the pattern. But ol' Daisy don't wanta get outa the way, seems like. Damn dog was so sweet and human. Like she had a soul, besides just the pattern. You think dogs got souls? My pastor says not."

"Um ... " A flight attendant was bearing down on us, I saw with relief. "Somebody gave you this as grief therapy?"

He nodded. "Makes it all not matter so much, don't ya see."

The flight attendant leaned over him and clucked at the cover of Dr. Brkczec's book. "I loved that," she said. "My fear group read it. Please bring your seat backs forward, gentlemen."

*

I rented a car at the Springfield airport, borrowed a phone book at the Hertz counter, and found Morris, Gerard, and Verry on something called the Chestnut Expressway. I asked the counter girl for directions. A pimply kid who was bringing her a handful of car keys did a double-take and opened his mouth, but the girl waved him off and told me, right on West Bypass out the terminal road, left on Chestnut Expressway, and it'd be a mile, mile-an-a half on the left.

"Left outa Parking, hang a left off the Expressway at Campbell. You get to National, you gone too far."

"Campbell good, National bad," I said. "I get it."

The temperature on the rental lot must have been in four figures, under a silver-white haze of humidity. A dust devil accompanied me through the ranks of baking cars until we found the one that was mine for $17.95 a day. It was a Saturn, which figured. I loaded my stuff in the back, and the dust devil moseyed on down the row, looking for new fun. When I'd waited a plausible length of time, I walked over to a "courtesy phone" attached to the outside of the car wash. I called the counter and told the girl the car wouldn't start.

"Oh, fer..." she said. "Hang on. Timmy'll be with you in a sec." Before she remembered to hang up, I heard her say, "Shit fahr." It made me feel at home. Her voice came over a squawker on the chain-link fence, telling Timmy to assist the customer in slot 43.

I sweated for another five minutes, watching a big cloud of gnats dipping and dancing over the grass outside the fence. Gnats joined the cloud, gnats departed, the cloud danced on, keeping its pattern. I squinted to see if I could make it look like a marching band, or a dog. Or Lee Morgan. Trouble was, I was too advanced. I was already seeing the Nothing.

When the pimply kid showed up, I told him I'd figured out what I was doing wrong, gave him a fiver as if I had more of them than I could count, and asked what it was he'd wanted to tell me about Morris, Gerard, and Verry. He giggled, wiped sweat off his face, and spat.

"Pretty slick, fella. Morris is dead. They jus' keep the name, like. Gerard's about a hunnert'n eighty, creeps around in a black suit with this silly tie like a shoestring. Nobody can tell if they's anything going on in there. Verry, shee-it, man, they knowed what they was doin, they named him. He's old, too, maybe forty I guess, but he's like a black belt karate, very hard, very smooth, mister macho all the way. He's got a wife, and he's humpin that Darlene that works for him, plus God's own number a women from over't the College."

"I see. You know Mr. Verry pretty well, sounds like."

"Darlene useta live down from me. Her mama does yet."

The kid leaned on my car and spat again. Some of it dribbled down one of the tires, and some of it hung on his chin. He wiped it off, leveling a hard gaze at me over his sleeve.

"You got business with that man, you better have your shit lined up. Daddy of some girl at the College come inta town from outa St. Louis somewheres, that he was sticking it to. Thought he was gonna whup Mister Verry for it. Great big guy with tattoos and all, looked like a truck driver, something. He come through here the next day and handed in his keys, I never seen a fella look as whupped on as that man done. Shee-it, he was half the size he'd was the day before. I give you a look, cause I was wondering if you was gonna end up the same."

I told the kid I was Amos Verry's dad, and winked at him, figuring he'd spend a couple of days wondering if I was kidding, and then forget about it. I also changed my game plan. Hang a left on Campbell, nothing. I poked the Saturn into the hazy blaze of sun and asked the first cop I came to for directions to Suellen's motel.

The Harley was parked outside Cabin Three of the Shady Stop Motor Hotel. I was pretty sure Suellen and Paula had picked the Shady Stop for the retro funk of an old-time Route 66 kind of place, not to mention it was probably the cheapest lodging in five states. It was a curvy line of separate rustic cabins perched on a wooded limestone knoll that had probably been on the edge of town, back in 1947. Now, I-44 blasted past on one side, and a service road on the other. The cabin in the middle, a little bigger than the others, served as the office. It advertised Running Water, Color TV, Moderen Accomodations.

Cabin Three had a striped and only somewhat rusted metal awning over its west-facing window, and a roaring AC stuffed into the south-facing one. The shadiness was provided by a very big oak that had worked its roots under the sidewalk and buckled it good, forfeiting on this grounds alone Shady Stop's compliance with the Americans with Disabilities Act. I picked my way over the rubble, and knocked.

Paula Vanek came to the door barefoot and sweating. One look at her face told me that what I'd been telling myself all the way out there — that Suellen would have turned up on her own — wasn't so.

"Hap, Jesus. I thought you were her, but thanks for coming all this way. This is my fault, goddamn it. I should have watched her." She stood back and gestured me into Cabin Three.

It was one room, with a sort of housekeeping alcove that featured a sink, a fridge, and a little 3-by-4 table topped with chipped enamel in a stenciled floral pattern. I hadn't seen anything that '40's since - well, the '50's. A soft-looking double bed with, sure enough, a nubbly chenille spread was flanked by a couple of rummage-sale lamps, one of them with a nautical motif, and the other Art Deco.

I put down my suitcase, and accepted that we weren't in for

a short, happy ending. "She's a big girl, Paula. I expect she's all right. Tell me what you know."

Not an awful lot, was the answer to that. Suellen's appointment with Amos Verry two days ago now, was for a quarter to twelve. So, he said, they could beat the crowds at this little restaurant that all the courthouse regulars used, and get a booth. Paula had an idea about going to the Greene County Courthouse while the lunch went on, and seeing what she could find about Trudi's death by posing as an anthropologist.

"You are an anthropologist, I thought."

"Yeah, but I don't pose as one, most of the time."

Suellen had said she needed ladies' supplies, and asked Paula to drop her off at a CVS a couple of blocks from the restaurant, which Paula had done, and driven the Harley on down to the courthouse. And that was the last she'd seen of Suellen.

"Did you go to Verry's office?"

"That same afternoon. Out of the office, what this Darlene Feely said. I think she was lying, but I can't be sure. She has a pretty dead face."

"What's your take on Verry?"

"I haven't seen him, mind. People I talked to downtown say he's a nice enough guy for a lawyer. Funny, even way out here in the country, people don't like lawyers. I thought that was a bicoastalism."

"I hear he's a - he's quite the ladies' man."

"A cocksman? Is that what you were about to say? That's what one of the courthouse women called him."

"Close enough. Anyhow, have you tried to get hold of him since then?"

"Sure. He's been in St. Louis since the afternoon Suellen disappeared. I checked with his secretary, and I verified it through the airline."

"How did you do that?"

"I called them and said I was Darlene Feely, and Mr. Amos Verry had instructed me to find out how much it would cost to extend his stay another two days. She coughed up all his flight numbers and everything."

"Very slick. They probably aren't supposed to do that kind of thing."

"They aren't, no way, but I'll tell you. The more rules you put on certain people, the better it suits them to help you out. The kind of people that feel guilty about all the petty bureaucrats they work with. I happened to get one of those."

"Well," I said. "Good work, I guess. Not that it gets us any closer to Suellen, though, does it?"

She deflated a little, and admitted it was so. "Strong, independent people can get the delusion that they're bullet-proof. I wish the hell I'd just kept an eye on her."

"What other leads do we have to work on? Maybe we can divide the labor."

"I haven't done much on the cop front yet, except to report her missing. Somebody that's not a local goes missing, they put that pretty low on the list. But they'll pay more attention to you than they would me. You could work on that."

"Fine. When does Verry get back?"

She looked at her watch. "In about an hour. Want to see if we can nab him at the airport?"

I thought that over. "OK, but reserving the option just to watch, and not nab, if that seems the better course at the time."

She shrugged drily. "There's a market for that. I charge the same as a regular trick."

Amos Verry's plane from St. Louis was late, and eventually posted as delayed over an hour. We were getting nothing out of sitting in the little airport watching a bunch of Midwesterners come and go, making modest wry Midwestern jokes about airlines. We drove downtown to the offices of Morris, Gerard, and Verry.

The suite opened off of an interior courtyard, with an anteroom that housed two large commercial green plants – I mean, they weren't fake, but you knew no one gave a fig about them – and a woman at a desk.

"Miz Feely?" I asked her.

She looked offended. "I don't think so."

"Sorry. I was really looking for Mr. Amos Verry."

"You would haftew consult Miz Feely." Perfectly straight face.

"Gladly. Where would I find her?"

"Second door. She's not in, I don't think."

But she was. Darlene Feely stood a fortyish five feet in flat shoes, a brown page-boy, and a crisp little June Cleaver dress with a Peter Pan collar. There was no nonsense to her, she let you know, without your having to ask.

"Mr. Verry will be sorry that he missed your visit, Mr. Maryland. However, he has been quite, quite busy with his case load this summer, and of course his campaign, and now with this airplane delay - " She lifted a small, clean hand at a stack of neatly slit mail and a worried-looking lady sitting next to a sullen boy whose attention and soul centered on what a pair of silver earphones were pumping into his temporal lobes. His eyes were half-closed and a little crossed. He didn't tap his foot, or anything else - unless his spine - at what he was hearing.

"His campaign?"

"Mr. Verry will announce very soon that he will accept the Democratic nomination for state senate next year. He has very good lines of communication with the people of this area, which I am pleased to be able to assist him with."

"That must be satisfying for you. I guess our immediate concern is an appointment he made with my - my ward, Ms. Ransom."

She pursed her mouth. "He was quite vexed - "

An inner door opened behind her then, and Darlene Feely clapped her mouth shut. A man emerged, looking a little like Strom Thurmond, in another twenty years. He was cadaverously thin, with wisps of grey hair slicked across his skull. An asymmetric string tie slumped under his grin of welcome.

"Got guests, have we, Miss Feely?"

"Yes, sir. Miz Hill is here with Mr. Edmond Hill, for their appointment with Mr. Verry."

The cadaver bowed in a courtly way to the waiting mother-and-child, and turned to us. "I had reference to the folks with whom you were in converse." His eyes were of the palest possible blue, steady on mine within bony sockets.

"Hap Maryland, Mr. Gerard," I guessed. "Dr. Vanek and I are trying to locate our friend Ms. Ransom, who apparently had an appointment with Mr. Verry, and seems to have disappeared."

Gerard tutted absently and extended a hand. "René Gerard. Sorry to hear about your friend. Have to watch yourself like a ...." He trailed off. "I have no doubt she will resume her intercourse with society in due ...."

Gerard pivoted creakily toward the Hill family. The motion seemed to throw him off track for a moment. He looked back at us, getting his bearings. "Due course. Perhaps you'd like to begin with me, Mrs. Hill."

"We had our appointment with Mr. Verry," Mrs. Hill said. She didn't look like she was about to waste time on René Gerard.

Gerard grunted. "Quite wise of you, I'm sure." He turned back and gave Paula an appraising glance.

"Young Verry was quite vexed, I expect Miss Feely was about to say, when your friend did not appear."

"Us, too. She hasn't called or come to this office?"

Darlene Feely reinserted herself into the conversation by stepping between Paula and Gerard. "No."

That was so pre-emptively unhelpful that it made me quit giving her the benefit of the doubt. "And you've heard from no one who's seen her?"

Her eyes widened minimally. "No. I expect you will find that she is pursuing her inquiry in other directions."

"Did she say anything about that to you?"

"I would need Mr. Verry's approval before I could discuss that with a third party. I do hope she has come to no harm."

Paula shrugged as we walked down the sidewalk. "Almost certainly lying, Hap. But about what, it would be hard to say. We don't have the standing to grill her. Or Verry for that matter."

"No. But if somebody disappears, seems like the person they had an appointment with is a prime suspect, wouldn't you say?"

"Why don't we call the cops, and see if they'll let us instruct them on that?"

So I did, when we got back to Paula's cabin at the Shady Stop. The Springfield city police bounced me to the Greene County Sheriff; but there, I got a bit of luck.

"Yeah," the guy on the phone said. "Butchie kind of a lady, was it, lookin for information about her momma, sposed to've got killed. She was here. I told her we didn't have nothin on that, far back as 1990, which she said it was after that."

"When was she there?"

"Oh..." He seemed really to be thinking back. "Couple-three days."

"Well, whether it was a couple or three makes some difference. She went missing, two days ago."

"Hang on."

He covered the phone, not efficiently enough that I didn't hear a half-muffled query about that dyke, was in here, when was that? A couple of voices off-mike said something, and there was a small detonation of cop laughter. My informant came back on the line, snorting a little.

"Guys here think it was Monday."

Three days ago. I wrote "Monday" on a pad and showed it to Paula. She shrugged. I came back on the line.

"Look, Captain," I said, feeling like a chain gang, "I'm out here at the request of her, her stepfather, who's a cop back in Fayetteville, North Carolina. He's worried about her, and he's too sick to come out here himself, or you can bet he would. Would it help to have him call you?"

"Naw, frankly, sir, I doubt it. 'Fwe knew something, I'd have no reason not to help you out."

I gave that the silence that was all I could think of, and he relented a little. "Where was it her momma was sposed to of been killed?"

"Branson, I think."

"Well, there you go, see," he said brightly, sounding suddenly as helpful as one could imagine. "That ain't in Greene County. I dunno why she never said that. You might do better in the county Branson's in, which is Taney. County seat ain't there, though, it's over'n Forsyth."

"We need," Paula said, twisting the neck on a bottle of Gatorade, "a better approach than running around in circles." She swigged neatly and kicked her rusty metal chair back against the wall of Cabin Three. Below us, heat glittered off broken glass in the service road ditch.

"Such as?"

She shrugged. "Isn't there someplace we could go that'd be, like, a guide to the politics and stuff? Is Amos Verry right at the heart of this business, or is he just incidental, because it never happened here, it happened in some other county? Or what? We keep on at this rate, we'll never find Suellen."

"Maybe she'll find us."

"Trouble with that is, she knows where to find us. Me, anyhow. Right here at Shady Stop. I have to think, by this time, she hasn't shown up because she can't."

I didn't like the sound of that. "Trouble is, I don't know what else to do, but try to go where we think she went, and try to pick up some sign of her."

"We chased out to the airport for nothing. We went to Verry's office, which I'd already done, and learned nothing. We called the cops and learned we weren't even in the right county. All I'm saying is, before we fly off to - to whatever that town was, maybe we ought to do some more research."

"More research."

She laughed. "You know what I mean. Isn't there somebody who could give us some kind of orientation?"

"Forde Morgan gave me a name of a guy on a local paper, said he'd know what there was to know. Now, all I have to do is remember who it was." I shrugged. "Which I can tell you right now, is not going to happen. I'm getting to the age where I'm starting to lose short-term memory."

Paula made a face, and let her chair slam down onto the broken concrete. "Crap." She stood, and opened the door to Cabin Three. "Come in here."

I followed her into the cabin, pummeling my brain about the name Forde had mentioned, and I had not written down. Feeling about as cogent as a cloud of gnats. Hoping Paula might know some kind of magic that anthropologists use to stimulate the memory of aging informants. She shut the door behind me, and stood with her back to it, hips cocked, shoulders thrust back, looking up at me through her eyelashes. Her eyes were still green, so I deduced, a little rattled, that green was their real color. It made an odd combination with the IPA hair, which, on the basis of the here-and-there grey ones, was also genuine.

"Do you remember now?"

"No. What - "

"Shut up." She unbuttoned the top button of her blouse. "Now?"

"No, damn it. Stop this. What the hell do you think you're doing?"

"Jogging your memory." Another button.

"Is this supposed to be funny? It's not."

She made a little pouty face, and undid the last buttons. The blouse swung open to reveal a strip of contoured, lightly sweaty skin, not interrupted by underwear. "You're not helping me. How about now?"

"God damn it, *Doctor* Vanek, if I did this to you, you'd sue me blind."

"No I wouldn't." She sucked in on the contours and started wiggling to loosen the button on her shorts. I looked elsewhere, anywhere. Christ's sake, whatever else, at least Lee was modest around strangers.

"Well, anyway," I said, suddenly furious. "Knock it off. You may be the world's greatest scholar, for a hooker, or maybe you're just the best little whore that never got tenure. Maybe sex is something between a useful tool and an obsession for you, but I am *off limits*, got that?" I pushed her aside - her shoulder was just nicely muscular - and started to reach for the door knob. And stopped.

"Saffel. Len Saffel, damn it. He's something or other on the local paper. Now will you for God's sake get dressed?"

Paula smiled, patted my cheek, and pulled up her shorts. "Sure. Now, was that so godawful hard?"

9.

Len Saffel looked I guess like somebody who might have come calling on your Granny with a banjo and a box of mints. He wore white shoes, a little smudged with printer's ink, and white trousers held up by cream-colored galluses with little satin clocks on them. His brow bore a pink crease that would have exactly fitted a straw boater.

"Amos Verry," he said. "Oh, my. I do hope you have not done anything to disconvenience Mr. Amos."

"I've never even seen him. He had an appointment to talk to - " I gestured at Paula, sitting demurely buttoned up in a side chair, feet together, earnest face. "To Dr. Vanek's friend and my ward, and she has now disappeared. He also performed some legal services for the missing woman's mother, some years ago, shortly before she died. It's her death that Suellen was here to talk to him about. She was killed in a brawl that started with a poker game."

Saffel pulled a keyboard off his desk and started tapping on it. A data base screen appeared on the monitor in front of him. "That here in Springfield?" He sounded like it would be hard to imagine.

"No," Paula said. "In Branson, we understand."

"Uh huh. Mr. Verry gets around all this part of Missouri pretty freely. What was the deceased lady's name?"

"Trudi Ransom," I said, and spelled it, gritting my teeth.

Tappity-tap. "Not registered in Greene County courthouse. That's here. Deceased April 14, 1995, Stone County."

"Where's that?"

Mr. Saffel cocked an eyebrow, making the crease on his forehead tilt. "Where a lot of folks from other counties go to their reward, seems like. Kind of a rough stretch of country between here and the Arkansas line. West of Branson. You happen to know why she would of picked a high-price fella like Amos Verry?"

"Trudi had a thing for guys with money," I said. "She's the kind of woman who could give any man a sort of a look, and they're reaching for their wallets." I avoided looking at Paula. "I'd guess he was paying for her, as much as the other way around."

"Our Mr. Verry strike you as a man who'd have to use hookers? No offense intended, but it sounds like you're describing this lady that way, and if anything … " He stopped, seeming to reconsider. "Was this Ransom woman a pro?"

"Not... exactly. Just a woman with a good instinct for quick money."

"Ah, well. There they have something in common. Let me tell you a just little about Amos Verry."

Saffel swiveled around to face us, and leaned back. The back of his chair knocked the mouse off its pad, and it fell off the desk, to twirl and swing for the next five minutes while Saffel - who gave it a single dirty glance, and did nothing to rescue it - told us about Mr. Amos Verry, Esquire, LLB.

"Amos Verry is one of these guys that's cut a little bigger

than the rest of us, or than the place where he lives. Like Babe Ruth, Bill Clinton, Al Capone. He came out of one of the old quarry towns in Stone county. Smart, good athlete, good looking. I expect he about had his pick of the country girls down there. Fella like that, he can move out and up, and get knocked down to size in a bigger setting. Or he can stay where he come from and get runty, like Ross Perot. Get used to seeing things come his way, get lazy about thinking what it is he wants next.

Len Saffel shrugged. "Course, Amos Verry's case, seems like he wants to get laid, about more'n anything else he can think of. 'Scuse me, ma'am."

"Think nothing of it," Paula said, avoiding my eye.

Saffel grunted, and flashed a quick reportorial glance across the space between us.

"Anyways, he went up to Rolla to learn to be a mining engineer, and switched off to something else. Word I had was, he found out he didn't have a head for it. Politics, beer, women, and practical jokes come a lot more natural to him than rocks and calculus.

"He went on to Mizzou, buckled down and got a law degree, just about the time Mr. Morris, who was the founding partner in Morris and Gerard here in Springfield, took a stroke and had to cut back on his work load. Gerard was getting on, too, so they were tickled to hire a smart young fellow to help out. He married Morris's daughter Florrie, and in a couple years, it was Morris, Gerard and Verry. A year after that, Mr. Morris passed on. They kept the name, but if Amos gets his way it'll be Verry and

Gerard in another year. Or maybe just Verry. He's got a truckload of ideas that's prob'ly got old Morris spinning, and Gerard would hate, if he once understood everthing Amos wants to do."

"Florrie Morris Verry?" I asked, not meaning anything really.

Saffel grinned. "We've got used to it, and I guess so has she. Whatever qualms it might of given her, I believe she felt she could live with, as the price of hooking up with a comer like Amos." Saffel shook his head. "Legal and business deals that walk awful close to the edge of sharp practice. Tax advice over the internet. Anybody looked at it hard, I expect more'n half what Verry wants to do would turn out illegal, or unethical, or regulated to death. But he'd do it anyways, long as he could, for the payoff. There's them that say he's got fingers in dirtier stuff. Vice, prostitution, rackets. I wouldn't know; or, more accurately, I'm not gonna tell a couple strangers everything I think I might know in that direction.

"Mostly, he likes to operate on the up, as a - " Saffel broke off with a tiny smirk. "As a respected member of a respected firm. Only thing holding him back is, Greene County's got some pretty sharp judges, and they slip Gerard the Yes or No - mostly No - on things he wants to have cover on through the legal practice. By the terms of Verry's contract, Gerard can always outvote him on any policy matter."

Paula stirred and broke her silence. "Sounds like a recipe for trouble. Or an assassination."

"Not yet, would be my judgment on that, ma'am. Amos still benefits from the connections he gets from the name, which is pretty well known outside of St. Louis."

I nodded. "I understand he's running for - what was it, Paula?"

Paula didn't try to jog my memory, thankfully. "State senate."

Saffel smiled. "Y'all getting up to speed right smartly. Don't believe even I've known that longer than a week. Thing is, this is pretty conservative country down here, except for the quarrymen. Amos has pretty much voted Republican right along, but he has got to run as a Democrat, which is all that was available, even for him, who generally takes what he wants and asks later. He's gonna have to walk very careful indeed, he wants to win election as a Democrat down here."

"Even if the rackets don't hurt him, won't his reputation as a, a...." I glanced at Paula.

"A Lothario," she said.

I grinned. "Exactly. Won't that make it tough for him?"

"Don't know how he's planning to handle that. You'd think so. Thing is, Florrie knows the score, but she's devoted to him just the same, and she builds him up in public ever chance she gets. Course, so does Darlene Feely, 'cause whatever he wins, she gets a cut. I dunno how he keeps the college gals quiet. Anyway, guys admire him because he gets what he wants, and he's a black belt in karate. One thing and another, he could go a long ways. We're not that far from Little Rock down here."

I nodded. "But, seems to me, we're pretty far from finding Suellen. Thanks for the information, though, Mr. Saffel."

He raised a hand to show us how little there was to it. As he stood, he scowled. "There <u>was</u> something about a lady got killed over west of Branson, Stone County, some time ago. They never found the fella that done it, something like that."

"Hard to believe it could be Trudi's case. The whole thing was caught on videotape."

Len Saffel looked startled, and rescued his mouse. "Wait a second."

He woke his computer up, and went back to the main query screen. A series of images flashed across the screen: ribbon-cuttings, wedding photos, a funnel cloud framed by the windshield of a car, all the stuff a newspaper is likely to have in its morgue. And the screen filled with the image of Trudi Ransom.

"That your lady?"

I sighed. "That's her. Looks like one of the images out of the videotape of her murder." Trudi was in the same nipple-grazing peasant blouse, and her piled-up hairdo was long familiar. On the other hand, she may have dressed that way five days out of seven.

He nodded. "That's what tipped me. There's a related file. Wanta see it?"

"If it's the tape, not on your life. I've seen it a couple of times, and that's - "

Paula spoke up. "Hap, sorry, but I haven't seen it. Would you mind?"

I shrugged, a little grumpily. "I thought we were looking for Suellen."

"We are. I'll have a better feel for the whole thing if I see this. You don't have to look."

So Paula and Saffel went through it. And after a few minutes, so did I, and it's a good thing I did.

"Holy cats," Paula said. "Will you look at that. That wouldn't fool a baby."

I peered over her shoulder. We were getting to the nub of it, the place where Trudi rubs the side of her nose. Immediately, the guy opposite her said something that was lost in the low-fi scrape and whang of the country music. Trudi cocked an eye at him, and winked, and it wasn't long after that, that the attack came, the spurting blood and the hideous zoom-in on Trudi's dying face.

When it was over, I asked Len Saffel for a copy of the face shot of Trudi. While it was laboriously printing, I asked what he knew about the video, and got the same answer I had before, that some tourist had been making a vacation videotape, and had happened to catch the fatal scene.

"Tape was confiscated by the Stone County Sheriff," Saffel said. "According to this file."

"Mr. Saffel, that is one hell of a data base you got there. No wonder you know everything that's going on. Thanks for your help, and we've got to be going."

"My pleasure. Say hi to Forde for me, and tell him get up outa that chair and join the human race."

"Once in a while he does, but only so he can sit by himself on a riverbank, pretending to fish. C'mon, Paula."

"What's the rush?" Paula wanted to know, when we were back on the Harley. "You got someplace special to go?"

"Hush," I said. "Put on your helmet."

Suellen had equipped the Harley with a pair of crash helmets with built-in intercoms, which I figured would let us talk with a little more privacy than we'd get standing in front of the newspaper office.

When we were mounted and in radio contact, Paula said, "OK. Now, what is it?"

"Find us someplace we can sit and think. Let me just give you something to chew on, though, while you're driving. That's not the same tape I saw."

"What? How do you know?"

"In the one I saw, the camera panned around the room after Trudi signaled by rubbing her nose. In this one, it stayed right on Trudi. While we're finding a nice cool bar somewhere, why don't you see how many different explanations you can come up with for that, and where they all lead?"

Paula took a sip of Wal-Mart chardonnay and started ticking off fingers. "One: There were two tourists with video cameras there. Two: You didn't remember right, which I'm discounting at the start. Three: One of them's fake."

I sampled my insipid "microbrew" and looked around. We were in a place called the Slaughterhouse Grille down by the stockyards, and there was a scattering of what might plausibly have been cattle breeders at the bar. No one close enough to hear us was paying any attention. I pointed at the last finger.

"Bingo. And if one of them is a fake, ..."

"Which one? No, wait.... They both are! Could be, anyways. Holy shit!"

"Keep it down. We haven't eliminated the possibility that there were two tapes of the same death. Just, I guess I would find that a little surprising. The close-ups at the end were almost identical. I don't think there'd be room for two cameras to crowd in like that, even if we admit that there could have been two tourists that heartless in one room."

"No, and I never saw any other camera in that tape he just ran. What about the other one?"

"Nope." I thought about it. "Two cameras, and neither one ever gets into the other's field of view, while they're jostling in to get a close-up? I don't believe it."

"OK, so it's two separate incidents. I suppose it's possible one of them is a real death, but I doubt it like hell, and they can't both be. Where does that leave us?"

"I don't know. I can't think straight right now, I'm so disgusted with that goddamn woman. Jesus! When I think how Suellen suffered about that! And all the time, Trudi was selling her a goddamn lie that she had to know would break Suellen's heart."

Yes, and I'll record something here that I didn't care to bore Paula with. I had been mourning Trudi just a little myself. Which tells you something about hatred, doesn't it? But there was a time when I thought she and I were working side by side, and if it was a prickly sort of working, full of digs and put-downs and one-upping, still, I admired her guts and brains. I thought she was "authentic." I certainly knew she was as hot as a dimestore laptop. I didn't even hate myself all that much for sleeping with her the one time. I was depressed and lonely, and I guess she was, too.

If so, the tearful bed we shared was the ticket, because she recovered right after that and sold me out, and my son, and damn near killed Lee while she was at it. So she made a perfect hated one, and I was happy as a clam hating her, steeped in the chill and tangy broth of contempt. And when I heard she was dead, ... Well, there had been a little pang.

Suckered again. I sipped the sweet, watery beer and snorted. "I can't stand liars and game-players."

Paula drooped her head and looked up at me soberly, slantwise. "I'm sorry."

"Not your doing."

"Not that. I meant, I'm sorry about jerking your chain before, when you couldn't remember Len Saffel's name. It was just, I knew all you were thinking about was how you were never going to remember it. I figured you'd remember OK, if I just took your mind off of forgetting for a couple of minutes. It worked, but I didn't mean to ... to, whatever." She tossed a hand. "Tease you, insult you. I know you're off limits. I apologize."

She really did look repentant. "Aw," I said. "Forget it. I'm a crusty old jackass. You did what you could with the materials at hand. That's what I tell all my clients to start with." I shut up kind of abruptly, since I didn't want her to think I considered her a client. I was still miles from wanting to get into her tenure ruckus.

"Anyhow," I bumbled. "I'm sorry I called you a whore."

"Hey." She tossed off the rest of her wine, grimacing. "I am one, remember?"

"And you vote."

She stood and grinned down at me. "Bet your ass. I gotta use the Ladies'."

As she walked out, a bulky guy with crisp little grey waves in his hair, a good-sized bandage over one cheek, and one of those Texas style, sucked-in upper lips walked past us. He'd been in time to hear the last thing Paula said, and he snapped his head around for a double take. It made him bump into the waitress, and he made elaborate avoidance moves while she juggled a pair of beers on a tray. Somehow, it ended with his patting her ass. The bandage, and whatever interior damage it may have covered, didn't seem to cramp his style much. The waitress showed him a millimeter of tongue.

"Good afternoon, Mister Verry."

"Afternoon, Cindy. 'Scuse my clumsiness."

"You're surely excused, sir."

Paula was far enough toward the Ladies' that she missed it. I went after her and caught her at a little hallway off the entrance that housed the facilities.

"When you come back," I muttered. "Get a look at the guy that just came in, but don't talk to him. That's infamous Amos."

The restrooms were paired up in the hallway, which was painted to look like cattle chutes in a stockyard. I headed for the door marked with a male symbol. When I'd been in there long enough, I came out and looked around for Paula.

It took a while to find her, because of the way Amos Verry was cozied up against her at the bar. He stood with one elbow up next to his martini, hinged out from the bar and angled toward Paula, who was draped backwards, both elbows on the bar, head thrown back and looking him right in the eye that wasn't partly eclipsed by bandage. My God, the Pope would have cozied up. When she saw me looking, Paula put a hand on Verry's bicep and whispered something; I thought I lip-read "wee-wee." She walked past me without a glance, headed for the Ladies'.

OK, I thought. You don't have to draw me a map. I looked around the bar, and at my watch, taking the attitude of one stood up by a date for drinks. Amos Verry looked past me at the swing of Paula's marvelous butt, and rolled his free eye, muttering something that I didn't catch, but which convulsed a little circle of hench-guys. I looked at my watch once more, and headed back to the cattle chutes, fuming.

Paula was there with her finger to her lips. She pressed the key to the Harley into my hand and muttered, "See you back at the ranch."

"I told you, don't - " I said.

"Tsht," she reasoned, and ended the discussion by flouncing through the door of the ladies', beyond whose ringéd cross I dared not press my case.

I grunted, and went back into the gents'. While I was there, taking advantage of the facilities this time - you can only resist the power of suggestion so long, at my age - I tried to think of a way to tell Paula she was playing with fire.

And decided, to hell with the jade. I was here for Suellen; Paula Vanek was not only a grown-up, but a professional, who fancied herself well able to handle horny men. Fine. Maybe she would learn something we could use to find Suellen, and get her and ourselves the hell out of this part of the world. Meanwhile, I would take the Harley back to the crazy little motel and see if they had a cabin for me, and maybe a bar that would stock a decent brand of beer.

When I came out of the can, I didn't glance in the direction of the bar longer than to see Paula and Amos Verry lobbing body-language bombs at each other and laughing like a pair of drunks in a fistfight. I wondered if that was part of Paula's pre-transactional interview, and if so, how Amos Verry was adding up in her personality inventories. She seemed to have lost a lot of the shadowed weariness that I'd thought was part of her appeal. Probably it was inhibitions.

I found myself on the street, staring peevishly at the Harley with the key in my hand, host to a rainbow of mixed emotions, each of them at least forty percent indignation.

OK. Start with finding the ignition. Shove the key in. Wham! Good! Helmet: still there, as was Paula's. She might need it where she was going, but she would just have to ride this skateboard without pads. It would be nice to keep that radio link, but probably what she had in mind for the next little while wouldn't do as well in a crash helmet.

*

I won't embarrass myself with a bruising account of driving that Harley back to the Shady Stop Motor Hotel. My only other experience with powered, two-wheel transport was a little motorbike that Lee and I rented on a vacation in Bermuda. Enough of the basic controls were the same - with the exceptions of the Harley's touchy and unpredictable clutch and its orders-of-magnitude greater weight, power, and speed - that it was fatally easy to get it going, and damn near impossible to keep it under control. I popped wheelies twice, the first time dumping myself onto the road, to the great amusement of a watching drunk.

By the time we got there, around seven o'clock, the Harley and I were both scraped, overheated, weary, and short-tempered. I pulled up next to Cabin Three, shaking with relief and fatigue in the blazing tag-end of a Missouri dog day, while trucks that had damn near killed me roared past on the Interstate, and cicadas shrieked about the heat; *Jeez, 103 degrees.*

I kicked down at the stand, missed it, and gave myself a last nice gouge on the ankle.

"Tsht," I snarled, showing that I was able to learn from younger colleagues. After a little more explicit language I felt silly, so I stood the fuming Harley on its little stand, stripped the helmet from my sweat-soaked head, and limped over to the Office-cabin. It was locked and empty.

There was a sign on the door, *Gone to diner, back in 15 min.* It was smudged and dog-eared, and had probably been put up and taken down thousands of times. God knew how long it had been up this time, or what "*15 min*" really meant. The Shady Stop Motor Hotel didn't do so damn much business, evidently, that it could afford backup staff. I looked for a way to express exactly how I was feeling, and not spoil it by making myself feel silly.

"Damn it," I muttered. It was so superlatively short of what I was thinking, that the self-control involved in saying only that was as painful as if I'd pounded the fake-stone walls of the office with my naked fist. It gave a grim kind of satisfaction. I limped back to Cabin Three, trying to think of something useful to think. *Cold Beer* said a sign on the window of a little store on the service-road side of the Shady Stop. Good enough. Start there.

The D & J Deli looked very unlikely to stock Pilsner Urquell, and such proved to be the case. But they did have Sam Adams, which I will drink when I must. And it was cold. When I got back to Cabin Three, I didn't even dither. My suitcase was in there. I walked around to the window that didn't have the air conditioner in it, and jimmied it up with a screwdriver from the Harley's tool kit. Silly woman didn't even lock her windows, Jesus Christ.

I put five of the Adamses into the little refrigerator in the self-catering alcove, and took the sixth into the bathroom. I stripped and added my stinking, sweaty clothes to the pile of female stuff that was mounded on the back of the toilet. I took a shower, leaning against the wall, sucking beer and ignoring the green mildew, as I'm sure I was meant to do. The soap - a cake about the thickness of a credit card that had already laid down most of its short life at the hands and bodies of Paula and Suellen - did not lather in the limestone water of this region. A scuzzy mixture of sweat, soap scum, and oozy blood from my scraped ankle swirled reluctantly around the drain, putting me in mind of Hitchcock. Fine, c'mon in, Norman.

I selected the least wet and skanky towel, and used it, quitting when the towel and I reached a standoff as to which of us was drying which. I visited the controls on the air conditioner, and found them already twisted around to "MAX" to produce the mildewy, clogged-filter breeze that was the best the thing could do. I sat on the bed with the towel around my waist and a fresh beer in my fist. I turned on the nautical bedside lamp, and by its parchment glow dug a ballpoint and a pad of paper out of the desk drawer. I leaned back, and every joint in my body creaked and pinged with relief. I pulled the lamp closer and wrote a Roman I at the top of the pad.

Now, I thought. Let's think this through.

*

A car door slammed in the wilderness of my skull. The scream of rubber on the service road woke me in time to hear the rattle of a key in the door. Shit, there I lay with nothing but a towel - but no, not even that, it had escaped while I slept, and it took some half-panicked fumbling before I could sort it out from the chenille beneath it. I re-wrapped, and the door opened.

Paula Vanek came into the room, and stopped with a gasp

of fear.

"Sorry," I said. "It's just me. The Office was ..."

I trailed off because I wasn't getting through. Paula was staring at me as if she'd never seen me before, her face a study in fear and something even more wrenching.

"What?" I said. "Paula, what is it? What happened?"

Paula said nothing, still. She began to shrink before my eyes like the Wicked Witch of the West, drooping and knee-buckling until she was a little mound on the floor of the cabin.

I never seen a fella look as whupped on as that man done. I jumped off the bed and shut the door behind her.

"Paula, hey. What's the matter?"

"Hap?" I could barely hear her.

"It's Hap, Paula. Can you stand up? Let's - "

"Hap?"

"Yes, it's me, it's Hap. What happened?"

"I, I ... oh, my God." She began trying not to cry, gritting her teeth against the sobs, sounding like someone on the rack.

My cue to scoop her featherwise in my manly arms and carry her to the bed, hey? Listen, I squatted on the floor next to her, and got her arms around my neck, and I lifted with my legs, not my back, and skinny as she was, she still felt like a good solid chunk of woman to me. For one thing, she was so damn limp, she was barely more than a dead weight.

I laid her out in the dim light of the nautical lamp, and put a finger under the corner of her jaw. Her pulse was heavy and fast, as if she'd run all the way from Big Spring. I shifted the hand to her cheek, and found it clammy in the barely tempered heat of the room. I went into the bathroom and ran cool water over a washcloth, and smoothed the sweaty hair away from her eyes. She flinched at its touch.

"Paula, what happened? Did he rape you?"

She shook her head. But when she'd done that long enough to convey the message, she just kept shaking it from side to side, as if begging me not to ... what? Ask her any more questions? Touch her? Do anything more to her than had already been done?

I took off her shoes and skirt, I checked her for blood, bruises, and obvious broken bones – all negative, as far as I could see – and I wrapped her in the chenille bedspread, tightly enough to give her some support and security. I left the little lamp on, but moved it as far from her as its cord would allow, and I settled into an armchair with my feet up on the bed, and monitored her breathing for as long as I could stay awake, cursing Amos Verry, cursing Paula. The green numbers on the clock radio read 1:51.

At some point, I woke up enough to wrap myself in the spare blanket, and when I did that, Paula woke up and went into the bathroom. She emerged a long time later, smelling of toothpaste, and re-wrapped herself in the bedspread. And that was the last I knew until daylight.

10.

She was up when I woke in the relative cool and quiet of dawn. The discouraged air conditioner had prevailed at last, and Paula sat at the enamel table, hands wrapping a cup of instant coffee. The weariness was back in her face, deeper than I'd ever seen it.

She tipped her head sideways at the jar of Flavor Crystals and a pot of hot water. "Coffee first, or you want to put some clothes on? Christ, you snore."

I took my suitcase and retired with some small dignity to the bathroom. When I came out, she was pouring boiling water into a mug. She looked like a ten-year-old girl telling herself to be brave and plucky, like on TV. The coffee she handed me had circular waves on its surface.

"Here you go." She patted my arm. "Hap, thank you for taking care of me. I came to in the dark, and there you were, by God, sitting up with me like you were my mother or something, and I had a fever. That helped." She smiled. Pluckily. "It helped a lot."

I didn't tell her I was sitting up because I wasn't about to lie down with her, and had nowhere else to go. "Forget it, you'd do the same. What happened to you last night?"

She shuddered. "That bastard. I expect you can figure out the first part of it without much trouble. He bought me a couple drinks and took me to this little motel out by the airport. Cheesy little plastic place, but hell, we weren't moving in. He looked a little surprised when I named my fee. I never go into one of those transactions without everything agreed up front. He kind of grinned and shrugged, and said he hadn't thought I was that kind of girl, but OK."

"Hold on," I said. "You don't have to tell me too much of this."

"I need to talk it out. Does it bother you?"

I thought about that. Would I be bothered if some zookeeper unburdened himself about getting his pandas to breed? "Go ahead."

"So we went to bed. It was a little rough, but nothing I couldn't handle all right. He seemed to have a good time, though I gotta say, he didn't exactly make the earth move."

I opened my mouth to say, "And you?" and buried it in the mug, sloshing scalding pseudocoffee into my mouth. I sucked air and swore.

"OK," I said, over the rough spot on my tongue. "But then...?"

She said nothing for a moment. Her face was as hooded and tough as a state trooper peering into fresh wreckage. When she spoke, it was trooper testimony.

"I said, I hope that was as nice for you as it was for me, and that'll be $400. He kind of laughed and shook his head, and said, Well, if it was that nice, maybe you don't need my money, do you, sweetheart?"

"Uh oh."

Paula shook her head. "I told him, Sorry, sir, we had a deal. You don't look like a welcher to me." She took a few long breaths. "That was probably a mistake."

She was silent long enough that I risked another sip of coffee. "Uh huh," I said, gently.

"He got mad. He said Amos Verry wasn't the kind of guy that had to buy women, hadn't for years, and he wasn't going to start now for a two-bit whore he could get busted for vagrancy and solicitation and into the lockup so fast it'd make my head swim." She snorted, which I took as a good sign. "Guy has a gift for fresh and inventive language."

"Ya," I sighed. "Is there some prostitute wisdom about cutting your losses and getting the hell out?"

She gave me a weary look. "That's all it's about, pal. But there was no getting out from this one. I had offended Mr. Verry. I challenged his manhood, I guess, by implying that anybody'd think they were owed money after the privilege of getting pronged by the biggest stud in Greene County, Missouri. He proceeded to retaliate."

"He assaulted you?"

She choked a laugh, a single *Ha.* "He damn well demolished me, Hap. The first thing he did, he took all my clothes and wadded 'em up and threw them out the front door. I was right behind him, saying, Hey, what the, and he turned around and pinned my arms behind me and walked me over to this connecting door to the next room, and one of his buddies from that bar is there, with a big, tough-looking woman. 'Have a look at this,' he says, and he's shoving me at them. 'It wants 400 bucks. What do you say?' And these people look me up and down good. The guy says, Aw, give her twenty-seven fifty; and the woman says, Fifteen bucks tops."

She stood then, and began to pace. "Then he says, 'Well, maybe we can maybe persuade her down.' And he and his friends started in, and they kept at me for hours and hours, and they never once let up."

She wrapped her arms around herself. "It wasn't that they were hitting me, or almost anything that crude. I checked myself this morning, and there's nothing you could show a cop or a doctor. They just made life hell for me, physically, and mentally, and - I don't know. Spiritually. Almost all of it was from Verry. The others were there mostly to keep me from getting away. Otherwise, they mostly watched, which was bad enough. He figured out things to say or do to me that made me feel like shit. Like, he picked me up like a rag doll, and he shook me and threw me down on the bed so hard, I bounced off onto the floor. He did that ten or twenty times, Hap. Hoping I'd sprain something, or break a rib maybe. He knows these, these wrestling holds, where you're helpless and immobilized. He teased, and he prickled and chafed and tweaked, and humiliated, God..."

She looked at me, wide-eyed, shaking, sweating with the memory. "He just kept it up and kept it up. He put on some pants while the woman was holding me with my face against the rug, so then he's dressed and I'm the only naked one, and that makes it worse. I had to beg him to let me go in the john and vomit. I tried to get to the phone, but he's so strong, and quick, he made a game out of that, which I lost, of course. There was just nothing I could do but take it, and keep on taking it."

She slumped into her chair, laughing in a way that was hard to tell from sobbing. "And the crazy thing is, he never got tired of it. It got to where I was begging him for my life. He was laughing and killing me little by little, and I think I'd be dead, or it'd be going on still; but some time after midnight, he got a call on his cell phone. He kind of signaled the other two to keep me quiet, and they held me with my face in the rug again. And when he hung up he said - "

She grinned wanly at me. "Get this, Hap. He says, 'C'mon, Florrie, we got a busy day tomorrow.' He told the other guy to take me for a cruise. He and the woman left."

"Florrie? It was Florrie Verry?"

Paula nodded. "Don't think there's that many Florries in Springfield, do you?"

"Doubtful. How lovely that she shares his interests."

"Oh, and does she ever. There was a TV on in that other room, with a black-and-white picture of a bed that looked kind of familiar. When Amos talked, you could hear it coming out of the TV."

"Jesus." Not that one hadn't heard of such things. But for God's sake, in Missouri?

"Oh, yes." She was silent for a while, and then took a long breath. "OK, well, there I was with the last guy." She shuddered.

"An armed and dangerous Irishman named Arthur, who had the job of driving me out in the country and dumping me, before he could call it a night. Arthur looked tired, and sort of unfulfilled. I persuaded him to bring me here instead."

"How - no. I'm not going to ask. Come here."

"I'm all right."

"I can see that. This is for me. Come here."

She stood and walked toward me, as wary as a wild animal. Her forehead was rough and swollen with what might have been rug burns. I very carefully took one of her hands between mine, and examined it. The tips of her fingers were red too, maybe from clawing at things to keep her balance or her dignity. I began, with a pitying gesture, to fold them into her palm, and to enclose the folded hand in mine. Thinking, There, there, little lady. Telling myself, This is nothing but sympathy, This is just being a decent human being; while something sat in the back of my head and called me eighty kinds of a fool to show the least tenderness to a chuckle-headed academic prostitute. Well, she wasn't having it in any case.

She took back the enfolded hand and stepped away from me. "What do you mean, it's for you? I appreciate your evident concern. But if you have any notion of that leading to anything else, let me set you straight, Dr. Maryland. What happened to me is strictly one of the hazards of my line of research, as if Jane Goodall had been roughed up by one of her gorillas, because she wasn't careful enough. I'm not some damn little damsel."

"Heaven forbid," I said, stiffly enough. "Do you think that's what happened to Suellen?"

Her eyes narrowed. "No, and I'll tell you why. After I'd - "
She broke off, and lifted her chin defiantly. "After I successfully
bargained with Arthur, he told me Verry was looking for a woman
to beat up, because the last one he'd hit on had made a fool out of
him. It was just my lucky day he got me instead of that waitress."

"What makes you think it was Suellen?"

She looked surprised that I didn't get it. "Well, timing for
one thing. We know he had a lunch date with her three days ago
now, and that's when she disappeared. I'd bet my ass he came on
to her. Maybe she played along for a while, to see what she could
find out. But when push came to shove, I'd guess it was him that
got shoved, wouldn't you think? After the stuff she was into with
that Neville guy?"

"You think maybe that bandage on his face came from
Suellen?"

Paula grinned, and for that few seconds, she really did look
all right. "I hope so. Anyhow, the buddy said part of the
embarrassment was that it was a lesbian that roughed him up."

"Ah. Did the buddy know what happened to this lesbian?"

"I asked. He just laughed and asked if I was a lesbian, too.
Don't think I wasn't tempted to tell him yes, but I'll tell you, Hap, I
couldn't have taken one more thing. But when he dumped me out,
he said something like, Your freak dyke friend has gone to join the
other freaks."

"What do you suppose that means?"

"I think we ought to see if there's any kind of lesbian

organization here, or maybe in Branson, or Stone County. But this is by far the biggest town in this part of the country. Let's start here."

I will say this: I would have been at a loss to find and penetrate the lesbian community of Springfield, Missouri by myself. Paula took the obvious shortcut of Harleying us to the neighborhood of Southwest Missouri State, dropping me at a used book store, and rumbling down to the corner of Grand and National to see who turned their heads with some appreciation.

I moseyed back to the mysteries and found an early edition of A Purple Place for Dying on sale for a buck. You want to get those when you can, so you don't have to pay all kinds of money for the reissues with the Carl Hiaasen introduction that, once you've read it, you don't need to read it over and over.

By the time I'd done that, and read a few pages, I heard the Harley grumbling outside, and Paula walked in with what I guessed was a captive lesbian in tow. She was a thirtyish woman, skinny as straw, with a blonde pigtail that reached her knees.

"Hap, meet Patsy Fogg," she said, and Patsy held out a skinny hand. Her wrist was about an inch around, coated with straw-colored fuzz. "Patsy's secretary of the local Human Rights chapter. Hap's my old man."

"Paula's just being literal there, Patsy," I said. "Did she tell you who we're looking for?"

"Yeah," Patsy said, and looked a little resentful. "It's not like we have regular sabbaths."

"We know. But I'll tell you, we're kind of grasping at - we're trying everything we can think of. We had some slight evidence that Suellen might have joined a lesbian group, just in the last day or so."

"You got a pitcher?"

"You'd know her. Buzz cut, very fit and strong, let's see... an inch or two taller than Paula, here."

Patsy reached behind herself and retrieved her braid, so she could chew on the end. "I don't think so. Around here, it's pretty much the same faces - " She frowned. "Wait a sec. She into martial arts?"

"Yes. Something called... damn. I know it means 'Land Hard' in Korean."

"Yeah, I wouldn't know about that, but I know who would. You got a couple minutes?"

"You bet. Shall we come with you?"

"Huh uh. Wait here." Patsy went out through the front door fast enough that her pigtail was sticking out behind and almost got slammed in it.

I winked at Paula. "Pretty good. What did you do, pose as an anthropologist?"

"More or less. I hope this isn't another dead end." The shadows were deep under her eyes, and the momentary rush of finding herself alive and safe this morning was wearing off. I tried to think of something to do or say that wouldn't be another hug, and gave it up when it was obvious the moment had passed.

"They have comfy chairs and reading lamps back there.

Why don't you pull a book off a shelf and pose as a customer?"

She blew a short razzberry. "I'm fine."

"Good for you. Lee was always saying that."

She tipped her head, as if considering how to take that high a compliment, and turned to a shelf of travel books. I went to the cash register with my Purple Place. And by the time I'd done the small business, Paula was in a comfy chair with Byways in Fife and the East Neuk, and Patsy was back.

She had a kid with her who looked like he might be higher up the Land Hard scale than a Gray. In fact he was himself black, and as knottily constructed as Suellen or Neville on their best day.

"This here's Royce," Patsy said. "He might of seen your friend."

"Pleased to meet you, Royce. Suellen's a maybe couple of inches taller - "

Royce held up a hand. "Fi' foot seven," he rumbled. "Hunnert thirty two. Thanks, Patchy, I'll take it from here." He watched Patsy Fogg out the door, and turned to us. "Yeah, blonde buzz cut, leather wristbands, attitude a yard long. Thew a white boy lawyer out the front window of Miz Mary Alice's Bikini Club a couple nights ago."

"Hot damn," I said. It was like somebody saying they'd seen Aslan. "That's got to be Suellen."

He shrugged. "Told me her name was Happy. 'Call me Hap,' she says, so I done. We'd arm-wrestled for beers, which I beat her of course, but I tell you, that was one strong dyke. Told me she'd a beat me if she'd had a chance to work out the last week.

So I says, fine, chickie, you work out, and I'll see you here in a week. We was gettin on pretty good, for a sort of a odd couple, see what I'm sayin. The lawyer boy come in - "

"Amos Verry?"

Royce nodded, a little cool about being interrupted. "That's the man. Know him?"

"Not personally."

"I do," Paula said; her face had the trooper look again. "Go on."

"Mist' Amos Verry ain't the man to trifle with in this town, what I hear. Miz Mary Alice runs her place a little loose, and you gotta be on your guard, you go there, or else tough enough that nobody messes with you."

Royce flexed an arm thoughtfully, reassuring himself and us that he was that tough. "Anyways, he enjoys slummin around places most gentry stay out of, like he was sayin, Watch me, I go where I damn please. And he does enjoy chasin skirt, wherever he finds it. He had a couple chickies with him I never seen before, and he brings his lady friends over where we're sitting. He's sayin, Bet you little girls never met a hunnert percent purebred lesbian dyke before, well, I'm gonna show you one. Suellen - "

Royce broke off and looked surprised. "Tha's right, that's what he called her, Suellen. She was havin me on, with that Happy talk."

"Keep talking," I said.

"He says, 'Suellen's momma was a client of mine, that wound up in a bad place.' And he starts to add, 'And she damn well had it coming, the slut'."

He tilted his head, wanting to be accurate. "Well, he said it. He got that far. He was fixing to elaborate, but Happy Suellen jumps up, and she gets Mist' Verry by the collar and the nuts, and she frog-marches him straight on towards the front, knockin tables over, goldfish flyin, beer, women gettin it down their fronts. An' I tell you, Bam! Straight out through that mullion window, musta caused a million bucks damage."

Royce looked thoughtful. "Understand, I coulda done that, but for a chickie to have that kind of balls, shee-it... Mista Verry ends up out on the street, and your friend runs back past me, and she says, 'God sake, call Paula an' tell her I gotta get outa town, this very second. This place got a back way?' Course, it does, anyplace like that got at least two. I showed her one, and time I got her out the door, Mist' Verry's coming back in, and I see he's carryin. Now, shit, I ain't scared of him or nobody, but I ain't Superman, neither, bullets don't bounce offa me. I got shot one time, and I'm here to tell anybody it don't feel so - "

"For Christ's sake!" Paula yelled, and she grabbed a handful of Royce's sleeve while two or three poetry shoppers glared at her over their slim volumes. "Why didn't you give me the message?"

Royce drew back his head, peeled her fingers off his sleeve, and gave her the full urban-legend stare. "Cause the dyke din't give me your contact information, chickie," he said. "She was far too flustered about getting out a Miz Mary Alice's with her ass in one piece. So to speak." He brightened. "You Paula?"

Paula fell back into the comfy chair. "Yes. Christ, we almost found her, and now she's gone again." She turned to Royce. "And of course, you have no idea in the world where she was going."

"Course I do. Think I'm some shuffle-foot darkie? I axed her. She's goin to Branson. I gave her a lift out where she could hitch."

*

I returned the Saturn to Hertz with a sense of relief, and we droned the Harley south on US 65. "I think we have to conclude," I said, "that Amos Verry kept his lunch appointment with Suellen."

It was a good few seconds before Paula's voice crackled in my helmet. "Why'd he pretend he didn't?"

"Well, how about, he's embarrassed about the encounter in - what was that place? Aunt Alice? Or something else that happened at the lunch that made Suellen blow up without much provocation later."

"Miz Mary Alice. Ya, maybe. Seems thin to me, but Christ, the guy's a psychopath. Which doesn't mean there's no explaining him. Just, I don't think we've got enough information to account for things he might do."

"I'd think you had all the data you cared to get."

Paula arched her back and said nothing for a mile or two. I watched the scenery over her head - you sit up pretty high on the back seat of a Harley - while the highway plunged between limestone bluffs into the hill-and-hollow country of the southwest corner of Missouri. Something else was bothering me worse than Amos Verry's foibles.

"You want to chew on something, try this. Why didn't Suellen get in touch with you after her lunch with Verry? Why hasn't she up to now? Doesn't she know you'd be worried?"

Paula let some more road slip under us. The sun blazed from straight overhead, and the wind of our passage was dragon's breath. A little rest area baked at the side of the road, and Paula took us under the pine shade of a picnic area.

"I think he told her something that upset her so much that nothing else mattered."

I thought about that. "What, that her mother's death was a fake, and she's alive somewhere? Why wouldn't she come skipping back to Cabin Three burbling over with the great news? Why wouldn't it make more sense to go down to Branson with you and the Harley, instead of hitching by herself?"

Paula pulled off her helmet and took a long drink from one of the water bottles. Her hair was soaked with sweat and matted to her head. The rug burns on her face were bright red. "Maybe she was as mad about being fooled as you were. Madder, or more upset anyway, since it was her mother, not just an old girl friend. Anyhow, it wasn't like she totally forgot me. She told Royce to get in touch with me."

"But without telling him how. I think Verry must have told her something else. She was already wrecked after she just talked to him on the phone about her mother's supposed death. What else could there be? I have to wonder if she was intending to go back to Shady Stop, but she needed a drink, and she was pretty well along when Amos Verry showed up. She loses it with him, and then gets scared and beats it without going back to you."

I thought for a moment about how wise it would be to raise what was really bothering me, and then plunged ahead. "Also, remember what Len Saffel said about the rumors that Amos Verry is also connected to much bigger, organized-crime kinds of stuff, including prostitution. Thing is, we may be out in the sticks here, but Springfield isn't Gabbro, and Kansas City's not that far away. You're talking really serious warfare when you tweak around with those guys. Maybe serious enough that he quits kidding around with "I'm gonna show you a 100% lesbian dyke, ladies," and comes after her with lethal force. And succeeds, maybe."

Paula scared the hell out of me then by grabbing my arm. In the corner of my eye, I saw somebody coming toward us, which was a little alarming, given that the rest area had been deserted when we pulled in, and there was no place to hide. I spun, and snorted.

A dust devil, bigger than the one in the airport parking lot and bulked out with limestone dust, dead leaves, and two or three scraps of newspaper, moseyed across the baking pavement, whispering and gossiping. It sucked in dust and spat it out, and it looked at least as solid and permanent as wispy Patsy Fogg. I wondered if it was the one from the airport, grown fat and footloose since I'd seen it. But no, those things die at night. Don't they? Just another pattern that it would do no good to form an attachment to. We watched the baby tornado dance and snuffle down the edge of the road, sowing havoc among the ditch dwellers, rattling a home-painted sign for Wonder Cave. An 18-wheeler raved by, engine-braking down the grade while doing 70, and when it was gone, so was the dust devil.

I said, "Suellen's mother was not a girl friend, thanks. Maybe Suellen was trying to protect you, not leading Verry to where you were staying."

Paula shook herself and let go of my arm. "Maybe. Yeah, and let's think about that, how he shows up at this dive with a couple of straight women, sounding like he knew she was going to be there."

"Uh huh. Maybe people tell him things. Maybe he has an army of spies and sycophants. And who were those women he was escorting around anyhow? New blood that he maybe suckered off of farms to make it big in country music, and they're going to end up on street corners in Rolla or KC? He can't let a Suellen Ransom show him up in front of a couple of rookie recruits. Christ, Paula. We've got to quit spooking ourselves, guessing. We're out on a limb over our heads."

She grinned. "Without a paddle. Let's go, then. What was that you were telling me about her, her guardian guy. How'd it go? Blunder on - "

I nodded. Wet Parsonage's crime-fighting formula. "Blunder straight ahead until somebody jumps you. The one that beats you up the worst is the one that did it."

She put on the helmet and gave me a plucky face through the shadows and the rug burns. "See? We've already made a lot of progress on that."

11.

We drove into Branson in the early afternoon. We were pretty hungry, and we didn't have far to seek for lunch options. The town consists of a compact rectangle, maybe five by six blocks of houses, stores, and a train station down by the White River, that is adequate to the town's native population of a couple of thousand souls; and a sprawl of theaters, mini-golfs, motels, and tourist traps splayed out over miles of ridgetops, radiating in four or five directions from the "old town" and dominated by unrelievedly congested miles of such stuff along US 76.

"Lordy," Paula muttered in my headset, while we rumbled past the offerings. "What do you want first, Christian books, go-karts, country music, or lunch?"

"Well, I was hoping to pick up a quilt for these cold nights. Let's get some lunch."

The place we found was crowded but cheap, and had singing waiters. The freckled young lady that took our order reappeared in about ten minutes with a couple of gigantic burgers, haystacks of fries, six or eight slices of tomato and pickle each, two towering milkshakes, and a chubby sidekick, with whom she proceeded to croon "Jesus Loves Me As I Am" in close harmony as soon as she'd dropped the vittles. Paula and I listened in appreciative disbelief, munching like contented cows.

"Know what?" Paula managed at last.

"Mmf?"

"I think it might be a little tougher to get in touch with the lesbian community here than it was in Springfield."

"If there even is one. I think we'd be talking about a 'community' of about three, the majority of them still in the closet."

Paula looked around at the fresh-faced employees and the jam of clientele. Most of the customers were overweight, a lot of them grossly fat. It was as if all the lard in the great Midwest had melted in the furnace of the summer and pooled against the Ozarks here at the bottom of Missouri. Maybe I'm being unfair, but my Lord.

"Four, counting Suellen," Paula said. "Remember, she was dead set to get down here, so she had a place in mind to go. No, listen, this place isn't so different from anywhere else. There's probably plenty of un-straight folks out there. It's just going to take a little longer to find them. What do you say to the waitress?"

I looked at Freckle-face, now laying her gigantic offerings before a family of four that must have run to a half-ton on the hoof, counting a seven-year-old in pigtails. The waitress was grinning at the massive Head of Household, giving him a little hip-twitch to pump up the tip. While I watched, she asked them if they had a favorite hymn.

I grinned. "No way."

"Put money on it?"

"Sure. I'm so broke, I'll even take your money." I reconsidered. "Just, not half of it, mind."

"Five bucks says either she's gay, or she knows somebody that is."

"Well, 'knows somebody,' that opens it out a lot. But if you need motivation, sure, you're on. Maybe you'll catch some luck."

What Paula caught was a slap from a freckled arm and a ruckus that had the manager firing the waitress on the spot, and hiring her back on the same spot when tearfully apprised of Paula's insulting –

"I just asked her a question," Paula said. "I'm an anthropologist, for Christ's sake."

"Ma'am, then you will have to do your anthologizing somewhere else. I am asking you to apologize to Christie here, as I am doing myself, and then to leave Uncle Sam's forthwith."

"We haven't paid," was all Paula could think of.

"No need. Sir, you are with this lady? Will you be so good as to escort her from the premises? And to prevail upon her to keep her filthy questions to herself if she cannot apologize for them? And if I may say so, sir, you seem a decent sorta fellow - " All this time, the manager was gracefully hustling us out - jeez, not even the front door, but out through the kitchen - "And I most earnestly request sir, you encourage her not to take the Savior's name in vain. A day is coming, perhaps sooner than we can know, when she will be calling it in earnest."

Genteel shove, introducing us to a midblock vista of trash cans and parking lots. We were in a kind of half-alley, bounded on one side by the backs of stores and restaurants. A rat looked up from his work, a little resentfully, and trundled into the shadow of a trash can.

"Wait - " I said.

Slam.

It was a steel door with a keyhole but no knob. I commenced banging on it with my fist and foot. An image lingered on the edge of my retina, a little smeared from the speed of our passage through the steam and clamor of the kitchen: the half-seen and fragmented sight of a pivot, a sudden bending over a sink full of pots, a head drawn down between muscled shoulders, a rose not quite hidden by a greasy apron.

"Shit," I said. "Suellen's in there."

"What!"

"You heard me, anthologist. C'mon, you guys, for Pete's sake, open up."

The door clicked and swung open. Filling it was the chubby guy whose tenor had filled in the harmonies on "Jesus Loves Me." He looked bigger than I remembered, and not so much chubby as muscular and relaxed. Maybe not so relaxed now.

"Sir?"

I looked past him. The doors to the dining room were swinging to, and there was no one at the sink.

"Never mind. C'mon, Paula. Front door, quick."

I sprinted down the alley, and Paula followed me; which goes to show what kind of smart cops we made. By the time we cleared the end of the block, I heard a door slam in the alley, and the snarl of a light motorcycle engine.

"Shoot," Paula gasped, "Whyn't we split up and go both

ways?"

"Never mind, she probably cut back through one of the other buildings. We can still catch her on the Harley. Thing is, why?"

Paula figured that out by the time we had the helmets on. "The good news is, nobody kidnapped or killed her. The bad news is, she didn't contact me because she didn't want to."

We listened with mouths slightly open to catch the faintest thread of Suellen's bike before Paula started the rumbling mill beneath us. I thought I heard it heading west out 76 past the endless blocks of ticky-tacky.

Paula got us on her trail, and I think we made a whole lot of tourists mad, the way we slammed past the patiently creeping SUV's on the shoulder, mothers on the sidewalks snatching their chubby offspring out of our way, fathers yelling and shaking fingers at us. A lucky glance showed Suellen blocks away from us on a side road, and I pounded Paula's shoulder, just about spilling us, before I remembered I could talk to her through the helmet mike.

"Back! She cut down that street by the BP station!"

Paula leaned us into a desperation turn that had me sure I was going to lose a leg; but she straightened out, and roared down the side street. Luckily, we were in the new part of Branson where there is little or no grid of streets once you're onto a ridgetop, and there was no place Suellen could shake us by turning into.

"Got her now," Paula crowed.

"Fine but why should we have to? Why the hell's she

running away from us?"

"Maybe she'll tell us. She's pulling over."

As we gained on her, it was clear that her motorbike was an underpowered little Vespa, better for delivering pizza than outrunning a Harley.

"Hold it, Paula. Don't push her by getting too close."

"Right."

Paula stopped fifty feet from where Suellen slumped against her sputtering scooter.

I got off the Harley gingerly. "Suellen?"

"Congratulations."

"What's the deal?"

Suellen shut off the scooter and sat in the street next to it, kneading her head with trembling hands. I squatted next to her, and saw tearstreams converge on the point of her chin.

"I don't know what the deal is, Hap," she said, and her voice shook with the effort she made to say it calmly. "I don't... bloody... know. Something really, really bad is going on down here, and I ... Jesus. I don't know what I'm doing. Paula, I'm sorry I made you worry. Hap, I - "

She pulled back from me then, pivoting on her butt in the roadside dust. "Hap? Oh, Christ, you … did you ..." She seemed unable to say it.

"Paula called me, Suellen."

"And you came out here because you were worried? Oh, God, I am the worst, the rottenest troublesome bitch - " All her dislike of showing weakness dissolved. She threw back her head then and howled with grief and perplexity, pounding her breast hard enough to cripple anybody else. People like to tell me that I don't show my feelings enough, I should go around like some human mood ring, turning magenta when I'm feeling blue ... well, whatever. I'll tell you, if I ever take that seriously, I'll sign up for lessons with Suellen. Boy, did she express herself then.

And what she expressed was sorrow, anger, mortification, guilt, ... Jeez. All the emotions that had taken her over since the unwelcome and ill-auguring phone call from Amos Verry that started this mess. In fact, name anything but sunniness or tranquility, and she ran through it on that Branson back street. And here is the story that emerged, some of it in an expository gusher, some in response to questions from me, or to sisterly clucking from Paula.

Amos Verry did not in fact keep his lunch appointment with Suellen. No, but as Suellen was getting ready to slam out the door of the little café and stomp down to Morris, Gerard and Verry to wreak some indignation, a waiter came up to her with a cordless phone.

"Miz Suellen Ransom?

"Yeah? Gimme the goddamn thing. Is it that asshole Verry? Listen, Verry, you asshole, you think - "

"You grew up with a dirty mouth, you know that?"

"Yeah? Who the ... who're you?"

"Your mother."

Silence. Some attempt to consider whether this could be so.

"My mother is dead."

"You wish. Ask me something only I would know."

"Well... Well, why'd you wait five years to send me the beanie baby?"

"I don't know. But anybody could say that."

"Who'd you ship me off to, and why?"

"Wet Parsonage, because you were pregnant, you little slut. Ask me something tough."

"All right, then, Mommy. Who got me pregnant?"

"The Very Reverend Henry Baxter. On his Sunday School bus, so he'd have better dreams about the end of the world. The less said about that bozo, the better."

Well, Suellen said, she'd never known Reverend Baxter's first name, but it was that evangelistic old fraud who'd gotten into her pants a few days before his own private version of The Rapture had snatched him off to heaven; had left Suellen gravid and, in a few weeks, on a bus headed for North Carolina. Nobody else in the world knew those things.

She'd tried to play it cool, finding that the mother she'd thought was dead, whose murder she at first took in stride until she saw it on a snuff porn Web site, was on the other end of a phone line. She acted as if she'd never torn herself apart with guilt and grief, had come out to Missouri for no special reason but to maybe tour a cave and take in a country music show. She asked Trudi where she was. As if, maybe she'd drop by. And another voice came on the line.

"Amos Verry here, Suellen. I seem to keep standing you up, don't I?

We don't have a lot of time for pleasantries here. Your mother has a very urgent message for you, which I'll let her tell it in her own words."

A muffled silence, and a few heavy breaths. *"Ya, this is mommy again. Fuck off, kid."*

"What?"

"Three words, for shit sake. Fuck. Off. Kid."

"Wait a second. I came all the way out here - "

"Well, you always were the dutiful child, weren't you? Where were you five years ago, when I coulda used you?"

"You were - "

"I was dead, right? Sure, who wants to muck around with a corpse? Can't say I blame you, honey. I sure's hell wouldn't of bothered, it'd been you got killed."

Now, that was surely the literal truth, but it hit Suellen right in the guilty spot where she had spent the last weeks hurting. Her knees buckled, and she found herself on the floor of the café, incapable of protesting, of reminding Trudi that, for Pete's sake, it was Trudi who'd washed her hands of Suellen before she even knew whether Wet Parsonage would take her in, or would send her to reform school.

Verry came back on the line and said sympathetic things about how it distressed him when family members quarreled, but that maybe it would be the best thing all around if Suellen took her mama's advice and fucked off.

Suellen tried to fight up through the avalanche of guilt, to quiz Verry about Trudi's apparent death and, if she was not dead, her whereabouts; to wring from Trudi the most trivial acknowledgement, anything that would let her get some footing. The mass of the event, of Trudi's cool sarcasm and Verry's lawyerly condescension was too much for her, as if leagues of mud and boulders were piling on, compressing her, flattening the springy fibers of her life into a seam of muck a quarter-inch thick. It was too much, it was impossible. She crouched at the foot of the cashier's counter, clutching her head, going crazy with grief and guilt. The waiter who'd brought the phone disappeared, and no one else seemed to give a damn about her. Lunchroom customers stepped over her to pay their tabs.

Then, at the very end of the conversation, Trudi said something puzzling. Her voice took on the transparent heartiness of one bucking up a reluctant child. "Run on home, honey," she said. "It's for the best. Say hello to my brand-new grandson."

I shrugged. "Grandson? You don't - "

"Duh," Suellen sobbed. "Of course not. So guess what I just now figured out? That *wasn't Mom*, it couldn't of been. Or maybe they've got her, I don't know, like hostage or something. Maybe they found out that stuff about Reverend Baxter from her before they killed her. Maybe they got somebody who can mimic her voice."

"OK," I said, doubtfully. "But if that's what's happening, why would they take a silly chance like talking about a grandson?"

Suellen was silent on that, and then brightened grotesquely. "Disinformation! Mom caught on to what they were doing, and she planted a false fact, that she knew I'd catch. Hah! Dead or alive, she's still outsmarting 'em."

The power of hope. I didn't see, even granting Suellen's doubtful theory, that it implied any chance Trudi was still alive. The only evidence of that was the fact of the two videotapes, and all they proved was that one of the deaths was faked, not that both were. Or that Trudi had not bought it in some other way afterward, if only to shut her mouth about something.

And whatever was going on here, death and deception seemed to be pretty much the warp and woof of it. Still, Suellen didn't yet know about the second video, and, though I hated to feed false hopes, I filled her in on that. She got the implication right away. She was delighted.

"Sure, see? And here's something else. Either the guy that called me in Gabbro wasn't Amos Verry, or the one I talked to at that diner wasn't. It wasn't the same voice. So who was it with Mom, anyways?"

Paula groaned. "Good Christ, what a mess. Look. I think we need to settle down somewhere with a round of beers and a pencil and paper, and see if we can figure out between us what we know, and what we're guessing. And what we've been conned about, maybe there's a pattern to that, too. C'mere, Suellen. C'mere, Hap."

She peeled her helmet off, and pulled Suellen up off the road into a sweaty embrace. And when they'd done with that, and Suellen had gulped and sniffled some more, they pivoted open and extended an arm each to me. Sweat, muscles, tears, heat, interesting soft points of contact, on a backwoods street in the Far Gone of the Midwest. It made me remember being alive.

*

Paula had a credit card that wasn't maxed yet, and we used it to get a "Unit" at a Residence Inn that would accommodate the three of us in a decent configuration. We parked the Harley and the little Vespa – which Suellen had borrowed from one of the singing waiters in exchange for Land Hard lessons – by the door, and took turns at the shower. Classy place like that, there were actually three fluffy, dry bath towels. I found a market and paid cash for a dozen Urquells. The luxury did bugger-all for our mental acuity.

Halfway down her second beer, Paula tossed her pencil onto the grid of contradictions before her, and crossed her ankles over it.

"Crap," she summarized. "Some geniuses we are. We come out here to find out who murdered your mom, and so far we're not even sure she's dead."

"I came here for Mom," Suellen said. "Dead or alive."

"OK. And I came here to help you out, and Hap came here to help me out."

"But we don't know why she swallowed that fly," I crooned.

Paula giggled. "Maybe we'll die."

That's the thing about Urquell. It tastes so great going down, you forget what it's doing to your brain chemistry. That, and the relief of finding Suellen again - and, for Suellen, the emotional workout she'd gone through in the past days - had us all a bit giddy. Damn giddy, if that's a permissible construction.

But we did establish one new thing, by getting Suellen to compare the phone voices of Amos Verry with what she heard during her brief and violent encounter with him at Miz Mary Alice's Bikini Club. "The second phone call sounds more like him than the one in Gabbro," she concluded. "Let's concentrate on that one."

"OK, fine," Paula said. "But who was the other guy? Why did he say he was Verry?"

I held up a hand. "That sounds to me like something we'll find out down the line somewhere, if ever. Maybe in the process of finding Suellen's mother, or her ... or evidence that she really is dead. If the second call was probably Verry, then we ought to concentrate on him. We know he's at least a thug."

"Ya, plus he's mad as hell at me, after I threw him out that window. We better figure he's the threat."

Paula sat back and ruffled a hand through her hair. "OK, but what threat? How do we even know there is a threat? Sure, he beat me up, but he probably beats up prostitutes all the time, if they don't give him a big discount. Or if they don't come up with their take, if Saffel is right about that."

"Because," Suellen said, sounding like Al Gore explaining something to a Republican, "He's in and out of this thing all the time. Whoever called me first said he was Amos Verry, when come to find out, he probably wasn't. I come out here, and Verry says he'll see me, and gives me the runaround, and then sets up either a fake phone call, or a pathetic one, from my mother, that tries to get me to go back home. He does beat up Paula, and maybe that's no accident. Maybe he's sharper than he acted in that bar. And besides … "

Suellen got up off the big bed where she'd been sprawled, and hoisted herself up on the breakfast bar. Her face was a study in rue. "Besides, much as I hate to say it, he's the lawyer my mother picked in the first place. You gotta say, right off the bat, anybody that's associated with Mom is probably a bad guy or a fool."

Nobody disagreed with that. What we did agree on was to finesse Amos Verry and focus on Trudi; either to find her, or to track down a clean story of her death, including who dunnit, why, and what happened to him. Just that was so daunting that, against every instinct, I found myself hoping that we'd find Trudi Ransom alive and grifting. As far as I was concerned, that would give me a chance to kill her myself and go home happy.

12.

We started off the next day, Hap Maryland and his all-girl detective agency, combing the environs of Branson for evidence of Trudi according to the slightly drunken plan we'd worked out the night before.

As the oldest and stodgiest, I took the old downtown, including the old White River Hotel, a scattering of restaurants and law offices and general stores, and a family resort straight out of the fifties, with cabins and a huge pool and a rec hall. Charming stuff, and much easier on the senses and sensibilities than the newer precincts, where Paula was puttering the Vespa up and down among the tinsel and the two-story banjos and the tour buses. Suellen, an honest-to-God next of kin, took off on the Harley for Galena, the county seat of Stone County, to have a look at the death certificate Len Saffel had found on his data base. We gave ourselves the day for it, planning to meet at the Unit for beer and debriefing at the end of the afternoon.

I posed as a reporter for the *Leipziger Spiegel*, a German tabloid, the invention of which was almost my sole accomplishment for the day. I showed people the picture of Trudi in her peasant blouse I'd got from Len Saffel, and told them I was doing a "where-are-they-now" about once-famous Germans. This month's subject, I said, was the well-known gymnast and cabaret singer Trudi Gernreich (Ransom).

I told that lie to waiters in restaurants, to realtors, to the ticket-taker on the Branson Scenic Railway, to staffers in tourist traps and fast-food hells and legitimate infrastructural businesses, and even to a couple of tourists who looked like they'd been coming to the family resort for years. I described Trudi as ageing but still fit, a lithe and muscular knockout with a pile of blonde hair, and an ekcent rahzzer like mine. Guys in particular would take the picture and study it at length, frowning, reluctant to give it back. For a while it was kind of fun to watch their eyes gravitate to the edge of the blouse and nestle there, but by the end of the day it was as much a bore as the Midwestern Christian cheerfulness, the commercialism, and the heat.

The only response other than blushes, winks, and shrugs was the fleeting reaction of a deputy sheriff in a Taney County Cruiser. We had decided not to get more cops into it unless we really had to. There seemed to be so much we didn't know about this place and Trudi's niche in it, and all we truly did not need was for some desk sergeant to say, Yeah, they never caught her killer, and what were you doing on the evening of April 14th, 1995? Or, We got an open warrant on her and her grifter boyfriend, you got some ID?

But this guy either overheard me, or got informed that some kraut was going around asking questions, because he cruised up beside me as I trudged along the riverfront park, looking for a rental realty place somebody had referred me to.

"Offer you some assistance, sir?"

"No, sank you, offitser."

He sat there in his whispering squad car, just looking at me, and I saw this was not going to end it. "Ferry vell," I shrugged, "Vy not?"

I offered the standard baloney, of which I had almost convinced myself in the course of the morning, inventing the particular section of the *Spiegel* that was my beat ("German athletes of yesteryear") and an editor, Sachsenhausen, who was a bit of a bastard about expense accounts. The deputy heard it out with the stoic politeness of one who is lied to hourly, and took the picture of Trudi. That's when I saw just a momentary tightening of the corner of his mouth. He handed it back and looked at me with such blandness that it was obvious that he was about to enjoy giving a liar some of his own back.

"Can't say as I seen nothin on anybody like that. Might want to run a ad in the Advertizer. Looks a little strong for a milk carton."

It took me thirty milliseconds to remember to look puzzled about that, and the cop nodded at me a little grimly, touched his hat, and took off. It was awfully hard not to fantasize that he was headed for the nearest Amos Verry clubhouse to blow my cover with the Big Guy.

About two o'clock in the afternoon, I decided that I'd sucked the place dry, and that nobody would be less wise if I got back to the Unit and had a shower. I had talked to someone in just about every public space in the core downtown of Branson, and not too long after lunch people began knowing what I was going to ask before I asked it. That didn't stop some guys from having a good careful look at Trudi's picture; even in a smeary frame from a video, her death star quality came through. But even as they were looking, they'd be nodding, finishing my questions for me, and handing the picture back with a regretful shrug.

The Residence Inn was a long trudge uphill from the riverfront beat I'd been walking, and I was barely functioning when I got there. Paula came in while I was in the shower; she again raised herself in my estimation by handing an Urquell through the curtain.

When I came out she had the TV going, local news and a Springfield Chrysler dealer who was prancing around on his lot in a Speedo, fanning himself, promising deals too hot to bear. Sucking in his gut was making it hard for him to yell, but not impossible. His naked flank left a smear of sweat on a PT Cruiser. I traded my wet and exhausted Urquell for a new one and sprawled on the couch.

Paula took her turn in the bathroom, promising to be out in three hours, tops. Through slitted lids, I watched the parade of crap, half-listening to the hiss of the shower, not much thinking about the woman luxuriating under it. Cooling off, getting clean and fluffy. Water beading and sliding . . .   The TV showed a line of tornados sauntering across Texas, leaving tearful resignation and an infestation of on-the-scene anchors. Patterns, I thought. Just these graceful moving patterns of air that will rip your ass right off you, and spit it out again ten miles away. Pity the poor Texans, left with The Nothing. I sort of passed out, not sure if the tornados had been real, or had human faces.

When Paula came out, looking a sight fresher than she'd gone in, I was semiconscious. I roused myself and asked her what she'd found out, and got the answer I expected.

"Nothing much. This place is like a big old tub of cotton candy, all puff and no weight. You try to bite into it and it's gone, except your chin is sticky. Ninety percent of the people you see are tourists, and all they care about is, are they gonna get in to see Glen Campbell or whoever, and is this really a better deal on a quilt than they could get at home. Nobody knows from nothin about no Trudi Ransom, huh uh. You?"

"I think maybe I got a bit of a reaction from a deputy sheriff. Blanks otherwise. I hope to hell Suellen finds a good solid death certificate and a grave."

Paula scowled at me. "Why'd you ask a cop? I thought we were staying away from them."

"Other way around; he sought me out. It was just clear as day, he'd got sicked onto me by somebody. Probably the Chamber of Commerce, for stirring up trouble."

"Crap. Cops give me the willies."

I grunted and shrugged, and thought, *Well, considering* ... "How'd you get into your particular ... line of research?"

She snorted. "Johns always ask that. What's a nice girl like you doing, hooking?"

"OK, sorry," I said. To hell with her. "I'm not a john."

"Ya, shit, I'm sorry, Hap. That was bitchy, wasn't it?"

"Yup."

"I'm sorry."

She threw herself down on the bed, and I picked up a copy of the *Sunny Day Guide to Branson* that was sitting on the TV. I was a couple of pages into the saga of Boxcar Willie when Paula started talking to the ceiling.

"I was the brightest kid at St. Olaf. Everything was easy and delightful and funny, and every day something else would happen that would make me laugh. If there's such a thing as emotionally overprivileged, that's what I was.

"I dated a guy who seemed like the same, and we had a high old time, singing in the madrigal group and sledding on the hill behind my dorm. We stayed celibate, which made us kind of famous in those days. When we couldn't stand it any more, we got married. He was a Business major, but he didn't take it too seriously. I mean, he didn't live or die the Corporate Dream. After we graduated, I was going to get a master's in Ed, and he was going to get a good job and we'd be rich and happy, and screw every night.

"Well, he got a good-enough job with a middling kind of a company, and we put the program into action. I registered at Saint Bonnie's and started taking stuff like *"The Child and Her World,"* and Steve got a promotion, and then missed one. The screwing was OK. But the Reagan Recession came along, and Steve's company started losing contracts, and they started laying off people. Steve worked his butt off then, and I hardly ever saw him, seems like. He lived and died Interactive Services Limited, which was the name of his outfit, and he never talked about anything else. I started going out for coffee with the *Child and Her World* prof, just to have something else to talk about.

"Steve tripled his sales from the year before, and ISL gave him this cheesy Chinese desk clock that must have set them back $17.50 a gross. It had a little rotating globe of the world and a fake-brass plaque that said, 'World Class Salesman' on the base. He put it on the mantle in our living room and once in a while I'd find him just standing there, twiddling the globe. Watching the little world go around and around. The faculty coffee dates kind of eased over into cocktails. The time we had a quick screw afterwards, was the first sex I'd had in a month. Two days after that, ISL laid Steve off."

Paula shifted restlessly on the bed. I sat as quietly as I could, giving her a listening look when I thought she was about to glance at me. But she was focused on the ceiling, unspooling the video of her American dream. "The way I found out about that was, I came home from class and found Steve with his brains blown out and the pink slip on his chest."

"Aw, Jeez, Paula. That's ... Aw, Jeez."

No answer. Behind me, something rattled in the darkness of the freezer, tumbling ice for the tall, stiff ones that market surveys had shown to be favored by Unit dwellers. After a while, Paula sighed. "You do run on, don't you? Me too. Shit, we could talk it over for a week, and get no farther than 'Aw, Jeez.' Anyway, I was so guilty and miserable, I kind of went numb. People that knew us couldn't get over how wonderfully I was taking it, and what a gutsy girl I was. Got tired of that and went into a support group for numb people. Met a guy there, his wife died of ovarian cancer a month before that, he wasn't feeling much either, which we learned to believe was our brains telling us they had more shit to feel than they could stand, so they weren't gonna feel any of it. I doubt that's so, but it gives you some kind of belief to go on with.

"By the end of a year - to cut to the chase on this - this guy and I were telling each other how great we were for each other, spending whole weekends in bed. Which, let me tell you. Better, longer, more amazing sex never existed in this world. He was a kind of an outdoorsman, so we'd go for hikes and screw all afternoon in virgin timber; or we'd go hang gliding, which if you've never done it, you spend a day thinking you're gonna die the next second, but you don't, and then you do it again. That's kind of how sex was, with us."

Paula was silent again then, and sighed. "One Sunday he asked me, didn't this seem like really It, and shouldn't we make it official, and I said, God yes. I was so recovered from Steve, I'd forgot all about being numb. The whole thing was so much bigger and deeper than what I'd had before, it made Steve's death and my guilt, seem like - I don't know. Like your grandfather died. Sad and all, but you get over it.

"We went shopping the day after we got back from that trip, and he bought me a ring. The second weekend after that, we were hang gliding in the Smokies, and a funny thermal scraped him into the face of a cliff and crumpled one of his wings. He spiraled two hundred feet down in about ten seconds. I was watching from the next glider over, and it took me fifteen minutes of maneuvering to get down to him. The whole fifteen minutes, I was thinking, why am I hanging on?"

We heard Suellen's card in the door. Paula got up and headed for the bathroom. "Anyways," she said over her shoulder. "Nothing much has scared me since then. And that's what got me into the line of research I'm in."

Suellen's day was as frustrating and fruitless as mine, and as Paula's. She gave us a five-word summary, plunked a brown paper bag on the counter, and headed into the shower. We were a cleanly crew, there in Unit 117. Paula came out, wiping her nose with a Unit hanky, and I tried to think of something better than Aw Jeez, but still noncommittal. Failing, I kept my mouth shut, and Paula flopped back onto the bed.

When Suellen came out, absently towelling the buzz cut and rummaging the kitchen drawers for where we'd left the bottle opener last night, she elaborated to the point where it was obvious that we were not taking a fruitful approach to the problem of finding Trudi, her body, her killer, or her gravesite.

"Can you believe it? There's no record in Stone County of her death at all. Isn't that where you said she was supposed to've died?"

"So said Len Saffel, who was only quoting his data base. Which, we should add, is legendary."

"Ya, well, legends are one thing, I guess. I looked like a goddamn fool, going into Galena on this pilgrimage for my sainted mother, and come to find out they got no record her ever even being there, let alone buying it."

Paula popped open an Urquell. "Meaning?"

"Here we go again," I said. "I could do this in my sleep by now. Either she isn't dead, or she died somewhere else, or she died there and something happened to the record. If the last of those, either it's just an honest screw-up, which happens, or somebody fudged the record. How'm I doing?"

Paula groaned. "Why doesn't anything in this ever just play out the way it should? God's sake, is that too much?"

Suellen pulled a jar of honey out of the paper bag. "We still got any of that bread?"

"Here," Paula said. "Where'd you get the honey?"

"Little roadside stand. It's jimsonweed-blossom honey, made by bees that were stoned out of their skulls. Exoskeletons. Is this the last beer?"

"Hap'll get some more, right, Hap? 'Al's Apiary, New Branson, Missouri.' That's kinda far out for this country, wouldn't you say?"

"New Branson?" I said, heading for the door. "Sounds like whoever settled it didn't get far at all."

"Naw, I meant calling a bee business an apiary. Sounds hoity-toity, for Missouri. Get a case this time, don't be so cheap."

"I'm about broke, so it's your money anyhow," I said.

I was halfway out through the maze of neighboring Units when it hit me. I stopped like a mime in a glass factory, and sprinted back to the door I'd just shut behind me. I couldn't get my card into the slot fast enough. When I burst into the Unit, Suellen was crouched by the sink, staring at the door.

"New Branson!" we yelled, in ragged unison.

Paula's voice lazed out of the bathroom door. "Huh?"

Suellen and I started hollering at the same time. "New Branson! Grandson! The grand New Branson!"

Paula stuck her head around the corner and bonked it with her fist. "I'll be damned," she summarized. "The brand new grandson?"

13.

Nothing short of rushing right out to New Branson - wherever that was - would do. Off we went, then, Suellen and Paula on the Harley, I putting along behind on the Vespa in the blazing heat. The first thing, of course, was to get directions, and that turned out to be tougher than you'd think. There was no listing of "New Branson" on the highway map. The desk clerk at the Residence Inn and the money-taker at the 7-11 both swore ignorance of any such place. I thought Suellen was going to punch out the 7-11 clerk, a matron with curlers in her hair the size of coffee cans.

A trucker leaned an elbow on the counter, shoving aside a rack of cave-tour brochures. "New Branson," he ruminated. "That's more of a idea than a place. A region, like. If'n it's got a downtown, that'd be if you folla 76 west, out where it hits 13. What they meant by naming it that, it's acrost the line into Stone County, see."

"Thanks." I found the intersection on the Touraide map. It bore no name at all. "Pretty small place?"

The trucker rubbed his jaw. "Ain't no good answer to that. It's unincorporated, so it don't have no legal boundaries. One way of looking at it, it's most everthing from here to Galena."

The intersection of 76 and 13 had occasioned a strip mall,

which I guess is what the trucker meant by "downtown." There was a Mailboxes franchise and a holy-roller church, a couple of empty fronts, and a roadhouse called the Roselight. We converged there, hoping for a cool drink and somebody who knew Trudi Ransom just fine and – speaking for myself here – could lead us straight to her grave. By the time we were there, the sun was getting close to the yardarm, and a bunch of pickups had gathered at the Roselight, probably with the same ideas of cool drink and conversation. It looked like Trudi's kind of place, really; I first met her at a roadhouse in the red light district of Fayetteville, North Carolina.

In fact all of New Branson - all that we could see from the strip mall, at least - seemed a lot more Trudi's kind of country than Branson proper. Commercial, still, but a sight less slick and wholesome. Weedier, rougher, less prosperous, with more room for an inventive grifter to function, if maybe less loose cash to target. Not a sign of a realtor or a tour bus.

"Ladies, wait" I yelled from the Vespa. They waited.

"What say," I said, "we think about what we're going to do here, instead of just blundering ahead?"

"What's to think?" Suellen shrugged. "Either they know where Mom is, or they don't. C'mon, this looks like Mom's kind of place. She could be sitting in there right now."

"Wait. If she is, she'll be there two minutes from now. But maybe she isn't. Maybe Amos Verry is, or somebody who reports to him. Remember, he tried to shoo you away from your mother, and she cooperated in that, right up to the end. Maybe there's some good reason, that has to do with self-preservation, that we might want to be a little more subtle. Ask indirect questions. Sometimes you find out something you didn't know you were looking for, that way."

"Ya, I can just hear Wet. Whatsa matter, Hotshot's got cold feet?"

Paula raised an eyebrow. "This is the Wet of the famous detective method? I think I been beat up enough for one week. Give us an example of subtle."

I shrugged. "Well .... OK, how's this: after we've been there a while, we ask the waitress about a place called the Grand Something, maybe the Grand Theater, that somebody in Branson told us about, and could she give directions."

Paula cocked her head. "The Grand Something?"

Suellen grinned. "The Grand, New Branson. Pretty cute, Maryland. Course, I don't know that Mom's that cute, but it's the first un-dumb thing anybody's said since we crossed the Mississippi. We could give it a shot."

We did. Paula looked a little hurt at Suellen's remark, so I very circumspectly patted her far hip and said, "Suellen includes herself when she says 'anybody' of course." Paula uncircumspectly bumped my hip with hers. We went into the Roselight.

Its architecture was that of a hollow brick or a roach motel, making a space that could have been used for anything from a rape crisis center to a Ford agency. What might have been the show window, in the latter case, was bricked solid except for a brace of air conditioners. There was a bar down one side, a lot of tables, and a smallish dance floor with a raised stage for a band. The pine-plank floor was sprinkled with a gritty mix of sawdust and plain dust and dirt. Doors on either side of the stage said "Men" and "Ladies" on signs I expect they got from K-Mart. I took it as encouraging that the stage was not protected by chicken wire. The Roselight lived up to its name with an all-black paint job, relieved by neon beer signs and, on the ceiling, a winding pink neon rose that looked quite a lot like Suellen's tattoo. It was dark after the glare, and we stood in a little triangle by the door, waiting for our night vision to kick in. Suellen got there first and led the way to a table, where we were joined by a waitress in a sort of cowgirl getup, with white leather boots and a fair amount of jiggle.

"Draw you guys one?"

"Whatcha got?" Suellen asked. She was always quick at dialects.

"Bud, Bud Lite, Miller, Miller Lite."

"Oof," Paula oofed. "How about dilute frog piss?"

"Outa that," the waitress answered, unsmiling. "You guys wanta look at the import list?"

"If possible," I said, playing the diplomat. "You have Heineken's?"

"We don't carry no foreign imports. Coors, Rolling Rock, or Gansett. Got a special on Coors up ta 5:30."

Suellen scowled, craning around the room. "Nazi frog piss. You know any of the others, Hap?"

"The only one I don't know is Gansett," I said, "so let's try that."

The waitress brightened. "An excellent choice, sir. Happens I'm from there myself." She struck a hipshot pose, hand raised in greeting. " 'Hi, neighbor! Have a Gansett.' First beer I ever drunk."

"Gansetts all around it is, then," I said, "And one for yourself, if the boss'll let you."

"I'll hafta bill you for it now, and drink it after my shift, but thanks." She scooted her white boots off in the direction of the bar.

Suellen whistled. "Hap, you smooth bastard," she said. "Every whore in Stone County's gonna be eating out of your hand."

"That's a stimulating notion," I said. "I just used exactly the line I used when I first met your mother."

"Ya, so speaking of which, whyn't you try the Grand riff on her?"

"All things in due course. You don't get anywhere laying down your cards the first minute you walk in a place."

The Gansetts arrived, and turned out to be "Narragansett," a New England strain of the national bland-beer disease. When the waitress had been paid and handsomely tipped but uninterrogated, Paula cleared her throat. "I have every confidence in Hap's impeccable timing. But speaking of cards, how's this place look for where that video was shot?"

Suellen paled - or, seemed to, in the dimness - and looked behind her at the blackish depths of the Roselight. "Nah. Jeez, though, don't give me the creeps. The place in the video had like rafters and stuff, and lanterns hanging down. Like a set for a Western."

A cowboy band had been setting up while we talked, and they launched into a string of very presentable stuff, including "Cool Water," "A Whiter Shade of Pale," and "Victim to the Tomb," which has always been a favorite of mine. Truckers and ladies danced, kicking up clouds of sawdust and assorted grit. We did not. The Gansetts drained pretty much of their own accord, sending Suellen and Paula into the blackness looking for the Ladies', and bringing the white boots - and now I could see their utility, they gleamed in the dimness like running lights - to ask about refills.

"Sure," I said; and when she came back with them, I asked about the Grand.

"Why," she frowned. "I dunno. What kinda place was it?"

"You know, I really couldn't say. It might be a theater. It was just a quick conversation with these folks. What they said was, they'd been over here to New Branson, and they said, You just gotta go to the Grand. Their bus came along right then, and they never had a chance to tell me what it was. I wouldn't of come here just for that, but we were here picking up some honey from Al's Apiary, and I says to the girls, shoot, let's see can we find it."

"Well," she said, "I don't think there's any such a place. Lemme ask, though."

She clomped off with a good piece of my last dollars tucked in her fringed apron, and hollered at the barlady, "Louetta, you ever heard of a place called the Grand The-ayter?"

"Shoot yeah," Louetta yelled back. "Used to be a burlesque house in St. Louis. My momma knew a girl, danced in the chorus doin' the War."

"Naw, he means here, dummy. Ain't that right, sir?"

I nodded, and walked over to the bar. So much for subtlety, jeez. Everybody in the Roselight knew now that this tourist was looking for something that probably didn't exist. But I ran through the "you gotta see the Grand" riff again. While the barkeep was pumping Bud and Miller and telling me about the danseuse her momma knew, I leaned against the bar and surveyed the Roselight, thinking it was about time for Paula and Suellen to be finished with their business. I got a creepy little flash when I realized that I was half-consciously imitating Amos Verry's bar-leaning pose.

And that turned into a solid shock when I saw Amos himself at one of the tables by the dance floor. He was over on the Men's room side, by himself, leaning back in the chair and facing the other side of the stage. Either waiting for a lady friend to emerge, or casing what did emerge for potential lady friends. Or, I realized, waiting for Paula and Suellen to come out, having spotted them on the way in. I didn't mull things over; I started toward him, but got blocked briefly by a customer arguing with the waitress over the math on his bar tab. It held me up long enough for Paula to come around the screen at the end of the dance floor, and for Amos Verry to see her.

He didn't mull things much, either. He jumped to his feet and started toward her, looking like a truant officer. Paula saw him coming, and from forty feet away, I could see her stagger a little.

Her head snapped around to the table where I'd been, and when she saw it empty, her knees buckled, and she went into a crouch amid the sawdust and the gum wrappers. That slowed Amos Verry a bit, and let me catch up with him.

"Amos," I hollered. "By God, Amos Verry. You goddamn skirt-chaser, whatcha doing down here?"

Verry tore his eyes off Paula and gave me a look. He didn't remember me from the bar in Springfield, I was glad to see.

He wasn't. I saw a quick blaze of fury in his face, and then the recollection that he was about to launch a political career, and maybe it wouldn't be good politics to kick every bothersome stranger in the nuts right away. "Sorry," he snapped, cordially. "You have the advantage of me, sir." He shot a glance back at Paula, which gave me a chance to see what she was up to. She was still on the floor.

Verry started toward her, and shot back at me, "Excuse me just a second, sir. Got a lady in some difficulty here."

Paula was up now, brushing off helpful strangers, turning to face Amos Verry. I grabbed his arm. "We need to talk about your campaign." He turned back to me. Paula began to wobble back toward the Ladies, holding her stomach. I thought about what she'd looked like after her big date with Amos, and I let that kick me into a don't-give-a-shit frenzy. I beamed and yanked on his elbow.

"You won't remember me," I promised. "I'm Tim Summerton, used to be the Democratic chair for Taney County. Got a academic job out East now." I pulled out Summerton's business card and pressed it on him. He barely glanced at it.

"Thing is," I said, "I was talking to Len Saffel the other day
–Len sends his regards, by the way – and he was tellin me how you
were getting ready to jump, and I said, Hot damn, that's a fella this
part a the state's been needing for a good, long time. I'd be proud,
sir, to be of whatever assistance I can be with your campaign."

Verry squinted at me, and started toward the Ladies'. "Got
a staff."

I nodded and got myself in front of him again. "Sure hope
so. I was wondering if you had all the financial resources you might
be counting on, got that all in your pocket yet."

That got him. "Never was such a thing."

I chuckled as venally as I could manage. "Thing is," I
confessed, dropping my voice and turning Verry away from the
stage. "They's a little group of us, that's working for a business-
friendly Congress out'n Washington, doing kinda some grass-roots
prospecting, don't you know."

"I'm not running for Congress."

I winked at him, and he winked back, in spite of himself.
"Not this time, you ain't. You figure to spend your life in the
Missouri legislature?"

He let himself think about it. Congress, shit. That's where
the serious money is. He shrugged, or maybe it was a little shiver of
anticipation. "I'd be open to any reasonable proposition."

"Good, good," I nodded, and glanced at the back of the
room. "Jeez, I gotta pee somethin awful. Something down there
ain't been right since my kidney stone. You hang onta that card,

Mr. Verry. You don't remember, but I was in your Engineering Physics class, oh, I think it was fifteen-twenty years ago, up'n Rolla. Bout the time I was ready to give up on it, you and me had a very enjoyable evening with a group a young ladies from the English Department. Heh. What was that one's name, Peggy Lou Something? 'Member her?"

I shook my beaming head in rue at the flight of youth and Peggy Lou. "Anyways, when my little group back home ast me, where we gonna find good reliable candidates in the Midwest, who knows anybody out there that's sharp, and attractive, and knows how the world works, I said, listen, they's a fella I use to know back in Rolla, Missouri. Lemme see if he's interested." I slapped his arm and headed for the Gents, the feel of bunched muscles tingling on my palm. "Might serve," I chuckled. "Oh, maybe not this time, but lemme see, lemme see..."

I rounded the corner behind the stage and found a slick and noisome kitchen hallway, at the end of which Paula and Suellen huddled, lit by an EXIT sign. I stuck my head back around the corner and saw Amos Verry scowling at Tim Summerton's card. I wiggled a finger at it.

"Gimme three-four weeks to canvas some folks," I whispered at the top of my lungs. "And gimme a call."

14.

I headed for the back door, as the white-booted waitress emerged into the hallway with a tray full of steaming grease. We avoided colliding, and she gave me a funny look. "I had a idea about what you might of was asking about," she said. "Gimme a second to get rid a this rat crap."

"We'll be out back," I said. "There's a fella in there thinks I owe him money." She grunted more or less sympathetically and headed into the twang and bonhomie of the Roselight.

The territory out back consisted of about ten feet of weeds and a drop-off to a limestone gully. A battered dumpster perched at the edge, looking as if solid waste removal at the Roselight was pretty much a question of a good shove and a rainstorm. Paula crouched next to the dumpster, retching while Suellen held her head.

"There," she said. "Easy does it."

"I'm aw ri," Paula gasped. "Just got a scare."

I waggled an eyebrow at Suellen. "You heard what this is about?"

"I heard." Suellen looked ready to go back into the Roselight and see how Amos Verry might fit through one of the front air conditioners.

"Hold tight," I said. "We need to think if this is just one of those coincidences, or he's in there because he was following us." I reconsidered. "Or, following you. He didn't know me before."

Paula slapped the sawdust and grit off her slacks. "Does now, though. Thanks, Hap."

"Forget it. I'm sorry I wasn't where you could find me."

"Ya," Suellen said. "Look, if we're not going to pull that asshole's face off, let's get out of here. Mom's not in there, and nobody I asked knew her."

"Wait a second. The waitress - "

As I spoke, the back door of the Roselight creaked open, and white-boots stuck her head out. She had a card in her hand.

"Call Sherine," she said. "She'll give you directions." The door slammed shut again, leaving us out back with the dumpster.

The card was about as simple as cards get. "Sherine," it said. "555-1756."

Suellen plucked it out of my hand. "Who's Sherine, for God's sake? A whore?"

"Doesn't say anything about securities or real estate," Paula said.

"Great. Who makes the call? You, I'd think, Hap."

I did, from a pay phone in the strip-mall parking lot. It felt so right.

"Sherine." There was music in the background; Stand By Your Man, I think. There was also another voice, saying, "C'mon, baby, hang it up, I ain't payin for no - "

"Gimme fi'teen minutes," Sherine said, and the connection broke.

We gave her twenty minutes, which we killed by easing the bikes out of the parking lot of the Roselight and buzzing off. We watched our tail pretty religiously, rounding curves and ducking into the woods to check for any followers, and saw none. If Amos Verry was looking for us, he was probably still in the Roselight, staking out the restrooms. A couple of miles up Highway 13, the road dove into a hollow, and joined a creek and a railroad track to march united on the settlement of Reeds Spring. Reeds Spring had a lumberyard, and the lumberyard had a pay phone. Sherine was receiving calls.

"Shoot," she said. "I bet I can see you from where I'm at. You the folks with the Harley, over't the sawmill?"

"That's right," I said, looking around. There were six or eight houses in sight, lining the highway. In one of them, a pale form waved from a front window. "I see you. OK if we come over?"

"I don't do groups."

"Us, either," I assured her. "Waitress, up at the Roselight, said you could give us some information about a place we're looking for."

"Yeah? Where's that?"

I cranked out the stupid little story about the tourists, the Grand Something, and the bus. Sherine seemed amused.

"I really need some fresh air after that dude. See that Weenie King 'bout a quarter-mile down the road?"

I looked. A giant hot dog, peeling weenie-colored paint, reared beside Highway 13 where it turned a corner in the middle distance. "Yep."

"Meet you there in ten."

We had time to get Mega-Doggies with sauerkraut and carry them out to the cement tables in the courtyard, under the giant wiener. King Weenie had a face painted at the top end, with reassuring, slanted eyebrows and what had been a broad smile, I suppose. Most of the smile had flaked off, leaving a rusty grimace of horror. It made him look like he was straining pitifully against the clutch of the guy wires that held him straight. The sun had just set behind the ridge to the west, and the Wiener ticked with relief at having made it through another day. While we watched Sherine stumping up the road toward us, a flake of faded red fell on the table, joining a smattering of others.

"Yee, shit," Suellen said, "that's prob'ly full of red lead. Keep your weenies covered."

Sherine slaunched her hot-pantsed self into the Weenie King courtyard, gave us a wave and a wink, and disappeared into the shack, to emerge in a minute with a good-sized cup of crushed ice. She looked about eighteen, flaxen-haired, still with baby fat around a ripe mouth that gave her a Renoir look. I did introductions.

Sherine's eyes got as big and blue as her chubby cheekbones would allow. "Wait a seckint. Are you that Suellen? The one in the paper?"

"Shoot, I guess," Suellen said. "About the hookers in North Carolina? That was in the paper here?"

"Listen," Sherine said, poking a straw at her cup of ice.

"You done every hooker in the USA a giant favor. My per trick gross jumped fifteen percent right off the bat, an' I'm gettin business I din't even know I was losing, to these little tarts out in the boonies that was lettin it go for peanuts. I'm on track to clear twelve thousand after ITO this quarter. You want any kind of favor from me, you name it."

Paula winked at me. "You think of any favors you could use from Sherine, Hap?"

"Ha ha. Just the facts, ma'am."

Sherine sized me up for a poor bet in half a glance and turned to Suellen. "He with you?"

Suellen patted my cheek. "He saves our butts every chance he gets," she said. "Give him what he wants."

Sherine got solemn. "I was gonna fub you guys off with bullshit. But I owe Suellen, somethin big. So ..." She seemed to steel herself. "So here's what you're after. Granny's Parlour, over by Galena."

Paula looked skeptical. "Granny's? What, it's a bingo parlor?"

"More to the point," I said, "We had an idea this place was in New Branson, which I understand stops at Galena."

Sherine flipped a hand. "Maybe. 'New Branson' is just a made-up name for a lot a sticks. I understood you were looking for someplace a little special."

Paula shrugged. "We don't really know what - "

Suellen lifted a hand. "Special what way?"

"Well, that's it, see. Granny don't advertise, 'cause she

don't want a lot of tourists from Branson gettin in there and - I dunno. Raising the tone, maybe. Gettin a shock, more likely. Bunch of fat farmers' wives, get the place shut down. She makes do with what business she can trust, charges a ton, and makes it worth their while. Gambling, top-class hookers, gay and lesbian interest, special acts. Certain amount of kiddie porn, to a point. Guys come from Springfield, Joplin, you name it, far as KC. But not a crowd of goddamn tourists, see what I mean?"

"OK," Suellen said. "Where is it?"

Sherine sucked air through her teeth. "You didn't hear from me, OK? Granny finds out I'm spreading word, it's my ass." A serene look chased the anxiety from her face for and instant; for as long as it took her to say "my ass." It was the satisfaction I'd seen on Royce's face when he talked about how tough you had to be to patronize Miz Mary Alice's Bikini Club.

"Anyways, hang a right on Chestnut Street, here, and follow the crick down to where it tees. Left there, and then look for John Holler Road on your right. Follow that back, and Granny's is up at the end of John Holler, set back into the hillside. It's in a place used to be a old mine, or a cave, something. Fella at the door, tell 'im you're a friend of Mister Verry."

She leaned forward, putting her cup of ice down amid the paper napkins and paint chips. "Now, listen good. Here's how they know if you're real. You look off over your left shoulder while you say that. Or, you can look to the right and say you're a friend of Granny's. You get that backwards, or look the fella in the eye, he'll turn you away, if he don't shoot you. Got that?"

She demonstrated, looking over her left shoulder at the giant weenie. In profile, she was more Renoiresque than ever. "I am a friend of Mister Verry," she said, carefully. She stood up and dumped her ice. "Shitsake, don't tell him you're a friend of mine."

We parked the bikes in the bushes a little way up John Holler Road. The road was woodsy and isolated, and it seemed unnecessarily gaudy to rumble up it on a couple of noisemakers. The sun was well behind the western hills by now, and it was dim and close in John Holler. Queen Anne's Lace, which had decorated the entrance, gave way to ferns and worts. Little hot breezes followed us in from the main road and fell away, disheartened. A trivial stream ran down one side of John Holler, aspiring to union with the creek we'd met in Reeds Spring.

"Granny's, New Branson," Paula said. "What do you think?"

"Pretty far-fetched," Suellen grunted. She seemed subdued, maybe a little snappish.

"I thought so," I said, "until I heard the password."

We walked in silence for a while, and then Suellen shook her head and spat a dill seed onto the road. "That mother's got his hand on everything that happens. What's the chances this particular thing's the one we want?"

"Shoot," Paula grinned. "If we can't find what we want at Granny's, we must be some kind of freaks."

"Well," I said, "we are, though." Paula bumped my hip again at that, and I kind of enjoyed it, even through the sinking feeling that I could get past the point where it would be easy to brush off her tenure appeal case, if I didn't look out. Loneliness is a bastard for getting into your self-preservation works, and bitching them up beyond repair. I gritted my teeth and vowed to watch it from here on.

"Sh. There it is. Who's gonna go give the password?"

"Yee, shit."

Granny's Parlour had no signs or parking lot. We'd been passing cars along the side of the road for a while, and to a car, they were missing their license plates. Looming beyond them against the hill was a mine tipple, one of those weathered mountains of industrial architecture, several thousand cubic yards of vernacular full of gables, pulleys, ladders, and lean-to's, splintered and repaired with sheet tin and tarpaper. The gathering dusk made mysteries of every angle and hollow in the façade. Light of a smoky and dubious color leaked from cracks in the cantilevered walls. An old-fashioned ceramic-lined billboard lamp, salvage from a Krazy Kat comic strip, hung over the entrance. Above it, a video camera panned mildly back and forth, surveilling the end of John Holler Road. Under that, a 300-pound biker in bib overalls and a ponytail lounged in a swivel chair, smoking. A ripe autumnal smell of burning leaves drifted on the fitful air. I took a breath and stepped forward.

"Wait." Paula said, and stopped me "I need to do this. If I poop my pants, just leave me here." She marched up to the biker and snapped her head leftward toward where we'd come from.

"I am a friend of Mister Verry," she said.

The biker raised an eyebrow a millimeter or so. "That right?"

Paula almost looked back at him, but caught herself, and nodded leftward. "Yes," she said, "but he didn't tell me what to say after that. Are you Arthur?"

The biker sighed and shook his head. "Chickie, chickie. As we speak, Arthur is beginning a painful process of atonement for displeasing Mister Verry. I expect it will take most of the night, and then somebody else, and I hope to God it ain't me, will have the job of doing for Arthur what Arthur failed to do for a hooker Mister Verry was also displeased with. Here on in, you never heard nothing about no Arthur. It was a unlucky name for you to remember. Call me Zuckerman. These geeks with you?"

"Yes, Zuckerman," Paula quavered. "Yes, they are."

"Well then." Zuckerman stood up, and seemed to keep on standing up for a long time. I think he must have topped seven feet. Paula stepped back, her store of guts about drained. "Won't you all just go on in and make yourselfs comfortable? Granny's always happy to see any real friend of Mister Verry's."

"Well, heck," Suellen said. I could hear the clicking of her dry mouth. "Why not?"

The interior of Granny's Parlour was a madhouse of tiny cubicles, crooked passages, tilt-floored ballrooms and hundreds of mirrors, in about half of which you saw no reflection, because, gilt frames notwithstanding, they were windows, and not mirrors after all. In a few of the cubicles we passed, I could see small evidences -

a Gucci'd foot, a tailored jacket on the back of a chair - of the owners of the cars out there on John Holler Road.

A fairly presentable young fellow - I took him or her for a fellow - bowed, gave us a table in an unused corner, and presented us with menus, nicely printed, a little grubby. There was a page of food, which was pretty sketchy; a wine list and a beer list that extended to imports from outside the US, and a short list of the house liquors. The following pages offered a menu of vices, from baccarat to bondage, in every conceivable permutation.

"My Lord and master," Paula said. "If this isn't..." Words failed her.

Suellen nodded. "The hamburgers look good, but I can't make up my mind between Eskimo and Turkish for the stripper."

"No contest, far as I'm concerned," I said, faintly. "The Turk's female."

Paula got us focused again. "Listen," she said. "We are absolutely in deadly peril here. Arthur is the guy who brought me back to the Shady Stop the other night, instead of killing me and dumping me down some ravine. I'm the hooker in that little morality tale. It took as long as from when Verry saw me in that Roselight place to now, for him to get word back to Springfield, and start killing Arthur. It's just dumb luck the guy at the door wasn't somebody that knows one of us. We have got to find out if Trudi's here, and get the hell gone as fast as we possibly can."

"Agreed," Suellen agreed. "How?"

"We could ask the waitperson when he or she comes back."

Suellen snorted. "Right, and then he goes and tells

somebody we're looking for Trudi. And we find out if that was a mistake when we start walking back down that road in the dark, and don't make it to the end."

"What," I said, "if we see what Granny can tell us?"

"Are you nuts?"

Paula shook her head. "More fundamentally, is there even a Granny, or is that just the name of the place?

"Well, maybe, but one of the passwords was being a friend of Granny's. See, the thing is, if there is an actual Granny, I get the idea that she pretty much runs this place, obviously in connection, somehow, with Amos Verry. Verry's busy overseeing Arthur's punishment, I hope, which means Granny's top dog for tonight. At least she won't tell some higher-up and put some kind of spin on it that'll get us killed. If it looks like a big mistake, we'll know right away."

There was a little silence. "And?" Paula said.

"Well … " I said. "Well, we run for it. Can't we outrun a Granny?"

Nobody could think of anything better, so that is what we did. When the presentable young fellow reappeared with an order pad, we ordered beer and cigars and – with fear and trembling – I put the question about meeting Granny.

"Oh, but," he smiled. "But of course. Granny practically insists on vetting all her new guests. Would you like to visit her now, while I'm getting your drinks together?"

"Well," I said.

"Sure," Paula said. "Do we go there, or does she stop by all the cubicles?"

The presentable fellow laughed silkily. "You haven't met Granny, have you? No, Granny doesn't get around much any more. If you'll follow me?"

He snapped his fingers, handed the order for beer and cigars to a half-naked little girl, and bowed us out the door.

Getting to Granny was a matter of corridors, stairways, turns and twists that I tried to memorize on the way in, so we could do them fast in reverse if we had to. After a minute of it, I gave up. We passed a humming utility room, an elevator, and a couple of closed doors from which giggles and hoarse screams issued. In a kitchen, a hairy chef wearing gladiator leather grinned at us and swung a cleaver as big as a flag, *Chunk!* and a rack of spare ribs fell into two gleaming servings. He tossed a bone chip to a waiting phalanx of rats while we passed.

We took lefts and rights and ups and downs, probably on orders to give us a runaround on the way to Granny's sanctum. We passed a suite of offices, a dumpster, and a storeroom that held cleaning supplies, a circuit box, hoses and a gurney. The paneled walls gave way to hewn limestone, and I concluded that we were in a passageway from mine or quarry days.

The presentable fellow stopped us with an elegantly lifted finger, and knocked faintly on the frame of the last door in the last corridor. Smoke lazed across the threshold, and light that looked somehow neither yellow nor rosy, but an unwholesome tone reminiscent of dirt or sewage, curdled from the doorway and shone into the corridor and up against the blank rock at the end of it. It illuminated our guide, rendering him no longer presentable.

"Granny?" he caroled. "Some new folks here to meet you."

"Bring 'em in," a voice called, and it was a voice I knew. Suellen gripped my arm and started to laugh and cry together.

"That's Mom," she said. "That's my Mom. Oh, my God, I'd know that voice anywhere. Mom!" She tore away from us and ran to the lighted doorway, yelling Mom, Momma. She swung around the entrance and stopped as if she'd been shot. She grabbed the door frame. I could hear the air hiss out of her lungs; I think she was doing her best to scream, as one does in a nightmare. The sweat on her hand squeaked as it slid down the frame of the door while Suellen crouched and stared into the room that held Granny.

"Mom," she whispered at last. "Oh, Momma, Jesus."

15.

The presentable fellow smirked, bowed, and silkily betook himself to other duties. Paula and I crept to the end of the passage where Suellen stood as if ray-gunned, gaping into the brownish gloom. With some creaky sense of chivalry, I lifted a hand to hold Paula back from whatever grisly sight awaited us. She snorted good-naturedly, and poked her head around the doorway.

Just inside was a wall of video monitors, giving silent views of what was going on in a sampling of the cubicles and - panning sedately - on the road outside. Some of what they showed was a little shocking, some of it funny, some horrible. One of them showed three beers and a box of cigars being placed on our table. Above the bank of monitors, I recognized the Western-style decor that had been the setting of Trudi Ransom's death video. The rest of the room was taken up by the principal horror. And that was Trudi Ransom herself.

A whole lot of her. The athletic ballbuster who'd entered my life as a topless bargirl with a waist like a rattlesnake had gone jumbo. Symphonies of tuba players had joined her marching band, and it was hard to see that anyone had dropped out. She lay propped on a divan the size of a flatcar tricked out with cushions and shawls into a parody of a Victorian chaise. In fact, it was a flatcar, one of the compact kind that they use in mines like this to haul machinery in and ore out. It was designed to haul a ton or two of stuff without breaking a sweat. Though the years had probably degraded its capabilities some, I suppose it carried Trudi Ransom's quarter-ton handily enough. It sat on rusted steel rails that led through a curtained doorway behind Trudi. Slung below it on an undercarriage, I saw a bank of batteries and a good-sized electric motor. By God, I thought, that's how she gets around. Anywhere the rails go, she can go.

Trudi was wearing some kind of a Tirolean muu-muu, is all I can call it. Ten yards of flowered blue nylon, with a peasant top bulging and hauling at a Clydesdale's dream of cleavage. A cheap-looking cigarillo was wedged between the fingers of her left hand. Perched on top of it all, fat lips sucking on a milkshake, sat a funhouse version of Trudi Ransom's face that made me look for the trick mirror. But there were no mirrors; it was all real, smelling of fat and baby powder, and now twisted with phony mirth.

"Glad to see Mommy again, are we, Hon? After all these years. I thought I told you to fuck off, and you not only didn't, you brought Hap Maryland. Jesus, what a treat. The only thing gave me a second's pause when I stuffed you on that bus was, Wet Parsonage might let Maryland get his hands on you. He boffed you yet? If he did, lemme tell you, it's a once in a lifetime experience, if you're lucky. Forgettable, didn't you find?"

"Oh, Mom. What happened to you?"

"One thing and another, sweetie. Thanks for asking, though. What took you so long to work up an interest?"

Suellen didn't say anything. She was waiting to wake up, and it kept not happening.

"She came out here to avenge your murder, Trudi," I said. "I thought she might need some help. You can picture our relief at seeing you blooming like this."

Trudi turned to Suellen. "OK," she said. "So you came, and you saw the freak show. When you going?"

"Mom," Suellen said. "Stop that. You're my Mom, you know. I still love you as much as I ever did, which was a whole lot. I want to help you get... get back to how you were. I want you to come back to North Carol - "

Trudi erupted in a nasal, adenoidal cawing, shaking like ... oh, gosh, I have to say it some time. Like a bowl full of jello. Her little feet kicked merrily at the ends of legs the size of oil drums. Tears of perhaps merriment plied the pink meridians of her cheeks.

"Back to lovely North Carolina? Where life treated us so great, we had to run for our lives? I think they got warrants outstanding on us yet, back there. Me, anyways. No, punkin, here's where Granny is, and here Granny will stay to the end of her days. Which could come down the pipe any minute, far as Granny cares." But she shut up then, and put the drink down on the divan. She squinted at Suellen. "You mean that, about 'as much as ever'?"

"Of course. You think I wanted to get on that bus, you stupid?" Suellen clambered up on the flatcar and did her damnedest to throw herself into Trudi's arms. Not her fault that she couldn't find an armhold and slid back, pulling the peasant blouse off one Brobdingnagian breast. Trudi's drink spilled, and a slow ooze of what looked like chocolate malt joined numerous other stains on the divan. Trudi stuck out a fat hand to keep Suellen from falling onto the tracks, and adjusted her neckline thoughtfully with the other.

"Well," she said. "I will overlook the epithet. I thought you were pretty much settled in there, though. Wet told me you were about to - "

"Listen. Wet thinks you're a bad influence, which you have to admit, he has a certain amount of grounds for. You can't pass messages to me through him. Forget Wet, forget everything. You're coming home with me, and we're gonna get you back in shape."

Trudi beamed at Suellen. "Sweet little thing. I wish it was that simple."

Suellen turned to Paula and me. "Well, it is, isn't it, guys?"

I opened my mouth and waited for something hearty to come out. We'll ship her air freight. We'll take her to a vet for liposuction, and starve her down to three-fifty, and when she can walk on her own again, we'll handcuff her and frogwalk her into court. I said nothing.

"Sweetheart," Trudi said. "If I leave this godforsaken corner of Missouri, it'll be to face a warrant for murdering Henry Baxter."

"Reverend Baxter? You didn't lay a finger on him, Mom. He got... he ..." Suellen trailed off.

Trudi snorted. "Your honor, the lucky devil got snatched off to heaven by an angel. Think the State of Minnesota's gonna buy that? They found our prints all over that bus, and they got an open warrant for my arrest. You're not in the clear, neither; how'd you like to spend time in a Minnesota boot camp for juvenile offenders?" She ruffled Suellen's buzz cut and beamed at Paula and me. "In't she the sweetest little offender, though? Always was. Don't you worry, honey," she said. "I got protection. I got a friend in a high place."

"Yeah?" Suellen asked. "Who's that, Amos Verry?"

Trudi looked surprised. "What made you think that?"

"Oh, Mom," Suellen groaned. "How'd you think we got here? He called me up and sent me that box of stuff."

"He never did! What box?"

Suellen rolled her eyes, gestured, and ran out of words.

"A box of Suellen's girlhood things, Trudi," I said. "A beanie baby, some photos, report cards. Stuff like that. Why is Amos Verry protecting you? And for Christ's sake, what was the deal with those death videos?"

Trudi smirked. "He's in love with me. Plus, of course, if he don't, - well, let's just leave it, I got resources he can't touch. The videos were never supposed to get out in public."

I put on an impressed face, and asked myself whether I wanted to know any more about that. No, I had to admit, I sure didn't. There was something about this whole business that didn't make sense to me, but I couldn't stop shuddering in horror at the sight of Trudi Ransom. It wasn't even that she was hideously fat; I had seen women at least half that fat, negotiating the attractions of downtown Branson. No, something had changed in her since I'd last seen her, all those years ago. Then, she was a cynical, lying hustler with a heart of brass, but there was still something likeable to her. Part of it was a kind of merriment that I couldn't resist joining sometimes, as long as it was directed at people and practices I found laughable myself. She was intelligent, self-reliant and oddly attractive, a good person to have on your side, knowing she would change sides at the drop of a bill. Now, that was gone. She looked stupid, coarse, and uncaring, no merrier or more likeable than a tank car. I was willing to believe that it began when she put Suellen on the bus to Fayetteville, all that time ago.

"Well," I said. "This has been heartwarming as all hell. Suellen, we found your mother, and she's alive and well, all five hundred - " Paula kicked my ankle, right where the scab from the Harley wasn't quite ready for kicking. "Ow, dammit," I concluded. "Now what?"

"I'm gonna stay here with Mom and get her straightened out."

"What's not straight, young lady?"

"Shit, mother dear. You're a helpless invalid under the blackmailing thumb of a four-flushing thug lawyer. Is that how you wanted to end your days?"

Trudi rolled her eyes. Even her eyeballs looked obese, popping from her face like boiled eggs driven from behind by the pressure of all that fat. They narrowed contemplatively at one of the monitors, savoring a scene that I cannot describe in an account that may some day be read by decent people. Trudi saw me looking at it, and winked.

"How simple it all seems to the young, don't you find,

Maryland? Like something you'd see on TV. And you, you skinny little mouse. Who are you? You look like you got a few miles on you. You ever known anything in this life that wasn't richer an' trickier than it looks to a kid?"

Paula raised an eyebrow. "Sometimes adults undersimplify things that kids see right to the heart of. Are you under Amos Verry's thumb?"

"No more than he's under mine," Trudi said. "I got goods on a guy that's got goods on him."

"Holy - " Paula turned to Suellen and me. "Tell you what, folks," she muttered, "this is fascinating and all, but I'm nervous as shit. Amos Verry is busy right now killing a guy that was supposed to've killed me. When he's done, he's gonna come after me. I gotta get out of here, and I mean way out. You can stay and put this gutbucket on Weight Watchers if you want, Suellen, and see if what comes out the other side is your mother. But we came out here to find her, or find out who killed her. I'm declaring Mission Accomplished. Coming, Hap?"

"You bet. Suellen, we'll leave the Vespa. See you back at the - "

"Tsht!" Paula's foot whacked my ankle again.

"Ow, shit. I wasn't going to say 'the Holiday Inn,' think I'm stupid? The ranch. Let's go."

We did our best to exit at speed, but it did involve some wrong turns and some backing and filling. It was distracting going, for things had heated up considerably while we were back there with Granny. We stumbled into furred and gloomy spaces where visitors were not expected, though not unwelcome. The screams from the closed rooms were getting urgent, and we barely escaped when one of the doors slammed open directly in front of us, revealing a middle-aged guy who looked like a biology teacher, wearing a corset and handcuffed to a teeter-totter.

At the uphill end of the tilted ballroom, a combo of nuns in Jiffy-Lube habits belted heavy metal at top shriek. The silky, presentable fellow - now female - was down to a G-string and a bowtie, refereeing a dodge-ball contest between the Turkish stripper and the half-naked little girl, using champagne balloons. As we passed, the little girl launched one at the stripper, missed, and hit the presentable fellow, who presented herself to a ringside table to be licked clean. Everyone we saw, from the biologist to the child, seemed jazzed up and hyper, as if Granny's Parlour was laced with aerosol uppers. I figured we wouldn't be missed if we left the beers on the table and skipped without paying.

Outside Granny's, Zuckerman was gone from the swivel chair. A hullabaloo of crickets and cicadas ticked and yammered in the breathless woods. Paula took my arm as we walked into the vortex of darkness beyond the gleam of the Krazy Kat lamp.

"Heavens," she said at last. "Did you ever see such in-your-face wickedness?"

"It's like somebody sat around thinking up things that would titillate a clientele of midwestern realtors. I bet I know who that was, too."

"Verry?"

"Egged on by Granny, I expect. And wouldn't you guess

that the cast of characters, like our guide, the strippers, all those staffers in all those rooms, right down to the little girl - whether she's really a girl or really as young as she looked - are some kind of captive string of sex workers that Verry and Granny run, enforced by Zuckerman and whoever else they've got for muscle. Maybe Florrie's friends, or Florrie herself, who knows? This thing is enormous, and I can't imagine how the hell they pull it off under Gerard's nose. Or I maybe he's in on it too. And of course, the cops, Christ!" I realized that I was jazzed-up myself, panting and uneasy, oppressed by the size and bloody depths of what we had found; and by something atmospheric that I couldn't name. It couldn't have been the heat; that had been a constant since I'd stepped off the plane in Springfield. Still, it irritated me, and so did the sense of hysteria, of some horror stalking us, that I couldn't shake.

"Cripes, it's hot," I groused.

"It is," Paula said, equably enough. But I felt the quiver of nerves in the hand on my arm.

I guess the darkness - which was almost absolute now, immune to night vision - made it seem hotter in contrast to expected coolness. No breath of air stirred the trees; we could have been inside an oven. We walked slower and quieter, straining for the threshold gleam from the crushed-limestone road underfoot, trusting to topography to keep us out of the ditch and the little creek. The bug cheering section grew quieter. Our footsteps grated and whispered on the stone. In the far darkness, a cow bawled again and again. A barely perceptible wind gusted and died.

I yanked Paula to a stop, and whispered, "Smell that?" My heart lurched and pounded.

"No... yes, shit. Hemp. Bloody Zuckerman's out here." Her whisper was thready with fear.

I pulled her close and breathed in her ear. "Stand absolutely still. He'd have to have night goggles to see us."

"Maybe he does."

"Thanks for that. Let's move very quietly...one step at a time... to the creek side of the road... and crouch down here for a couple of minutes. Maybe he's just out for a stroll."

"Ya, maybe. I can't stand the thought of getting beat up again, Hap." She started to cry. "Make them kill me, or stop this."

"Sh. We'll be OK."

We crouched by the side of the road, barely breathing, eyes, ears, and noses straining for sign of Zuckerman. After a few minutes of nerve-wrack, Paula put a hand on my shoulder to steady herself, balanced there on the balls of her feet. The gesture, the danger, the moody menace of the dead air, made me very aware. I turned to look at her. With full night vision now, I could barely make out, from a distance of six inches, the light grooves of her cheeks, her optimistic nose, the slight asymmetry of her mouth. With no warning, I was overcome with the conviction that no danger could compare to the desirability of that quirky, trembling mouth.

"God damn it," I murmured. "God damn it to hell, anyhow." She turned toward me, and that did it.

"Christ," she said, "Oh, Christ. I'm so scared." She

lowered her knees to the road. To kneel, evidently, so she could reach up and wrap her arms around me and pull me to her. "Hold me," she murmured. I did. We held each other, shivering.

"This is crazy," she whispered, and her teeth were chattering.

"Way, way ridiculous," I gasped. "Forget it."

She raised her head to see what I meant, and I was done for. Her mouth tasted of mustard and salt. My heart banged, upping the old blood pressure for any hydraulics that might follow.

"Hey," I said. "You don't taste like Gauloises." Kissing always makes me blather.

"I quit," she breathed.

"Good for you." I kissed her again, congratulatory.

"Listen," Paula said, when she could. "You're a fine fellow and all, but don't think I'm going to give it all up for you on a gravel road with a homicidal thug at large in the dark. If you don't take me back to that motel in the next five minutes, I'm going to scream."

"Don't," I said. "We'll get over this. It's just the ... the danger, I guess. And speaking of that, did Zuckerman stroll by just now?"

"No ... I think."

"Then he's still out here somewhere. Why don't you stay here, and I'll go get the Harley and - "

"And leave me here in the dark? I don't think so. We don't even know for sure how far away it is. I'm with you, Hap."

"All right. Then I insist on staying here, and staying alert and quiet, for five minutes, before we start down that road again. Count 300 seconds."

"Go."

While we were counting, we heard a small wind in the trees overhead, and a bigger one. A fat puff of cool air swirled around us. A front coming in, good deal; maybe the godawful heat was about to moderate. I entertained the notion that the weather gods had been holding out until I kissed Paula, before sending relief; dismissed it and went back to counting seconds.

I got there, and up to 323, before she whispered, "300." Fast pulse, I guess. We stood cautiously and began to walk, holding hands strategically, not to lose each other. When we'd gone maybe a hundred tentative paces I began seeing a faint blur of light that disappeared when I tried to look straight at it. Behind us, in the direction of Reeds Spring, I heard a faint roar.

"There's the end of the hollow, up there. The bikes should be - "

"Jesus," she whispered, and clutched my arm. "He's there too. Oh, shit, shit. I'm gonna pee my pants."

Where we'd left the Harley and the Vespa, I saw a momentary orange glow. The whiff of marijuana rode on the chill and fitful breezes that were starting to toss the underbrush. While we watched, a single orange spark arced into the little creek. Zuckerman was there, and toked, and he didn't give a crap whether we knew it or not.

"Hey, folks," he called, lazy and amused. "C'mon over here."

I touched Paula's lips and pushed her straight down onto the road. I knelt quickly by her, and mouthed into her ear: "I hear a train coming. Don't move until it's here, and then try to run past him down the road, under cover of the noise. If I can get away from him, I'll pick you up at the bottom of the Hollow." I left her with a little Don't Move pressure on the top of her head. The train's roar increased a little, and I could see the sweep and flicker of its headlight in the tops of the trees.

"Zuckerman?" I called.

"Tha's right. You the geek with that chickie, thought I was Arthur?"

"Jesus," I said. "'M'I gladda see you. Dark as a goddamn cow out here. My bike there?"

"Yep."

I followed the sound of his voice, stumbling in and out of the little creek, trying to remember if we'd left the bikes beyond it, not remembering. "Goddamn woman," I snarled. "Coon't get her into the spirit. Granny spirit. Frigid bitch."

"Sir? You having trouble with that skinny whore you come inta Granny's with?"

"Betcher ass. Bitch din' wanna play dodgeball. Dodge my balls, hah! Took off half a hour ago. If 'at bitch took my bike, 'mgonna killer."

The freight was getting nearer, and I had to raise my voice a little.

"Naw," Zuckerman said. "The Harley? That yours? Nice classic bike. It's right here. See?"

He reached out of the blackness and grabbed my arm. "And if you'll permit me to speculate, sir, I believe that could be the frigid bitch herself, creepin down the holler not twenny feet from you."

I spun, and saw only blackness. Zuckerman's massive hand twirled me effortlessly into a hammerlock that was followed by a knife under my chin. The yank on my hammerlocked arm made me gasp with pain.

"Paula," I croaked. "Run!"

Zuckerman yelled over my head, "You run, he dies, chickie. That what you want?"

I heard her footsteps, even over the growing roar of the freight, hesitate and stop. The damn little fool.

"What do you want?" she called.

"You, chickie. It was unkind of you to deceive ol' Zuckerman. Get that elegant ass of yours over here. Mr. Verry wants a word with you."

"Get the hell out of here, Paula," I yelled. "He can't see - "

Zuckerman slammed something into my eyes hard enough to make me see stars; and for an instant, a green and haunted picture of the woods around us, sliding and smearing with the motion of Zuckerman's hand. Night goggles. They went away again, leaving me straining into darkness that was broken now by the bobbing flicker of the freight's headlight.

"See?" Zuckerman laughed. "I can see fine. F'r instance, I don't know why you din't go ahead and boff her back there, man. I ever saw a woman ready to go, that was then. Tell you what, though, that was your chance with that one. She's gonna be a mess, time this night's over. C'mon."

He marched me back across the creek and onto the road. Paula stood in the flicker and glare of the headlight, looking as scared as it is possible to be, not saving herself.

"Paula, for shit's sake, run," I said.

"No," she said. "I can't do that."

"You stupid little whore," I screamed. "Move! Go!"

"Not that she's payin no attention to you, asshole," Zuckerman observed. "But shut your mouth." The knife dug into my neck, creating a streaming place that felt like a dentist's drill. Warmth puddled on my collarbone.

Paula just shook her head, standing there in the light -

Wait, I thought. Something's really, really wrong. In the first place, no headlight ever made that kind of a flicker, like all the nukes of World War Five going off. And furthermore, the train tracks don't come this close to John Holler. The thing sounded like we were standing inside the engine housing, and now the headlight was a constant sheet of lightning, and in the din of thunder, something ripped and slammed through the branches overhead and exploded on the road next to Paula, and then ten somethings, hailstones the size of baseballs and cantaloupes Pow, *Pow*, and then one hit Zuckerman and glanced off and knocked me half silly. The knife scraped across the point of my chin and Zuckerman collapsed behind me. Paula screamed at the spurt of blood, black in the glare and screech of lightning, and now you could hear the lightning, a steady snapping over the roar of wind and thunder.

And now it was smaller hailstones, but a hell of a lot of them, pounding us, making us stagger and cower in the constant strobe of lightning. The temperature dropped off a cliff, and it was winter suddenly. I grabbed Paula and yanked her into the creek bed, the only thing even a little like cover.

"Wha-?"

"Tornado," I yelled, and I couldn't hear myself. "Get your head down." I shoved her against the foot-high bank of the little creek and sprawled over her. I looked around for Zuckerman, and he was up now, braced against a splintered oak tree, fumbling with the night goggles, shit, when he gets those things on we're dead meat in any weather.

All the trees between us and the main road bent to the ground, groaning and splintering, and in the window of visibility that made, I saw the giant Weenie and the funnel cloud, waltzing across the fields in the strobe of lightning. The Weenie looked like Ginger Rogers. Ecstatic, free at last, trailing its guy wires like scarves, grinning and shedding pieces of metal big enough and sharp enough -

"Look out," I screamed, and shoved Paula's face into the mud. A sheet of tin the size of a desktop scaled at us like a frisbee, whup-whup-whup, and when it hit Zuckerman, it was the sound of a cleaver making a serving of ribs. The rest of the Weenie broke free of its partner and vaulted over us to crash into the woods on the far side of John Holler. And behind it, roaring with sorrow, came the tornado.

I found a tree root as big around as my wrist in the mud of

the creek bank, and I grabbed its underside with both hands, Paula under me and inside the circle of my arms. The tornado danced over us, flaying me with wires, or maybe it was only hypervelocity straws and grass. My shirt peeled away like paint, and I screamed, and then there was no air to scream with, only a mighty vacuum that hauled us straight into the freezing chaos and pelted us with debris. I held the root with all the strength I had, and gripped Paula with bare legs. One end of the root ripped out of the mud, and we whipped back and forth like a foxtail on a handlebar. Root and branch, I thought. The wrath of the Lord -

And it was over. We slammed to the ground, exhausted and half-conscious.

I was slithering over hailstones, choking on muddy water, filthy and ...

"Hey! Where's my pants, damn it?"

Paula dropped my legs and knelt by my head, panting and wide-eyed with shock. "Gone with the wind, pal. Sure hope the preacher don't come callin."

"Holy shit. How's come you're all dressed, then?"

She shrugged, and her fingers probed gently over my head, visiting a collection of bruises and abrasions that could have illustrated a first aid manual. "Some bozo saved my life, just now. Time I could see what was going on, he was drowning in the crick. I coulda shopped for pants, or I coulda hauled him out. Did I do wrong?"

"That's OK. Where's Zuckerman?"

"I think that's part of him." She gestured, without looking, at a barely visible huddle in the road. I looked long enough to know that I'd seen too much.

The woods that had sheltered us were gone, and so were the clouds that had blackened the world. A half-moon hung in the sky, and lit a scene of splinters and trash, broken glass, downed trees, and, up John Holler toward Granny's Parlour, half of the giant Weenie and a junkyard of demolished cars.

"Jesus, it went right up to Granny's," I said. "We better get up there and see if Suellen's OK."

We did. The Harley, crazily, was standing on its little kickstand, ready to go, and Paula weaved us up the hollow, navigating through the clutter of limbs and trash. Three of the cars were upside down. Alarms bleated and told us in stern voices to stand back. Two others were wrapped around trees, and a deflated SUV was making love to an overturned Buick. All of them were hideous with mangled metal and starred windows.

As we got closer to Granny's, we began to hear the moans and screams of the patrons. The whole outside and upper half of the crazy structure was gone, scattered to the wind. We walked in through Granny's floor plan, stepping over wrecked furniture and scattered bodies and the stumps of the flimsy partitions. Paula sucked breath through her teeth and began to fret about Suellen.

"Let's not borrow trouble," I said. I felt calm, my sanity standing erect as crazily and improbably as the Harley on its kickstand. "She was back in the deepest part of the place. Maybe it was safer back there."

"Hopeful bastard," Paula said. "Thanks for trying."

But so it proved. As we went deeper, the walls rose around us and became whole. And of course, nothing had happened to the limestone passages of the deepest stretch of Granny's. Suellen was not only safe, but sound asleep, cushioned on the sodden breast of her mother. I have to believe they drank something; I mean, who could sleep through the end of the world?

When Paula saw them, she began to laugh, and once she started, it went on and on, whooping and gasping on the floor outside Trudi's salon, pounding on her thighs, shaking, tears smearing the mud I'd forced her face into. I left her there with many a backward glance, and picked up a towel and a carafe of cold water from the deserted kitchen. I soaked the towel and brought that and a bottle of brandy back to her.

"Wipe your face with one of these, and drink the other," I said. "Probably either way would be an improvement."

Paula made a couple of gestures at it, and couldn't do it. She went back to whooping and gasping. I knelt beside her and gently sponged her face clean, and gave her a little snort of brandy, which they always do in stories, and I'm not sure why it's supposed to help. But it always does, and this was no exception.

Paula made the usual spluttering sounds, and actually said, "Thanks, I needed that." As if I'd slapped her. But I think she was just being -

"Listen," I said, and I knew that my calm was a deeper insanity than her hysterics. "What, you're working on your Pluckiness badge? For god's sake, Paula, cut loose. You're entitled."

She hiccuped, and rubbed the back of her neck with brandy. "Maybe," she sighed. "It's so hard to know what one's entitled to, before it's too late, haven't you found? Maybe that's the secret to power and riches. Let's get out of here before the paramedics come. You still don't have any clothes on."

See? I'd forgotten all about that. The rules were blown to hell with my pants. Luckily, there was a lot of abandoned clothing around. I dressed myself in Jiffy-Lube coveralls, and we scrammed. We met the first ambulance at the entrance to John Holler.

The storm had knocked out power in the stretch of Branson where the Residence Inn was. When we got back to the Unit, there was an earnest lass knocking on our door.

"The management and the entire Marriott Family regret the inconvenience, sir, ma'am," she said, handing me a packet. "Please use these candles safely, and extinguish them when you retire, or when power is restored."

We promised to be careful, and she let us into the room with a regular mechanical key, since the card gizmo needed power to work and the storm had apparently knocked out their auxiliary power. If any. I opened the packet and lit a candle, and looked at Paula.

"Damn good of them to come around at this hour. Why'd they think we'd need candles in the middle of the night?"

Paula tipped her wrist toward the candle and peered at it. "It's a little after eight thirty."

"No way. Your watch stopped."

She nodded weakly. "Way. Time crawls when you're having terror. Come here, you big damn hero."

She was sitting on the bed, I was at the breakfast bar scrunching the candle into a salt shaker. I walked over to the bed, finding the simple act of putting feet down in order almost more than I could handle.

"Jesus, I'm tired."

"If I try to stay sitting up beyond the next ten seconds, I'll ... well. I won't. Hap, you saved my life. Twice, from Zuckerman and the tornado. I've never met a life-saving guy, and you did it twice. For me. Honest to God, you are a genuine narrative hero. Do you have enough left to just hold me for a few minutes?"

"You saved mine, too, Paula. You met one and be'd one, all'n the same, ... the same...." I gave up and waved a hand. "Least I can do."

I did, and for more than a few minutes. As soon as we were on the bed together, she began to sob with exhaustion and relief, and in fifteen seconds I was bawling right along with her. The mortal fear of Zuckerman's knife, the hopeless, stubborn loyalty of Paula refusing to leave me to die, the baying chaos of the tornado: Now that we were safe, now at last they were real.

It took us maybe a quarter of an hour to pipe down. The last of it would have been impossible to categorize as sobbing, or laughter, or brute grunts of relief. We stopped and started again two or three times, each less frantic and more contented, and at some point it became the little croons and murmurs, the little rubs and entanglements that flourish at the top of the oldest, slipperiest slope known to humans. Paula raised her face to me in the candlelight. The rug burns were almost gone, though there was a pretty good residue of ditch mud in her hair. Her mouth tasted now of tears and Granny's brandy.

"Yes," she whispered. Her breath was warm on my mouth. "Yes, God, please ...." It was a prayer of theological rightness. We'd escaped death and perversion and atomization, and what was left was the grateful instinct to couple. She began to pull at the zipper of the Jiffy-Lube outfit.

"Wait," I whispered. "You didn't interview me yet."

Our eyes locked, and I saw the flare of annoyance give way to amusement. And then the amusement evaporated, and the eyes widened, and invited me to see more closely. Here is what I saw in the green depths of her eyes: I saw that what I had taken for some dramatic, possibly tiresome weariness was nothing but decency and humanity, seen through an overlay of well-earned sorrow. The decency and the sorrow drew me to Paula Vanek as dark matter draws galaxies over parsecs of empty space.

"We'll get to that," she promised. "This is off the books."

And did it occur to me to wonder whether that, or anything else she whispered from "Yes" on, might have been drawn from a repertoire of client-management protocols, arranged, say, in order of usefulness in various subclasses of prospective single-intercourse encounters?

Not at that time.

16.

I woke, or I dreamed of waking, in darkness. A match flared, and it was Paula at the breakfast bar, fixing a fresh candle. The light shone on her cheek, her hands, and on the edge of a breast. Something you'd find in the "Dutch, XVII C." section of a good museum. When she had the candle settled into the salt shaker, she stretched and wiggled her butt, getting kinks out, I guess. In the soft light, it was hard to see the hail bruises, but I knew they were there. Our lovemaking had been a medley of sighs and yikes, pleasure and pain alternating and blending.

"What art thou looking at?" She used some Northern European dialect. Dutch or Polish, maybe; nothing I would have understood by day.

"A very plucky girl. Prob'ly a world standard of plucky." My voice was furred with sleep.

Without moving, with no passage of time, she was back across the room, standing beside the bed. "Yes? I will pluck thee, pal." But she said it softly, as if not to scare me too much.

I fell back on the pillow. "I think I been plucked."

Paula stretched herself next to me. In the light of the candle, her body was tawny and shadowed, a sunset dunescape with freckles. Candleglo, I thought. This what you wanted, Lee? God, I don't blame you.

"Not half," Paula whispered, and her fingertips traced

patterns on my flanks that stopped my breath as efficiently as the tornado. "Oh, not all plucked by half, my splendid boy. There's a world of apples on thy tree. Now for example, I thought that first business was pleasant enough, but it went by kind of fast, wouldn't thou say? Want to try again?"

"Oh," I said. "Geez, Paula, you're dealing with a man of advanced age here. I don't know that - "

"Once a king, always a king, that it?" she purred, lapsing into English for the sake of the pun. "Look at the clock."

I did. "Yeah, exactly. A quarter of two, for Pete's - "

"Ya. C'mere."

I have to say, it was a new thing. Lee and I had often enough had doubles, and I'd kind of liked them. There's a kind of sweet soreness to the second time, slower and altogether different from the first. Pearly, D.H. Lawrence called it, and it's so. Paula led me through that, and into mapless lands beyond. She coaxed and teased and plucked and delayed and inspired. She taught me what would do that for her, and we did, inheriting each other's bodies, losing track of our borders. We circled the flame, weightless, electric, celebrating sex in Flemish hexameters.

And when she was at last drifting off, curled against my belly, I thought of one more thing, a kind of alternative afterthought subclass variant protocol that brought her gasping awake. "Well thought," she panted. "Thou hast the idea now."

The very last thing I remember, before sleep slammed me against the pillow for good, was looking at the clock.

"Christ," I muttered. "A quarter after three."

17.

I woke to the smell of coffee and the sound of the shower. Every corner of my body was weak and sore. I tried to go back to sleep, but I really had to pee. There seemed to be no alternative to invading the bathroom, and no real reason not to. When I was finished, and heading back to bed, a soapy hand came out of the shower curtain and yanked me into a place of steam and hissing water and gleaming skin.

"Good morning," Paula said. "I'm clean as a button right now, and you look like hell. Stand up here."

She soaped me up, and rinsed, and I began to feel a little better. Paula looked good in pink. I pulled her head against my collarbone, and her funny IPA hair squeaked under my fingers. She raised a finger, rather like the presentable fellow outside Trudi's parlor, and leaned outside the curtain long enough to grab the Marriott Bath Gel, and started over again on me.

"Aw, Jesus, Paula. Really?"

"Hush," she said. "This was on the agenda last night, I just fell asleep before I could get to it. Don't you want to feel all slick and swell?"

"I think I'm already feeling it." She smiled, and poured herself a fat handful of gel, and ... I astounded myself.

"Still," I said, thickly. "It takes your mind off the bruises and all. All right, then. You want to get slicked up, too?"

We were lucky somebody didn't slip and break his hip.

Suellen arrived as I finished shaving. Paula was sitting at the breakfast counter with a cup of Residence Inn coffee. Suellen looked from me to Paula and back, and started to grin.

"Well," she said. "Shoot. If that isn't sweet. Congratulations, guys."

"For what?" I asked.

"Don't give me that, you foxy codger. So, how was it, Paula?"

Paula smiled. "Hap saved my life twice last night, and that's no joke. The guy is a hero and a very superior fellow in just about every way I can think of. Also, he has the shortest refractory period I've ever run across, for a guy his age."

"Wait a second," I objected. "Just about?"

"You still snore."

"Well," I said. "You probably do too. I wasn't keeping score."

Suellen clapped her hands twice. "Could we settle down, here? We gotta figure out what to do about Mom."

"An exit strategy," Paula said. "We blundered into this with no clear rules of engagement and no exit strategy."

"The usual result of that," I said, "is that somebody starts clamoring to bring the troops home. I'd be glad to do that."

"It's not that simple. Mom needs me, and I need you." Suellen lifted a hand. "I know, that's not the same as saying Mom needs you. One of you, she hardly knows, and the other, she ...

well, she hates his guts. Which is mutual, I'm sure." She made a little Eh! of bafflement. "Help me out here, guys."

"Sure," I said. "Why do you need us?"

"I have to get Mom out of here. You saw her."

"OK. Is there a big problem with that? Other than Mom herself?"

"She says so. She's got herself into this crazy standoff with Verry and - get this - the guy she thinks she has goods on, which is Gerard. Verry ... God, where to start?"

I poured myself some coffee. "Start at the end, and go back until you get to the beginning. Let's say we just load Trudi's flatcar on a piggyback truck – OK, sorry – and ship her out of here. Aside from the cost, what's the worst that could happen?"

Suellen scowled. "Amos Verry will call up the Minnesota state cops, or attorney general, or something, and tell them he's got a wanted woman with a murder warrant on her."

"Why doesn't he do that anyway? What's he want Trudi around for?"

"Mom says Gerard won't let him. Something about harboring a fugitive, bringing disgrace to the practice, blah blah. Gerard can cut Verry loose any time, according to Verry's agreement with the practice, that he signed when he joined. He's a junior partner until Gerard dies or retires."

"Well, for Pete's sake," Paula said. "Why doesn't Gerard cut him loose anyhow? Verry's a thug and a crook, and I'd think Gerard would be glad to get rid of him. He can't be that far from retirement anyways. Not to mention, what's his motive for protecting your mother?"

"Well, it's not that simple. Verry gave Mom some kind of scandalous goods on Gerard, without necessarily meaning to, which Mom figures she can use to get Gerard not to can Verry, and thus not to give Verry no further reason not to bust Mom."

I thought through that labyrinth, and snorted. "That's the flimsiest, silliest nonsense I ever heard of. If Verry has some scandalous goods on Gerard, why doesn't he just blackmail Gerard himself? Why go around the barn like that?"

Suellen shook her head. "There's some kind of X Factor in play. I think Mom knows some key thing that Verry doesn't. It's unstable, I agree. I can't believe it's lasted this long. And I think it would fall apart if one of them took a clear look at the whole picture. The point is, they all believe it, and that's all it takes for it to work. It's like religion, I guess. Verry's not going to bust Mom, if he believes that busting her is going to get him canned from that law firm. He needs the respectability if he's going to run for the state senate, particularly as a Democrat."

She sighed. "And so forth, all around the triangle. But the thing is, I can't get Mom to tell me what the dirty secret on Gerard is. She figures I'd tell you, and you'd short-circuit the whole thing, and she'd end up on a prison farm in Minnesota."

"Me?" I protested. "I don't give a flying fig what happens to your mother. I thought I was well rid of her the last time she bugged out of town."

I saw then that this was not a subject on which I could just say any old thing that came into my head, around Suellen. "Shoot,

Suellen. I'm sorry. There, now. Your devotion to your mother is touching and commendable, and I'm, I'm … "

Paula cleared her throat, mercifully. "Hap sometimes lets the virtue of his plain-spokenness get away from him, honey," she said. "But I know he wouldn't do or say anything that would make you unhappy."

"Exactly," I said. "I withdraw that last remark, and I hereby promise to do what I can to get your mother out of this mess in a way that doesn't send her to jail."

Suellen sent me a sulky glance, which is not all that different from being eyed sulkily by a mother leopard. Sheesh. See why I try to stay clammed up? You open your mouth, you wind up deeper in the dip than you were when nobody knew what you were thinking. Look at what I'd just promised.

"Why … don't … we," Paula said, singing the words like a den mother coming up with a new crafts project, "try this? See if we can learn something about Gerard? Maybe one of us could substitute for Trudi in this, long enough to get her out of it, and then - "

"Ya, brilliant, Paula," Suellen snorted. "Verry finds out Gerard's guilty secret is, like, public knowledge, then Mom's got no traction against him. Off she goes to Minnesota."

"Well, we'll have to be very discreet. Maybe Len Saffel could tell us something, Hap. Could you give him a call?"

"Sure. I could try. Somehow, I don't see Saffel as a guy who gives away information over the phone. But I'll try, I'll try. What do we know that he'd like to know?"

Suellen looked up from her brown study of the floor. "We know who killed Arthur."

"Well..." I thought about that. "We know what a guy told us, which guy is now being autopsied in sections by the Stone County ME."

"Well, shoot," Paula said. "We know about this stupid, rickety, three-way blackmail standoff. We know that his video clip of Trudi's death is a fake. That ought to be worth something."

"Yeah," I said. "Come to think of it, what was that all about anyhow?"

"Oh, yeah," Suellen snorted. "Verry arranged for that as evidence that Mom was dead, in case the Minnesota cops ever came down here on their own hook. He knows some kind of amateur film director up in Kansas City, that came down for a weekend and shot it. The whole scene was supposed to be, originally, a tourist taking an illicit video of a colorful Branson tourist show, that was supposed to've gotten out of hand. Was the script. They had to shoot it twice, Mom said, which was a pain in the butt. Something went wrong with the Steadycam the first time, which is why the camera swung around like that. Verry also got a fake death certificate put into the Stone County records, which I guess was no big trick for him. He let it stay there long enough to get into the papers, and then he had it taken out. Yeah, go ahead and call your guy in Springfield, and then get off the phone. I wanta call Wet and give him the news about Mom."

And not a murmur from Suellen about the heartbreak she'd gone through when she first saw one of those takes. Blood is thicker than water, I guess; the bloodier the better.

"Well," I said. "Let's try it. Suellen's right, we'll have to be awfully cute about getting information about Gerard that nobody's supposed to know. I'd be surprised if Len Saffel gives us something that hot, no matter what we offer him."

But in fact, Saffel was mildly receptive when I phoned him.

"Listen, I'm always interested in exchanging information. How I make what they claim here is a living. But you think I'm gonna take serious information, or give it out, over the phone, you think again. Sure, come on up. You're down in Branson? How d'ya like it?"

"Um," I said. "What a place. This afternoon after lunch be OK?"

"I'll be out of the editorial conference around two."

After she'd wolfed a couple of grapes and a bowl of granola, Suellen putted back to Granny's on the Vespa to start the job of getting Trudi back to human dimensions, leaving me with Paula to kill a morning and eat lunch while we waited for our window of access to Len Saffel.

Paula, ignoring the maid service her credit card was buying, busied herself straightening the room up and making the bed. I have to think it was displacement activity, a way of keeping busy. I don't know how much of your life you've wasted noticing things like this, but the act of making a bed - the stiff-legged bend required to reach out and get things tidy without kneeling on the part you've just tidied - really showcases the bedmaker's butt. It's probably one of the little drops of glue that sticks marriages together through the rocky early years. And when the butt in question is world-class -

"What art thou looking at?"

We exchanged a look over the freshly smoothed linens, and laughed.

Paula stuck out her tongue. "Nah. We better let you get your strength back. I thought I detected the teeniest smack of reluctance that last go-round."

"In the shower? I thought I upheld a pretty good standard. For a guy my age."

"For a guy your size," Paula acceded, "you're in prime shape. I got to think the ladies of Gabbro County have let a David go unpolished. But even Michelangelo had to put down his chisel once in a while."

We drove the Harley up to Springfield by a back road that flashed through hollows and crested along ridgetops in clean and blessedly cool sunshine. I let myself see another side of southwestern Missouri, a country that the dam-builders and the retirement-cottage realty pimps and the lardbutt tourists hadn't got around to ruining yet. It was an Appalachia innocent of coal and desperation, carved out of clean and well-bedded limestone, a scrubbed and wholly Midwestern wilderness. Or it was the very same place as yesterday, and I'd gotten laid at last. I heard that cynical gloss in the steady snarl of the Harley, read it in the supple and elegantly forked body behind which I rode.

Goddamn sex. I thought I had got over it at last, and all I'd achieved was crabbed and beery isolation, now given way to sappy euphoria. I hooked a finger of each hand in Paula's belt and felt her haunches flex with the jounce and vectoring of the road. Paula wiggled her butt back a little on the seat, acknowledging the touch. Lee Morgan would never have done that; would never have ridden a Harley to scoot her butt around on in the first place. I patted a haunch and looked out over the valley.

The tornado that had saved our lives by killing Zuckerman had left a swath of ruin across hollows, forests, and fields. And still the birds sang and the freshness broke through, with the wildflowers blowing over it all. The hazy hell had become paradise through the simple agency of a lethal cool front. The trail of wreckage was easy to follow, and must have been pureed with people's lives, the tears of victims and their families, and the busy check-writing pens of insurance agents settling claims while the claimants were still in shock. That was part of the Nothing that lay behind a tornado.

And what of the Nothing that lay behind Hap Maryland? No one can catch that in the mirror. I had searched Zuckerman and Amos Verry, and if there was anything behind them, they kept it very well hidden. I had looked most searchingly at Paula Vanek, and found... well, Something. Not Nothing. Was that Something, that thing that wasn't Nothing, a refutation of Professor Brkczec? Evidence that there is a Something that makes sense of the random swirling of wind, or of events? Even marching bands spell out some message. Or was what I found in Paula's eyes just Hap Maryland, peering presbyopically at himself in the shining mirror of Paula Vanek's Nothingness?

And either way, so what? Have we proven something human that transcends the tuba players? A soul, for God's sake, that outmoded nonsense? The soul has been dissected for, and shown to be absent. I - who ought to know - have never seen or felt evidence of a soul within me. Can a marching band have a soul? Can a cloud of gnats, a dust devil or a tornado? A dog? If none of those, then how a human? And for heaven's sake, is that where it's been hiding all this time, while we've been praying over it? In the eyes of a woman who's getting ready to invite you into herself? I have not - to follow the Harley's logic, and let's not beat around the bush - coupled with a lot of women in my life. We should be talking to one of these superstud basketball players, I guess, if we want a good statistical sample. As for me, you can count my lifetime sexual partners on the bananas of a two-pound bunch. I was a virgin when I married Ginnie, the mother of my two children. Sex with Ginnie was by the book, and so was our divorce and her ritual dalliance with lesbianism. After that, there were a few one-shot stands, including the mistake with Trudi Ransom: selfish, embarassed, forgettable.

Lee Morgan was another order of woman. Serene and affectionate, so beautiful that my first sight of her left me awed and hopeless. I courted her as earnestly as a knight beneath the window of a princess, and when she astonished me by inviting me up, I was unsure whether my vigil had been of sufficient purity. With Lee Morgan, sex was iridescent, shimmering, the ravishment of Ravel or Debussy. It was a privilege, a joy ... And in the end, of course, a deception, since that magic implies, requires, and promises, fidelity. Sex with Lee Morgan was our special music, ours alone. Unthinkable that either of us could betray it. But she did. I do not remember searching Lee's eyes in the way I had Paula's. What would I have seen?

Sex with Paula Vanek was such a human thing. There was nothing in it that did not celebrate the human body and the mystery of that crazy little not-Nothing that sits behind our eyes - or below our navels - and makes the body do the things it does. So, to be fair, I do not know yet about myself, or about that fellow's dog. In both cases, doubt seems safest. Anyone can doubt that there is meaning behind the swirling nothingness of a tornado, or that there was a worthwhile purpose to these busy to-and-fro-ings in rural Missouri. I certainly doubted that there was anything but Nothing behind the fat eyes of one who sold out her child to save trouble. But I was sure that Paula Vanek held Something. I had seen it.

*

Len Saffel was in his office when we arrived at the Beacon building on Weaver Avenue. He was wearing the same white-on-white ensemble, maybe a little more inkstained, that we'd seen on our first visit. His attitude was a little scuffed-up, too.

"You know what word I got from down Branson?" he asked us. "I got word somebody went down there and started tweaking around the edge of Mr. Amos Verry's concerns, asking a lot a questions, posing as a Kraut journalist of some kind. From the description, I expect that'd be you, Mister Maryland. Then there's an open assault charge, with property damage, up here at Miz Mary Alice's Bikini Club, ended up with a couple stitches in Mr. Verry's face, and although they's any number of Springfield citizens that might have liked to see that, witnesses on the spot said the perpetrator was headed for Branson. A small-time goniff that works for Mr. Verry goes missing, but witnesses placed him in a car out by the lake with a slender, hooker-looking lady - their description, not mine - with short dark hair, Miz Vanek, which sounds like the same lady was seen getting along famously with Mr. Verry at the Slaughterhouse Grille earlier that evening. Then last night, a much more serious thug gets killed in the Stone County tornado, which thug also had connections to Mr. Verry. He has endured a run of poor luck since I talked to you folks, much of it closely connected to yourselves. You folks are getting a little hot to handle, seems to me."

I leaned back in my chair. "What would you like to know, Mr. Saffel?"

He leaned back in his turn, and looked out the window at a stuffed owl on the sill. "How much of that whole business can I get out of you, and how much am I going to have to give you?"

"Mr. Saffel, you can absolutely have the whole thing, as soon as I'm sure it's not going to bring Amos Verry's army down on us."

He shook his head. "Mr. Verry's getting a little short-staffed these days. So to speak. Give."

I gave Len Saffel a somewhat edited version of our adventures to date, leaving out as much as I could calculate, on the fly, might come around and bite us if it got back to Amos Verry. Saffel was silent for a time.

"That three-way blackmail standoff is the goofiest business I heard of yet, and you're looking at a guy that's been writing small-town stuff for forty years. I can't believe it'd survive one minute of contemplation by any of the parties involved."

I nodded. "There's something about it that doesn't quite jell. Sometimes, though, people get threatened and it sort of freezes their common sense. You must see that every day."

"That I do, sir. I think you just give me a headline and first paragraph for next week's column. Nevertheless, you'd think people in that position might lose some sleep over it, and one night along two-three in the morning, they'd come up with something. Any one of 'em for example, said 'publish and be damned' you'd think that'd bring the whole thing down."

"Maybe that's it," I said. "Maybe they all think it's too dangerous to fool with. Like Mutual Assured Destruction, but triangular."

He looked skeptically at his owl for a few minutes, and then came back to the here and now. "What if they was somebody with an interest in keeping the pot stirred up? Somebody with access to all three of 'em?"

"A ringmaster," Paula said, looking startled.

Saffel shook his head. "What you got here is the least thing like a ring there is. Neither Verry ner Gerard's the follower type, and it don't sound like your friend's mama is, either."

"Not a ring*leader*," Paula said. "A ring*master*, like in a circus. Listen, you think about these horses, trotting around in circles. Any one of them stops to think it over, or starts worrying about the rest of the horses, the whole thing piles up in a mess. It takes this guy in the middle cracking his whip, saying, Don't look at them, look at me. So none of them does."

"Hn," Saffel allowed. "That's a moderately amusing thought, young lady. You got any candidates?"

"One," Paula said. "Darlene Feely."

18.

"Darlene ain't here," the slattern snapped, and began to slam the screen.

Paula lifted a hand and tipped her head winsomely. "Gee, what a shame," she said. "We come all the way from North Carolina."

"Yeah?" The stained bathrobe turned to me. There was a rip in the bodice, repaired with a paper clip. "What for?"

"It's a bit of a long story," I said. "Miss Christian here is the case worker. I'm just her supervisor. Would you know when Miss Feely might be coming back?"

The door swung back an inch. "She works," the woman said, and lifted a hand to the grey straggle that crossed her brow. "Any god damn gov'ment snoop ought ta know that. Darlene is a perfessional woman in the legal perfession. She runs a group a the top lawyers in Missouri."

"Oh," Paula said. "We knew that. We aren't from the government, gracious. We're, ..." She pulled out an attaché case we'd bought for three bucks at a Salvation Army store. It bore the initials "LWC," and we'd given her the name Laura Christian to go with it.

Figuring that Darlene Feely would be working, we'd hoped to be able to size her up through her neighbors, out there at her trailer park. We invented a foundation that was looking for experienced females interested in training as paralegals. That was almost the extent of our planning, though, and we had definitely not figured on encountering her mother; the knock on her door had been window dressing for nosy neighbors. So I was hoping Paula had something pretty good in mind. Rummaging in the briefcase was a giveaway that her improvisor circuit was already running low, or else she'd forgotten the name of the foundation.

I raised a hand. "Hold on, Miss Christian. I told you last time, make certain to whom you're speaking before you give out information. That is the policy of the Minerva Foundation, and I will thank you to keep it foremost in your - h'm, your mind. Madam, you are Mrs. Euleen Feely of 41217 Battlefield Extension Court?" I rattled the numbers off serially, not using any short cuts like 'twelve' or 'seventeen'. Trying to sound like I was quoting from a case summary instead of the phone book.

"I am," Mrs. Feely said. "Not that it's none of your business, ya stuffed shirt. Lady here wants ta give me information, you keep your trap shut and let her. What was it, hon?"

Paula managed to look flustered and caught in the middle. "I'm s'posed to get a picture ID, ma'am. Mr. Hardacre is quite right."

Euleen Feely slanted a poisonous glance at me. "You come in here, Miss Christian," she said. "I'd have to get my purse. You can wait outside, Mister Wiseacre."

I stiffened and chewed the inside of my cheek. "Very well. Five minutes, Miss Christian."

I made it behind the next trailer where we'd parked the

Harley before I broke down. Mr. Hardacre, Jesus.

It was more than twenty minutes, and well worth it. Paula parted company with Mrs. Feely like a Welcome Wagon lady, and came back to the Harley with wide eyes and a barely suppressed grin.

"What?"

"Get that helmet on," she said. "I think I got the X Factor."

She made me wait for it, though, firing up the Harley and rumbling us back through the Airstreams and double-wides and the empty concrete slabs laced with wild carrots. The woman has a gift for stringing out expectations.

"First of all," she said, when we were back on Battlefield Road, headed for highway 65. "The scandal about Gerard is that he was caught with his hand on a little girl's fanny twenty-some years ago, and damn near got disbarred. Apparently he was one of these volunteer, Jaycee kind of guys that thinks kids are the future of America and all. He was giving a Brownie troop a tour of the Greene County courthouse, including the jail."

"And he copped a feel? Is that all?"

"Not exactly. One of the Brownies lagged behind, and when the den mother, whatever they call her, went back to check, they were in the solitary block. The little girl was in handcuffs over his lap with her drawers down around her knees. It was covered up, of course, but it cost Morris and Gerard a bundle. Morris was furious, but Gerard apparently was enough of a rainmaker in those days that he didn't want to break up the practice over it."

"Well, jeez," I said. "How rather amazing. Take twenty

years off Gerard, I get the same guy, pretty much. I'm surprised he'd be involved in something like that. And anyhow, how does that give Trudi Ransom leverage over him now, all these years later?"

"Silly question," Paula said. "She knows about it, and very few other people do. Journalistic protection of well-placed pedophiles no longer obtains, and Gerard would be ruined by disclosure. Here's two better ones, and I'll let you decide which one you want to ask first." She'd been a bit on the short end of the detecting up to now, and I think she was enjoying making a meal of this.

"How does Trudi Ransom know about it in the first place, and why did I find out by interviewing Euleen? She sends her love, by the way."

"I bet," I said. "What'd you tell her about life on the road with Mr. Hardacre?"

Paula scooted herself back against me and pulled my hand off her belt loop and wrapped it around her tummy. The Harley swayed a little, rubbing her back across my chest. Her voice purred in my earphones. "I said you were really a very nice person when you relaxed, but you were so shy around strangers that you sometimes came across officious. I led her to believe that it had hurt your career at the Foundation, and you were working real hard on your people skills."

"Poor Hardacre," I said. "Nobody understands what it's like to go through life with a name like that. Thanks for not making it Hardass."

"I considered Mr. Stiffley. OK, which question do you pick?"

"The first one," I said, "because I already figured out the second. That abused little Brownie has grown up to be no other than Darlene Feely."

"Very good, though it was kind of shooting fish in a barrel, considering who I was just talking to. The thing is, that is a very, very closely guarded secret. The little girl's name was withheld of course, and no one who was connected to it has much motivation to spread it around. I think that's the piece that Trudi knows; though God knows how she knows it."

"She used to be good at dirt. How did you get this scoop?"

"I have to thank you for it, Hardacre. Your tone put Mrs. Feely in mind of the lawyers and cops she dealt with back then. Apparently, they tried to make her believe the whole business was Darlene's fault, and she'd be lucky to stay out of jail. The more she told me, the more I admitted what an ordeal it was working with you, particularly on the road like this."

"You are a skilled interviewer, Miss Christian. Don't you think it would be kind of uncomfortable to have the Brownie you groped, serving as your office manager?"

"Sure must be. Wouldn't you think Gerard would do everything in his power not to have her around?"

"Which says that he has no power in this situation. Cripes! Who for Pete's sake would be so Machiavellian as to install the groped Brownie in Gerard's office?"

"Amos Verry would, but it wasn't him. It was Darlene

herself."

"Whoa. She calls up, and says, gimme a job, or I'm going public with a suppressed memory?"

Paula was silent for a minute, while she negotiated a ramp onto US 65. "Maybe that was how it occurred to her at first. But apparently she had a better idea. Euleen tells me that her daughter and Gerard are entirely reconciled, the best of friends, and engaged to be married."

My turn for silence.

"Uh oh," I said at last.

*

Euleen of course had called Darlene about this wonderful Foundation, and the opportunities it offered, and Darlene was expecting us.

"Really," she said. "The Minerva Foundation. I suppose I shouldn't be surprised, the way people take advantage - "

"Of their elders? Is that what you were about to say, Miz Blackpot?"

She fortified herself by sitting at her desk. Her starchy little office frock looked a bit wilted, even on as sparkling a day as this was. "Mister Gerard and myself are entirely committed to each other's happiness," she said. "Not that there is any call for me to defend myself on that or any other score. Did you have some actual business?"

"Yes, we did," Paula said. "What is it that Trudi Ransom

knows about Gerard that Amos Verry doesn't, and how did she find out?"

Darlene gave Paula a considering look. No way, I thought. And I was right.

"I can't imagine what would motivate me to answer such a question," she said. "Even if I had the slightest idea what it referred to."

A door opened, and Paula stiffened; but it was not Amos Verry, but Rene Gerard himself who ambled into the outer office.

"My little pea-patch," he greeted Darlene, vacantly. "My rambling rose. Let's see what these folks want and get them on their way, shall we? I believe we have a good deal of correspondence to generate in the Edmond Hill matter." He managed to make it sound like a debauch, and maybe that's what he meant.

Darlene frowned. "Sir, I am not at all sure that Mr. Maryland and Ms. Vanek have entirely earned our trust in the business with Miss Ransom. I earnestly recommend - "

"Nonsense, Pea-Patch," Gerard grunted. "We stirred this up, not knowing exactly what we'd get, and these folks are what we got. Part of it, anyway. I believe they'll do as good as any." He turned to us. "Where's your lesbian friend? I understood you had found her, and she her mother."

"Occupied elsewhere," I said. "What did you mean, you stirred this up?"

Gerard walked to a couple of connecting doors and opened them. "Where's Verry?"

Darlene smoothed her dress. "Mr. Verry is in Branson, Mr. Gerard." She sounded good and irked.

Gerard grunted. "Good for him. Chasing tornado victims, no doubt." He got himself to a leather chair and folded into it. He walked like one of these giant puppets that loom and topple in parades, barely under the control of the little fellows who run them.

"Morris and I made a huge mistake, taking Verry on," he said. "Morris thought he had a lot of energy and promise, and his rough edges would get smoothed off, working around us. Not sure it didn't work the other way. Morris, it doesn't matter to him, he's out of the game now. Don't believe I've got that far to go, either."

Darlene rose from her desk to stand behind him. She looked like someone who has an awful lot of leaves to rake, and the wind keeps scattering her neat little piles. "Nonsense, Papa," she said. "You been saying that for years."

"One of these days, it'll be true, mark my words." He turned to us. "Verry's an impatient kind of a fellow. His contract with the practice says he remains subordinate to either of the surviving original partners. I believe Morris thought that would be him when he wrote it, he was ten years younger'n me. Turned out otherwise, though."

He paused to wheeze a little. "Anyways, Verry thought he'd see if he could get some kind of leverage on me, see if he could speed my departure. He picks up this woman, Ransom, I think, while she's on the run from the cops. Verry's always been very susceptible to women. More cock than brains, one of his fraternity brothers put it to me. As part of a package deal that includes legal services she desperately needs, and I presume an episode or two of copulation, she agrees to be his cat's-paw with some information that he thinks might be sufficient to force me to resign, if it came from a third party. Couldn't blackmail me himself, you see, and stay in the firm. Never occurred to him Miss Feely here would keep me abreast of matters. Heh."

He leered fondly at Darlene, who sniffed and pinkened a little. *Sweet,* I thought.

"But you wound up in this crazy three-way standoff."

"That's right. From my point of view, it was a standoff, or lose outright. Miss Feely and I, we had to scramble a bit to get Verry and this Ransom to buy into it, but my little Pea-Patch is a very convincing talker, can be."

Right, I thought. If you've got a guilty conscience and a criminal heart, and not much else going on upstairs. "So Pea - excuse me, Ms. Feely here, has been acting as a double agent?"

"I have acted at every turn in the best interest of the Practice," Darlene said. "No more and no less."

"Ah, wait," I said. "Including getting Mr. Gerard to call Suellen, posing as Verry, and routing her return call to you, instead of to Verry. That's why the voices didn't match when Suellen talked to Verry later. What was the point of getting Suellen into it?"

Gerard sighed. "It appeared to Darlene that Verry could outlast us, that he had more resources and energy. That we would slowly end up on the losing side of the triangle, and Verry would take over the practice. I believed her, and I still do. Time is on his side. Having established it, we had to do something to break the cycle of blackmail in our favor. One thing I had on Verry, where he was vulnerable, was that business of faking Ransom's death, to protect her from the Minnesota authorities. A very stupid move on his part, a piece of senseless hubris that he very soon regretted, and attempted to undo. He sequestered her under another name in some dive over in Stone County, and keeps her pretty much incognito. Darlene researched it and informed me of it at once, of course. We hoped that bringing the daughter out here would force his hand."

"That was years ago," I said. "This go-around has been operating all that time?"

"No, Mr. Maryland. Darlene only joined the firm a year ago. It has been in effect since then, that's correct."

"Papa," Darlene said fondly. "I really do think we have reached the limit of conceivable benefit to confiding further in these people." She turned to me. "Mr. Amos Verry is in Branson, as I said. When his business there is concluded, I should very much imagine that he will wish to visit Granny's Parlour, to assess the damage. Are you entirely comfortable with that?"

"Bloody little Pea-Patch," Paula gritted. "She sits there in Springfield, and she opens the mail and answers the phone, since that's her job, and she may or may not pass on information as it suits her. In any case, she always reads, she always listens. She knows where people are and what they're doing. She tells us what

Verry's doing and she knows we'll go out and tackle him because we can't let Suellen deal with him alone. We're probably supposed to be grateful, she's warning us about him, but I expect she wants him pulled up short. I bet every person jack in this mess, including Gerard, thinks she's double-agenting exclusively for them. She's like a goddamn spider in the middle of a web."

"I liked 'ringmaster'. It's got the round-in-circles dynamism, and of course the whip, for us masochists. Is this all the faster this thing can go?"

Paula snapped my head back, taking us from eighty up to ninety-five. A limestone road cut screamed past, seeming inches from my knee. "Jesus," I quavered. "I was kidding."

"About the whip? Aw."

"About speed." We were silent for a couple of miles, and then both spoke at once.

"It would depend who's on the other end." "Five percent of johns ask for bondage, and not quite half of those ask for some kind of flagellation," Paula ruminated. "Say two percent of the john population. Indirect evidence suggests that upward of sixty percent fantasize about it, though there's a pretty big error bar on that number."

"Error bar, I bet. I've had the bejeesus kicked out of me more than once, and that's all I care to suffer, thanks. How does it correlate with prior experience?"

"Correlates neutral or negatively with recent experience," she nodded, "but strongly positive with childhood assault. Convert an early trauma to a turn-on; how's that for making lemonade?

Most devotees will tell you the whole thing's in the buildup - the bondage and humiliation and threats - and that the actual experience is deflating. It just hurts. Somebody who understands that can give you a good experience without the bad ending."

I rode silently for a few more miles. I began to see tornado damage; we were getting close. "That would be you, for example?"

She scooted herself back against me. "We could experiment. Come up with some data."

"You're making my error bar bigger than it needs to be as it is, thanks. You know, speaking of humiliation and threats, we're likely to have to deal with Amos Verry when we get there."

"I know. I hate how chicken I am about him. It feels like he knocked something..." Her voice died away in the helmet phones, and then came back, choked with tears. "Something important out of me. Please stay close to me, is all I can say."

"I'll be there, wherever that is. For what it's worth, I thought that important thing was very much there, when we were up against Zuckerman. Have you thought about a smart approach to this mess?

"No. I'll tell you, it's to the point that - Hey, I got it; why don't we blunder straight ahead, and the one that did it is the one we beat up the worst?"

I patted her haunch. "I don't think we have time for anything else."

But in fact, Amos Verry was nowhere around when we rolled up John Holler. The wrecked cars were gone and the wiener wreckage had been dragged into the woods, where I suspected it would stay until corrosion returned it to the earth from which it sprang. There was a lot of yellow tape across what had once been the entrance to Granny's Parlour, and across the first surviving interior doorway, which now served as entrance. In the warped ballroom, under a video camera that hung 90 degrees out of plumb from a bent mounting, the Vespa stood on its kickstand. Paula trundled the Harley in to stand next to it. We threaded our way back to Granny's lair, a more straightforward task than it had been last evening when things had been in full cry. We heard a thrumming motor, evidently an emergency generator, because there was light in the deep parts of the place, and a couple of the video monitors were on, showing the slowly waltzing exterior shot and a few empty spaces – including the ballroom with the bent camera mounting, whose floor was now posing as a wall, taking the place of a wall that had opted for ceilinghood. The destruction had brought out the rat population, and they were hunched around in little groups amid the wreckage, squinting against the unaccustomed daylight, probably telling each other they just didn't know.

Trudi's divan was in what served, I guess, as a bedoom, when her flatcar was at that end of the tracks. That was her world, a pair of rusty tracks leading from where she slept to where she leered at debauching realtors on closed-circuit TV. Suellen had scrubbed the place clean, possibly as motivation for Trudi to get off her fat butt and contribute something besides corpulence to the operation. She should have known better; Trudi could not be shamed into anything, because she had no acquaintance with shame. She was watching Suellen mop, sucking sulkily on a vanilla Slimfast which our entrance gave her an excuse to put aside.

"Wilkommen, bienvenue, welcome," she sang, a little thickly. "What's the latest from the straight world?"

"Death, destruction, and absurdity, Trudi," I told her. "You're smarter than you look, holing up in here. Not saying all that much, of course, is it?"

"Happy, happy Hap. Suellen caught me up on your sorrows and achievements since I last seen you. Condolences on the death of your wife."

"Thanks." I kept it to that because 'Fuck you' was more trouble than I wanted to take with her. I turned my back. "Suellen, we've figured out most of what there is to know about this stupid blackmail ring. If there's anything to it at all that doesn't defy logic, it's that Darlene Feely's in it to marry René Gerard. Preferably in the interval, which I expect will be short, between the pre-nuptial and his death. Beyond that, there isn't a goddamn thing to any of it."

Trudi sniffed and smirked. Maybe she was being sentimental at the thought of a May - December wedding.

"Feely's on my side, god damn it. She's the one's been keeping me up to date on this stuff, and she's the one told me it was her that Gerard molested when she was a Brownie. She don't give a crap for Gerard."

I turned to Paula. "What did you tell me? A classic example of the Feelian Fallacy. Every jerk in this mess thinks she's double-agenting exclusively for them."

Trudi banged her fat fist on the arm of the divan. The Slimfast tipped over and drooled, joining the stains of yesterday. "Listen, then, Maryland. She come down here a month ago and helped me pack up that box of crap that got sent to Suellen. Gerard din't know a goddamn thing about that."

Suellen shook her head. "I'm afraid that's not so, Mom. Gerard called me and told me it was on the way." She ruffled her hair and sighed. "Posing as Verry. But really, folks. I don't give a squat for any of this. I'm gonna get Mom into shape, and I'm gonna get her out of here. That's all that's left to do. Stand up, Mom. You can do that, can't you?"

Trudi smiled fondly at Suellen and shook her head. "Go to hell, honey," she cooed. Suellen flushed and turned away.

I'd had all I could stand of Trudi Ransom, and much, much more. "Suellen, for God's sake, listen to your mother. Hell would be a huge improvement over this wretched hole. Go to hell, go to North Carolina even, and leave her here. Give her a nickel for a phone call, she can live on her fat for a year, and maybe by the end of that, she'll have the tiniest, minimal goddamn decency to -"

Suellen spun on me. "Shut up, Hap," she snarled. "Amos Verry made her this way. If it takes a year, ten years, I'm going to stay with her and get her back to what she used to be."

I opened my mouth, and decided not to comment on that, for fear of Paula's editorial kicks in the ankle. I looked for Paula, and she wasn't there. But her voice came through the curtain from

Trudi's parlor.

"Oh, Jesus," she moaned. "Oh, Christ, here he comes."

We found Paula staring at the bank of monitors, shivering with fear. I put a hand on her shoulder and she jumped as if I'd stabbed her.

"Christ, Hap, don't do that. I can't stand this, we're trapped, oh shit ..."

She buried her face in my shoulder, and I held her and crooned, but I was worried as hell. About Amos Verry, certainly, though I was confident that we could probably avoid him and get the hell out of his domain; but far more about what he had done to Paula, which seemed to be settling deeper into her psyche. She was more frightened of him now than she'd seemed in the immediate aftermath.

"There," I said. "It's all right - "

There was a hum and a trundling sound behind us, and Trudi joined us at the monitors. "Hey," she leered. "This oughta be fun. I hear he hates your guts, the two of you."

"You hear wrong, twit," I said. "It's Suellen he hates."

Amos Verry was standing in what used to be the antechamber, shaking his handsome head, jotting things on a notepad. Getting ready to file his damage claim against God, I guess. He walked across the room and appeared at the bottom of the next monitor, the one with the bent camera, and walked straight up the side of the rotated ballroom and into a darkened doorway at the top.

And running stealthily after him came Suellen, zipping

along like Spiderman up the wall. She peeled off her tee shirt and disappeared in turn through the dark door.

From which Amos Verry now staggered, and though the monitors were mute, we could hear his yell of rage and fear echoing down the corridors. Suellen jumped out of the dark doorway, stripped to a thong, and proceeded to give Amos Verry a long session of Land Hard. I held Paula gently and stroked her hair while we watched. After a little, Paula giggled; and it was sort of comical, if you could forget that the thing ricocheting around the screen was a heartless bastard. The rotation of the frame of reference meant that instead of rising and falling as Suellen threw him around, Verry made little excursions from left to right, slowing as he approached the right-hand side of the picture, the former ceiling, and accelerating to crash into the left side. Suellen was always on him before he could pull himself up - or sideways - to defend himself. Her near nudity rattled him, I think, because he did almost nothing except to grab at her, in a half-hearted and tentative way, or at his own groin. It always ended in Suellen, moving too fast for him to react, grabbing an arm, or a leg, or with a foot in his crotch, and sending him on one of those eerie horizontal parabolas. She finished by holding an arm and a leg, giving him two or three turns of airplane spin, and throwing him the length of the screen. Her bark of effort echoed down the limestone corridors to us.

"Crap," Paula said. "Having me naked didn't seem to inhibit him like that."

"I expect you weren't doing that hee-yah stuff."

"Guess that's it. Is he dead yet?"

"Maybe we'd better intervene. We don't want Suellen up on murder."

When we walked into the ballroom, Suellen was towelling herself off with her shirt. When she saw us, she shrugged herself into it and spat on the pile of Amos Verry she'd left in a corner.

"Sucker wants any more, send him back," she grunted. I nodded and, thinking to get a quick word of sense into her ear, I walked with her toward the rear door.

"Listen, Suellen," I said. "That was terrific, but please listen to me. This whole business has gotten way out of - "

Behind us, Paula yelled, "Look out!" and there was an enormous *bang*. Suellen grunted, threw her arms out, and fell face-down on the floor. I crouched and turned to see Amos Verry, on his hands and knees, with a fat and smoking pistol wavering at me. The thing, I guess, he'd been trying to pull out of his pants pocket. His face was a mass of bruises and abrasions, and I can't believe that he was more than half conscious. His eyes were so bruised and swollen that we had to be vague shadows to him. Hitting Suellen must have been a matter of bad luck.

"Ou' th'way, jack," he snarled. "Gotta finish off dyke."

I have been shot at and beaten up a lot of times, and I don't remember ever being more scared than then. The wretched, evil setting, such a crappy place to get shot and to suffer; Paula's contagious terror, the nastiness and horror, Suellen's fate, all of it sucked the strength out of me. I raised a hand, as if I might try catching a bullet.

"Please," I whined. "Don't. Don't shoot."

Verry started to laugh, peering and swaying from his knees, and then Paula landed on his back, screeching like a fevered parrot, grabbing at the gun, riding him like horsie-playing child. Verry roared and raised himself to his feet, trying to shake Paula off while she banged at the sides of his head with small, wobbly fists while she rode him up. I ran over to them, turned Verry around to face me, planted my feet, and hit him as hard as I could.

What I intended as a martial-arts, blow-intensifying *Ya*! came out as a sniveling *Yuh*! of desperation. But I tried to remember what Travis McGee said about aiming for a point a foot behind the target's head, and I will say, it's very effective. There was a crunching sound from Verry's nose and a sudden sharp pain in my fist. The pistol fired again and powdered limestone showered from the ceiling. Amos Verry pivoted and fell full length on the floor with Paula riding him all the way down. He bounced; I saw Paula's hair flying around her face like an electric discharge of valor. When he hit the floor the second time, he stayed there, bleeding from a mashed nose. I toed his head sideways onto a cheek so he wouldn't drown in his own blood, and I reached down and pulled a gasping Paula off his back.

"Paula," I crowed. "That was the most - Oh, my God, you are the absolute bravest, most ... most ... "

Paula gaped at me, and began to hyperventilate, her face a mime of joy and disbelief. "I," she said. "I. You." It lasted about three seconds, and then she pulled out of my arms.

"Suellen," she gasped.

Fear shot through me. "Shit," I yelled, as if that would help. We ran to kneel next to Suellen, looking for blood, looking for a pulse.

Suellen raised her head and winked at us. "I'm fine," she said. "That's what you do in Land Hard when some jerk loses his temper and pulls a weapon on you. You surrender as fast as you can." She turned and jogged back into the depths to take more fruitless care of Trudi.

*

I took Paula out of there to get pizza. Amos Verry was unconscious in a puddle of blood when we left, and I decided while we were out that an adult was going to have to step in and get him some medical help. But he and his gun were gone when we got back. I suppose I should have worried about that more, but I didn't. I never seen a fella look as whupped on as he done.

We brought the pizza back to Granny-land, and used it to torment Trudi, who was confined to Slimfast by order of Suellen, unless she wanted to get down off her divan car and walk across the room for a slice of nice, hot Sicilian deep-dish, full of pepperoni and grease -

"Shut up, you rotten basserds," Trudi snarled. "Keep the shit. Gimme another Slimfast and go to hell. I hope you have a coronary on the way there."

"Two Slimfasts for supper, Mom," Suellen said. "That's it until breakfast time."

Trudi started to blubber softly. "Jesus, honey. You're gonna be the death a me. I gotta work into this gradual."

" 'Gradually,' Mom," Suellen sniffed. "That's another thing that's got to change. You could speak perfectly good English last I knew."

Trudi threw the empty Slimfast can at Suellen. "Insufferable brat. Is this the way Wet Parsonage brought you up?"

"That's better. Yes, it is. I'm going to leave a piece of this pizza over here, and walk these folks out. Don't you be trying to sneak a bite of it while my back's turned."

We had a quick strategy session with Suellen on the road outside Granny's Parlour, standing outside the sweep of the video camera, while the bug chorale tuned up for the late afternoon pops concert.

"I think our work here is about done," I said. "I'll help Paula drive the Harley back to Gabbro. I'll leave my ticket to Fayetteville on the dresser in the Residence Inn, if we don't see you before we leave. You can probably terrify them into letting you use it. It's open-return, so you can make a project of getting your mother back the way you remember her if you want. I don't think anybody's going to bother you. You've got about five serious felony-assault charges on Amos Verry if you want to trump anything he's got on Trudi."

The thing had been niggling at the back of my mind all through this caper finally crystallized, now that it was about over. "And besides, cripes, isn't there such a thing as habeas corpus? She can't be charged with killing a guy who disappeared into thin air.

This whole thing's built on a mistake."

"Well," Suellen admitted. "I sort of made that part up, to make a better story. I expect they found a body all right. Still, I don't think there's a chance in hell they can pin anything on Mom or me. We certainly didn't kill him."

She looked a little uncertain then. "At least, *I* didn't."

Paula and I took the Harley back to the Residence Inn and packed ourselves up; and fell into bed.

"Cripes," Paula said. "This place is too strenuous for me. Can we leave real early in the morning? Before anything else happens?"

"Bet your butt," I said. "C'mere, you big damn hero."

But a quarter to six wasn't early enough. We were patting our pockets for key cards and checking behind the shower curtain for a missing toothbrush when the phone rang. The voice was bloodless and alien.

"Hap."

"Yes? Suellen?" It could have been no one else, but the voice was not remotely right. I began to be afraid.

"Hap, Mom's dead."

19.

I stood in shock. Paula, sensible woman, picked up the phone on the breakfast bar.

"What is it, honey?"

Suellen was silent for a moment, and, shockingly, giggled. "Mom's dead, Paula. I can't believe it. That's it."

Paula put a hand on her forehead. "Oh," she said. "Oh, no, Suellen. Are you sure?"

"Somebody shot her," Suellen said. She sounded like it had happened in another country, years ago. "Amos Verry, I expect. Can you come out here right now please?"

"Where are you calling from?" I asked. Silly, old-fashioned question.

"Phones are still out here. I'm calling on Mom's cell phone. I'm still at Granny's Parlour."

"OK, we're coming right now. Are you sure she's dead? Did you call an ambulance or anything?"

"For what? She's cold."

"Call 911, Suellen. We'll be right there."

We rumbled out of Branson and down the country roads to Granny's in near silence. I expect Paula was thinking about as I was, Jesus, what next? That's a pretty callous attitude, I know, but I was about at the end of my string on this mess. When we pulled into John Holler, she said, "I hope to God Suellen's OK."

There was no ambulance or cop cruiser at Granny's when we pulled up, and in fact Suellen had still not called in the authorities. She was sitting on the ballroom floor when we walked in. Paula immediately started giving her female-to-female resuscitation, hugging her and rubbing the back of her neck. Suellen stared into the distance, and I would have been unable to put a name to the expression on her face. She wasn't crying and she didn't look angry, or baffled, or distraught. She looked, I guess, orphaned.

I left them and walked the corridors back to Trudi's lair. A splash of blood, dark and dusty now, looped across the threshold. I knelt by it. It was hard, but looked as if it might take the impression of a thumbnail. I didn't try. It had certainly not been there when Suellen was scrubbing the place.

Trudi was propped in about her usual position on the flatcar, resting the side of her head against the back of the divan. She stared at a video monitor that would have given a living watcher a view of Suellen and Paula walking the ballroom floor, arms around each other's waists. For a ghastly instant, I was sure Trudi would turn that bulging, obese eye on me and say something insulting. I might not have minded; but she was as still as furniture.

There was a dark hole in her forehead, just at the end of one eyebrow. I expect the shock wave of the entering bullet is what had popped her eye open to stay. The exit wound, if any, was pressed against the stained upholstery. The eye on that side was half-closed. I gritted my teeth and stared at Trudi Ransom's face, trying to remember. Futile. There was no residue of the cynical, sexy athlete I had known years before. It would have been an act of will to imagine anything but what was there: a woman aged, coarse, fat, and dead. Well, I suppose the part I would have recognized was long gone, holding a numbered ticket on the banks of the River Styx.

There seemed nothing more to do there. I walked back to the ballroom, wearily trying to imagine, or care, why Amos Verry might have decided to kill Trudi. The vanity of a man who knew she would have watched him beaten and humiliated by Suellen? For a man like Verry, it would be a kind of emasculation. But why not kill Suellen, in that case? Was he that afraid of her? I entertained a theory that Verry had sent a henchman with insufficiently clear instructions on a death errand that missed its target.

Paula was pacing the ballroom with a cell phone to her cheek. "Granny's Parlour," she said. "Well, it's just outside Galena. John Holler Road. That's right. Go right on up to the end."

Suellen sat against the wall where we'd found her. Her eyes were closed, and her arms relaxed on the floor. I sat beside her.

"Dead, don't you think, Hap?"

"I'm afraid so."

"Don't be afraid. I'm not. I'll tell you what, Hap. For me, Mom died the day she put me on that bus. I spent two whole days and nights on Trailways, thinking up ways to kill her. Grind her into little tiny bits. By the time I got to Fayetteville, you couldn't have found her with a microscope."

"Well," I said. "But ..."

"Ya. But after I got my feet on the ground, and I wasn't pregnant any more, I began to think she was right, I was a stupid girl to get myself pregnant, and didn't we have a wonderful time out there in the Midwest? So then a couple years after that, I hear she really is dead. So now she's dead twice, and I'm still a teenage kid. I felt guilty about that for a while, like I'd caused it, you know. Then I forgot about her for a long time, and next thing I know, guess what, she's dead <u>again</u>, this time on the good old World Wide Web. That was a tough one, you know? You saw how hard that hit me."

"I felt terrible about it."

"I know. I saw that, Hap, but I was so wrecked, it was like I didn't have room to let you know I knew you cared about it." She began to sniffle then, and I pulled her head onto my shoulder. "OK, so far she's dead three times, and it seemed to me like I just had to come out here, like I owed her something. Maybe just coming here and being here where she died. But the more I poked around, the less there was of her, and then all of a sudden she was alive again, exactly as mean and hateful as the day she sent me to North Carolina. Like no time had passed at all."

Suellen pulled back and stared at me, desperate for me to believe her. "She didn't used to be like that, Hap. When we were on the road together, she was strong, and smart, and sexy, and she always knew exactly what to do. I loved her, Hap."

"I know, Suellen. Your mom could be quite a package.

Almost as smart and sexy as you."

She shook off the flattery. "We were like sisters, that summer. We lived high when we had money, and we laughed and joked and figured out how to get some when we didn't. Guys, I don't care if they were twelve or a hundred, they looked at us and just about passed out, we were so hot and happy and, and ..."

Her eyes started to fill again, and she clenched her jaw, grieving for the sisters, for the one perfect summer on the road. But that time bore the seed of its own destruction.

We heard the blat and hoo-haw of an EMS truck jouncing up John Holler Road. Suellen sat up and blew her nose on her shirt-tail. Her voice became calm again.

"When I got pregnant, that was when she turned into this, this... what she was. She was furious, she called me a stupid little slut. She told me she couldn't be bothered with me any more. I don't think she even called W -" Suellen stopped and covered her eyes. She still hated showing tears. "... even called Wet until I was on my way to Charlotte."

I put an arm around her. "That's right, Suellen. She didn't. I expect she figured that way it would be too late for him to say no."

Suellen nodded, apathetic. "That's who she was, all along. And if he'd been on vacation or something, well, too bad. It took me a hell of a time to see it, but that was my Mom. I actually didn't figure that out until last night. She needed put out of her misery, Hap."

I looked into Suellen's eyes then, and got a scare. "Suellen,

Jesus. You didn't, uh...?'"

"What? Do it?"

" ...Well?"

"No. No, I didn't, Hap."

She got up and started pacing the ballroom. "Hell, I'm talking about my own mother. She was pathetic, Hap. She wasn't ever going to get off that flatcar. I was just going through the motions, really, talking about it, telling her the longest journey starts with a single Slimfast. She just laughed at that, and called me a supercilious little snot. I tried to talk to her about that summer in the Midwest, the stuff I just told you. She didn't want to remember it. Even think about it. Maybe she was feeling guilty about shucking me off, but she made it sound like it had been nothing at all to her.

"When I realized that, I went for a hike. I think I must have been gone an hour or two. I walked into Reeds Spring, to see if that Sherine was around, but her house got the roof torn off in the tornado. Everything was pretty dark. I took a kind of a roundabout way back. I was in no big hurry to get back to my big problem.

"When I got back here, the lights were off, except for a little glow from the monitors. She was lying there. I didn't try to wake her up, but I expect she was already dead then. I curled up in her room, but I didn't sleep much. If anybody'd come in, much less shot a gun, I'd have known about it. When I went in there this morning, I found her like that." Suellen shrugged a little shiver. "She hadn't moved."

Paula had gone out to meet the EMS techs, and I heard them coming through the antechambers of Granny's Parlour.

"OK, quick," I said. "Is there anything you want me to say, or not say?"

"I ... No."

"Where'd that blood come from, that's out in the hall?"

She turned and stared at me. "Mom. No, wait. Not out there. That isn't Mom's blood. It can't be."

"Not hardly. The entrance wound hardly bled at all. I don't know if the bullet's still in her, but if there's an exit wound, it's pressed up against the couch. That's not Trudi's blood."

Suellen shrugged and turned to the EMT's. "Maybe it's Verry's. Like his nosebleed came back, from the stress or something. That could happen, couldn't it?"

Well, I sure hoped so. I surreptitiously checked what I could see of Suellen. Usually, that's most of her, but this morning she was, for her, thoroughly dressed in a pair of jeans and a Branson Scenic Railway sweatshirt. Of course, it was a little chilly in Granny's, with the cool front and all. I was looking for fresh wounds that might have provided the blood in the hallway, and that she had chosen not to tell me about. I was relieved not to find any, but why was she so bundled up? Suellen was as close to a nudist as she could get away with, normally.

The EMT's took one look at what they had here, and called in a Stone County deputy and a second crew to provide the muscle it was going to take to get the decedent into an ambulance.

The deputy looked at Trudi, and at the scene, with some care, and talked to all of us, sorting out who was who, and what the rest of us were doing there. When he'd filled a couple of notebook pages, we got to the name of Amos Verry, and he held up a hand for us to stop.

"Sir, are you claiming that Mr. Verry had sump'n to do with killin that lady?"

"Honestly, officer, I have no idea one way or the other. He was her lawyer, and he was here yesterday under," I waved a hand. "Under somewhat violent circumstances, which left him with a bloody nose. There is that big splash of blood in the corridor outside Mrs. Ransom's room."

"Who give him the bloody nose?"

I sighed. "I did. He was unfortunately assaulting Mrs. Ransom's daughter."

"Assaulting her?" He didn't seem particularly surprised to hear it; I expect Amos had a pretty detailed reputation with the cops in this corner of the world.

"Yes. With a pistol."

The guy flipped his notebook shut, and replaced it with a cell phone. He talked a lot of numerical cop talk into it, ending up with a ten-four.

"Sir," he said. "I'm going to ask you and the two young ladies to stay right here for a couple minutes. There's a fella needs to talk to you about all this, on his way right now. I got to get back on the highway, but let me just offer this piece of friendly advice. That fella gets here and he don't find a young lady, a somewhat older lady, a dead one, and a middle-age fella with scars on his face, he's gonna be disappointed. And I'll catch up to you before you can clear the county line. Understand?"

"Goodness. Of course."

It took maybe twenty minutes, during which Suellen, Paula and I sat in silence against one wall of the ballroom, and the reinforced EMT crew sat against another and snorted and yocked about other visits to Granny's Parlour. Most of what I could hear concerned whom they'd pulled out of here, over the years, in one state or another of wreckage.

A car door slammed out on John Holler Road, and in a few seconds a man walked into the ballroom who looked so much like Harry Truman that it gave me the willies. He wore a pinstripe suit with a bowtie and a snap-brim fedora. His eyes twitched across us behind rimless wire bifocals. Maybe living in Missouri makes people look flinty and upright like that. Unless it turns them into fat idiots, of course. He stood facing us like a parade sergeant, and we straggled to our feet.

"You will be Mr. Harper Maryland," he told me, as if handing out roles for a pageant. "Which of you ladies would be Miss Ransom?"

Suellen raised a hand. "Me."

"Thank you. Miss Vanek."

"Here," Paula said. I could see from the narrowing of her eyes that she was fighting the impulse to tell him "Doctor Vanek to you, Sherlock."

He nodded. "I am Detective Sergeant Verlyn Rainwater," he said, and gave us two seconds in which to make the mistake of smiling at his Midwestern name. When nobody did, he relaxed a little, and twiddled a finger at Suellen.

"Miss, please accept my condolences on the death of your mother. Do you feel able to take me to her and show me exactly how you found her?"

"Yes, sir," Suellen said. She led him off into the bowels of Granny's; they were gone for probably fifteen minutes, during which Paula and I, with unspoken accord, sat down against the wall again.

I said, "It's kind of a relief to have a grownup step in, don't you think?" and Paula grunted.

"That part's fine, but you know, we're not making much progress getting out of here. Believe it or not, I have to start teaching again in two weeks."

"I think you're pretty much in the clear. I don't know about Suellen. Maybe you should take the plane ticket, and - "

"Huh uh," she said. "I'm with you for now. I guess if you get twenty-to-life or something, I might have to cut out."

"That could only happen if you fail to alibi me for last night."

She snorted, a little reminiscently. "The judge is gonna love it when I say you snore so loud, I'd have known if you snuck out."

I frowned, biting my tongue just in time not to tell her that Lee had never complained. "If it becomes necessary," I said, regretting the stiffness, "I will see what can be done about it."

She didn't answer that, and I don't blame her. We sat in warily companionable silence for the rest of the time Detective Sergeant Rainwater was gone with Suellen. The Medical Examiner and a police photographer filed past us, and then Rainwater was standing before us, looking like a haberdasher.

"Mr. Maryland."

I rose and followed the beckoning finger. Instead of taking me back to Trudi, though, Rainwater detoured into the kitchen. There, he leaned his narrow butt against the chopping block - I had a ghastly flashback of the sound of Zuckerman's demise - and stared at me without saying anything for quite a long time. While that was going on, I heard the EMT crew filing past

I never lose games of staredown, but I was conscious of Paula's fidgets. "How can I help you, Sergeant?"

He sighed. "Mr. Maryland, you are familiar with the term "Of two minds."

"Yes."

"That would describe myself quite accurately. On the one hand, we have a decedent for whom - and I say this with every possible respect to the grief of her daughter - not one decent eye will shed a tear in the entire state. Granny and her parlour were the bane of every honest cop in Missouri. Big parts of Kansas and Arkansas for that matter. Unfortunately, she was very heavily patronized by certain prominent and powerful individuals, and she was virtually untouchable. On the other - "

"Excuse me," I said. "I heard she was more or less at the mercy of Mr. Amos Verry."

"We will get to him. On the other hand, we have a young woman, a lesbian if you please, who accuses Mr. Verry - There, you see? - of killing her mother, and who offers for herself that flimsiest of alibis, that she went out for an extended late-night walk, during which she encountered no one, and which just happened to coincide with the likely time at which her mother was killed."

"You're not thinking of Suellen as a suspect, surely?"

"She spends the night with the victim, and reports her dead in the morning. Wouldn't you?"

I avoided the question. "You just spoke of her grief."

"It is not out of the question for a killer to grieve for her victim. Particularly when they are related."

"Well, Mr. Rainwater, I won't bother to expostulate with you. But let me tell you a little about what brought Suellen here."

"That's what I was hoping for. Please do."

I started with Darlene Feely's phone call and told him pretty much the whole thing, leaving out the stuff about marching bands, and the sex scenes, and rather soft-pedalling Suellen's repeated assaults on Amos Verry. Even so, it took a half hour.

Part way through it, Paula wandered in, acknowledged curtly by Verlyn Rainwater, and filled in some things about Suellen's mood on the trip out here, and what she had said to Paula when we first arrived here this morning. Which was pretty much what she'd said to me, about how many times Trudi had died for her before actually becoming deceased; but it was probably good that it came from another source.

When we ran down, Rainwater leaned against the

chopping block and studied the floor for a good long time.

"What you tell me," he said at last, "is very congruent to what meets the eye here. A good cop is always suspicious of what meets the eye, but sometimes a cigar is just a cigar. Young Miss Ransom is, of course, a hommasexual. For all that, she strikes me as an honest and forthright person, and in any case, she would have to be monstrous to approach the worthlessness of her late mother. I would be therefore disinclined to persecute her needlessly, even if I thought she might have been the perpetrator."

He smiled flintily at us to let us know he was kidding. "I have instructed the ME to sample the bloodstain on the corridor floor, and to get a blood sample from each of you. We will also obtain one from Mr. Verry. If that blood matches any of you, or Mr. Verry, that person will be a prime suspect. If it matches Mrs. Ransom, then I must conclude that she was elsewhere than where we find her now, when she was shot. She is so heavy that I believe no one of you could have moved her alone, and I would then be faced with a conspiracy and a ring of liars. That would be a positive development. I am very good at breaking down rings of liars, so you had better hope that it doesn't obtain. Please report to the room where I found you - the ballroom, I think it was called by the degenerates who ran this place - and get your fingers stuck. I hope you will confirm my gullible faith in you by giving blood samples voluntarily and without legal caviling. After that, you are free to go."

He looked at us over his shiny glasses. "As far as Branson, but no farther."

20.

"No," Suellen said. "Here's what I want, Hap. I want to finish this off by myself. If it's nobody but me and Mom, I can pretend none of this happened. Maybe it was her that got raptured off to heaven with the angels instead of Reverend Baxter, and left a devil in her place. Soon as I can, I'm gonna hitch up to Wisconsin, visit some of those places we were, back down to here, and get her straight in my head again. You guys need to get back to North Carolina. Do me a favor, take the Harley. Neville's gonna have a fit anyways. I told him I'd have it back this Sunday for sure."

I shifted discontentedly on the tiles at the edge of the Residence Inn pool. "Suellen, you could find yourself facing a murder charge. I'm not going to run off and leave you alone facing that."

"Hap's right," Paula chimed. She and Suellen were flattened on chaises, bikini strings dangling from bare backs, starting to give off that smell of skin and coconut oil that speaks of UV damage. I don't know why women do that to themselves, except of course that it feels delicious at the time. "I'm going to have a time problem in a week or so, but I don't have one now. I think we'd better stick around and make sure you're OK before we think about leaving you here by yourself."

She wasn't kidding about "by yourself." Loretta Lynn left town the night before the tornado, and Andy Williams wouldn't be back until Labor Day. Branson had settled into the late-August doldrums. The Residence Inn had almost no residents, and we had the pool to ourselves.

"Listen," Suellen said. "If that Rainwater guy thought I had anything to do with it, I'd be in jail right now. It's got to've been Verry."

A leather sole gritted on the pool deck behind me, and the Rainwater guy cleared his throat. "Do up your suits, will you, ladies?" he asked. "I need you facing me for this."

Oh, shit. I looked for a Miranda card in his hand. Suellen sat up first and tied strings second, but Paula was more accommodating. Rainwater squinted into the sundazzle on the pool until things were in order.

"I have preliminary forensic results. Ordinarily, I would not share them with suspects, but they are of a nature that hardly leaves you in that category. I am not going to tell you all of them in any case; just enough to give you confidence that I am serious about solving this matter, as little as I personally grieve the victim. However, I think you must now be counted as grieving family - at least Miss Ransom - rather than as suspects."

Paula and I couldn't help looking at Suellen. I still couldn't tell if grieving was a good word for what she was doing; or some mix of sorrow, relief, and ... some third thing that I could only pray was not guilt.

Rainwater nodded to himself. "First, then, I must ask you, Miss Ransom, or any of you, whether the deceased owned a gun or was in the habit of recreational shooting."

Suellen goggled at him. "Are you nuts? She was a total invalid. She never got off that flatcar."

"I am aware of that. Still, she could have had an employee supply her with a gun and ammunition for self-protection or in order to shoot the vermin with which the place is so rife. It would have been consonant with the persona she cultivated as manager of Granny's Parlour. I see no evidence of it in her quarters - no shell casings, pockmarks in the wall, desiccated corpses of rats behind the furniture, and so forth. Still, I must ask."

"Not that I know of," Suellen said. "It doesn't sound like Mom. Even when she was - even before, she never had a gun. I don't think she liked them."

Rainwater grunted, maybe a little surprised to hear of a tolerably positive quality in Trudi. "Nevertheless, oddly," he said. "There was powder residue on her hands. She had either been holding a gun recently, or someone attempted to make it look that way. And yet there was no gun on her person, or in the upholstery or appurtenances of the place she was found."

We sat there in the heat and the sunglare, and looked at him, waiting for more. When it came, it was on a different subject.

"The blood on the hallway floor matches none of yours. That is one of the reasons that I no longer consider any of you strong suspects in the killing. Also, a person in Reeds Spring actually saw Miss Ransom walking alone on Highway 248 toward Stutts around midnight that night."

He shrugged dismissively. "The prostitute Sherine Meyerhoffer, but still. She knows better than to lie to me. She sends her apologies for not offering you a ride, by the way. She was not in a position to request that the car she was in, stop for you."

Suellen blew a very short razzberry. "Did she say what position she was in?"

Verlyn Rainwater looked at Suellen; I swear, with a crumb of sympathy. "In any case, that hardly counts as an alibi, since the medical examiner is at a loss to establish even an approximate time of death for a corpse as grossly fat as that one. However, we can count it as corroborative. Likewise, Miss Vanek, the staff here testify that the door of your unit was keyed open at nine thirteen pm, and you were not seen to leave your unit until you visited the breakfast room the next morning. Mr. Maryland?"

I nodded. "I was with her."

"Again, corroborative, though hardly proof of innocence." Rainwater shrugged. "The fact that an alibi is lame or flimsy does not mean that it isn't true. Innocent people spend vast stretches of time that they could never account for in a legal and logical sense. Also, it is my judgment - and I am rarely wrong on this - that all three of you are behaving like persons who at least partly regret the death of Mrs. Ransom. So, to that."

Rainwater pulled up a chaise and laid his fedora on the pool deck beside it. Without it, he looked younger and more formidable.

"One scenario that would match what we found is that she engaged in some kind of struggle with her assailant, wounded him or her badly, and nevertheless lost the struggle. The attacker might then have retrieved the gun and fled. There are problems with that." He swept our ranks with a raised eyebrow. I could not see that his eye lingered over the bikinis a whit longer than it did over me.

"Well," I said eventually. "Was there a trail of blood?"

"Very good, Mr. Maryland. There was not. I can imagine scenarios that include the single good-sized hemorrhage and no other blood, but I must admit that I don't much like them."

"Could we ask," Paula asked, "about Amos Verry's blood?"

"You can ask anything," Rainwater said. "I can't tell you anything about that, nor would I if I could. We have no sample from Mr. Verry."

I could tell he'd planned to stop there; but the guy was more or less human, and I couldn't help thinking he kind of liked us. A very, very foolish assumption to make about any cop, I know.

"Mr. Verry," Rainwater said, "is not to be found in his usual haunts. He seems to have gone to ground, as the English say. Now, another avenue of investigation would involve gain. Robbery, life insurance and so forth. Miss Ransom, what did you stand to inherit from your mother?"

Suellen looked surprised. "I can tell you exactly. One beanie baby, some school junk, a key on a chain, my own diary, my birth certificate, and a jack of clubs."

I started to explain. "Amos Verry ... well, someone claiming to be Amos Verry - "

Rainwater stopped me with a raised hand. "Sent her those things. She told me. I meant things of greater actual value. For example, was there an insurance policy?"

Suellen shrugged. "You'll have to ask Verry, when you find him. He should know about that, shouldn't he?"

"But you know of no such policy?"

"Nope. Listen, if somebody told me there was one, I'd say he's lying. Mom had no ... " Suellen's eyes became bright, and she looked away. "That's not the sort of thing she'd do."

"No," Paula said. "But it might have been part of the blackmail setup."

Rainwater had been brought up to speed, such as it was, on the three-way blackmail standoff. He snorted. "That asinine business. I have a lot of trouble including anything relating to it in a serious theory. However. If there was such a policy, it will be a matter of straightforward police work to find it."

He stood and resumed the fedora. "Thank you. I think I have told you all you need to know for now, and more. As far as I am concerned, I will expect to find you here or at your home addresses if I need you. Not a one of you strikes me as material for the post office bulletin board."

Suellen adjusted her bikini top. "Are you sure enough of that, that you'll let me take off on my own? I have absolutely got to get out of this place."

"How far do you think you're going?"

"Wisconsin, Iowa, northern Missouri," she said. "That's the last place I was with my Mom while she didn't hate me."

Rainwater stepped closer to her, and focused the glitter of his rimless specs on her eyes for what seemed like five minutes, and grunted. "You will report to my office in Springfield tomorrow morning at 10 AM so we can photograph and fingerprint you for the poster. It will read, Wanted on Suspicion of Murder. You will check in with me by phone that afternoon at 5:30, and thereafter every morning at 9:30, and I don't mean 9:32. The day 9:35 goes by without a call from you, that poster gets faxed to every state bureau of investigation in the Midwest, and a lot of other places you couldn't guess. We'll have you by five that afternoon. Is that clear?"

"Yes, sir."

He showed her a line of neatly occluded teeth. "I look forward to hearing from you, Miss Ransom. You will tell me about your quest, and I will share what I think I can, about the progress of my investigation." His soles gritted on the concrete, and headed for the little gate that let him out of the pool area. With his hand on it, he turned back to Suellen. "Of your mother's unfortunate death," he said, evenly.

"Well, damn," Suellen said when he was gone.

"If you think of it," Paula said, "he told us almost nothing that we didn't already know."

Suellen hit the road at seven o'clock the next morning, after scarfing down the Residence Inn's free breakfast and loading her backpack with fruit and bagels.

"I'll be back home in a couple weeks, maybe a month," she claimed. "It's going to take that to even begin to get over this. You don't want me around while I'm doing that."

"Sure I do," I said. "But I'll survive. Call in every couple of days, will you? If you've got a nickel left from checking in with Rainwater. We should be back there by Friday."

Paula gave me a look. "Well," I said. "Sunday for sure."

21.

Paula didn't seem to be in a fat hurry to get back to North Carolina; she took a detour at Van Buren, Missouri to show me Big Spring, which is indeed good-sized. She seemed to want me to share in the wonders of the westward trip. For my part, I found 846 million gallons a day believable. After that, she gave me lessons in managing the Harley, so I was able to spell her as driver without badly endangering our lives. Every time we came to a little town whose name tickled her, she would insist on touring it. We stopped in Caboul to buy a disposable camera, and I have pictures of myself, Paula, or, once or twice where we could find amiable native help, both of us on the Harley in front of signs for Samos, Elsinore, and Alfalfa Center, Missouri, and later on, after we crossed the Mississippi, in Difficult, Tennessee. We accomplished that crossing at Fort Defiance State Park, Illinois, just south of Cairo. Fort Defiance - which no longer exists - was built, the sign said, at the strategic point where the Ohio and Mississippi join forces to meander south to the Gulf. We picked up a frugal picnic and sat ourselves at the very southernmost tip of the park, with the Ohio on our left and the Mississippi on our right. As far as I could see, we had the place to ourselves.

The two big rivers sucked and chuckled in the sunlight, greeting without mixing much, but maybe reminiscing about hundred-year floods. A duck cruised past on the Mississippi side, bound for the Gulf. There was occasional river traffic to watch, tugs pushing strings of barges upstream, diverging left or right around us depending on whether they were headed for Minneapolis or Pittsburgh. It gave us a feeling of power, which Paula acted on by waiting until it was clear which way a string was going, and then standing at the tip of the land like a traffic cop, directing the massive loads the way they were going anyhow. The crews seemed to appreciate the help, once or twice giving her a blast of whistle. I expect that had to do with the way she'd stripped to her bikini for extra visibility. She gleamed like a beacon in the southering sun. When she got tired of the game, we opened up the paper bag and started to chow.

"See how the waters don't mix?" I mumphed around my chili dog. "You can see the boundary between Ohio water and Mississippi water all the way down there, must be a mile."

"Uh huh," Paula said. She took a slug of cherry coke and disposed herself in skinny opulence on the southernmost five feet of grass in the State of Illinois.

"Mississippeh watah, taste like turpentine," she crooned. "You really think Verry killed her?"

I chewed for a while. It had been nice, not thinking about Amos Verry and not fearing him, for a few hours. "I don't think there's a lot of evidence of that, unless that turns out to be his blood on the floor. What was his motivation?"

"I don't see it, but there's a hell of a lot we don't know about him."

"I could imagine something about that blackmail triangle going sour, I suppose. The little we do know about Verry doesn't sound like a guy who would kill somebody with one clean shot to the head."

Paula shuddered, and closed her eyes. A couple of minutes later, though, she opened them and raised her head. "Who, then? Suellen?"

"I hate to think that, so I'm just not going to. How about what's-her-name? Little Pea Patch?"

"Good idea. I don't see her motivation either, but maybe Trudi stood to queer the marriage to Gerard in some way. We should have told Rainwater about her."

"I expect he'll get on to her pretty fast, trying to run down Verry. Hey, though, how about this, listen: Trudi does have a gun, and she kills <u>herself</u>. She's despondent over ... well, the loss of her wicked club, possible prosecution on sex-trafficking charges, maybe having to appear in public as the fat cow that she'd become. Even Suellen's evident determination to shape her up and bring her back to North Carolina. Heh; sudden self-knowledge. OK, Verry's got an insurance policy on her life as part of the blackmail. He can't collect if she kills herself, so when he finds her dead, he takes the gun, to make it look like murder; it's the opposite of the usual coverup." I half talked myself into it as I went along.

Paula stretched sleepily, giving me a review of the dunescape, now flickered by dapples of maple-modulated Midwest sun. "Ingenious, Holmes. What made the puddle of blood on the floor?"

"Hmm. Well... uh, the stress raised his blood pressure and started his nosebleed again."

She snorted with amusement at that. "The stress of a midnight visit to his own whorehouse for no reason but to plant a gun in her hand? God, you're sharp. C'mere, you."

"Jesus, Paula. Here?"

She looked around. "We're still the only thing in the parking lot. The next barge is about four miles down the river. You cannot, such is the nature of maleness, claim that you're not interested."

Well, it was very pleasant, in the breezes and river smells of that strategic prominence, Fort Defiance. The johnboat full of fishermen who slipped past the point out on the Mississippi side were just too late to spoil it, and of course they were way appreciative, whistling and clapping. I have a feeling they may have heard Paula some time before they cleared the point; sound travels a long way over water. We waved back and rolled apart. I felt sleepy, and oddly unembarrassed. The fishermen were way out there, coasting south at speed. Fort Defiance was our little garden, with no snakes and no prohibition about tasting whatever apples we might desire.

Sex with Lee had often left me with an odd exaltation, a feeling that I could see individual molecules of air, read the thoughts of dragonflies, feel the turning planet in its orbit. Now, I was content, almost drugged. I glanced at Paula, and she seemed in about the same mood; sleepy, content, the heat engine in her marvelous flanks ticking over at low idle. We nuzzled and dozed, as complete as Eden that first Sunday.

We may have slept for a few minutes. I drifted off in drowsy bafflement at the difference in their coupling coefficients. I may have dreamed of Lee. The next thing I heard was Paula's voice, with the faintest edge of melancholy.

"Am I as good as Lee?"

22.

I don't know how in thunder women do that. Or, having that weird power, why they choose to exercise it. And of course, they always ask the unanswerable question that you had better answer without the least hesitation. "Hm?" I lied. "Sorry? Are you what?"

"As good as Lee. I'm the one who should be sorry, for asking such a stupid question. No way, right?"

"What in the world would ever make you think that?"

"Oh," she said. "Nothing." But it wasn't nothing, or at least not that Nothing.

"Well," she said then, "it seems like I always have to start it. You always say, 'Jesus, Paula.' Almost always. You should feel free to just say No Thanks, Hap."

I don't like to be patronized, but I tried to keep a reasonable tone. "I would say that, if I thought it. You're every bit... Wait. You're very kind and tolerant to an old - to a much older man. You're wonderful in your own way, which is completely different from Lee. You're surely not going to ask me about what sex was like with Lee, are you?"

"No."

She started dressing, packing up the lunch trash. I could see she was hurt, but damned if I could see about what. If you're not prepared for any answer, don't ask a question.

"Paula, you're a wizard. You're ... OK, look, you're the Picasso of sex, she was the Ravel. How do you compare those?"

She sighed. "Yeah. Sometimes, you prefer music to painting, I think."

Oh, poor you, for God's sake. Was I right to call myself twenty kinds of fool for getting interested in another woman? I waved a hand and shook my head.

"They're both nice things. And, excuse me for saying this, but I think jealousy comes a little strangely from you." Before I was finished saying that, before I started, I knew it was a huge mistake. But once the words were lined up, out they came.

"Really?" Oof, in that falling tone of aristocratic disagreement, _Rea-leh_. "And what would make you say that, if in fact it had ever occurred to me to be jealous of Lee? She was a wonderful woman. I worshipped her."

"Ha," I barked. "Me too, Paula. Maybe even harder than you did. Come to find out, she played around on the side. But my point was, so do you. For a living." I was mad enough now that I didn't care what size mistakes I made.

"Ach, of course." She was white with hurt and anger. "There will always be a certain hesitation, dealing with a whore, won't there? A prudent and well-reasoned reluctance. Who knows what one might catch?"

"Oh, that isn't what I meant, and you know it."

She ignored that, slammed the trash into a Keep Fort Defiance Clean basket, and headed for the parking lot.

"I'll drive, please."

"Fine."

We didn't stop at any towns. We roared east on interstates all afternoon. Along about two o'clock, the windstream splashed something onto my shirt. I pressed a finger to the damp spot, and tasted salt on my fingertip. Very carefully, I hooked a thumb into her belt-loop and patted the flank under it. She did not scoot back or in any way acknowledge the touch. I sat back and watched the massive limestone road cuts go past. An hour later, she pulled into a rest area.

"We need gas, and I'm tired. Will you drive now, please?"

"Certainly."

When we'd gassed, and taken turns at the restrooms to protect the Harley from the klepto-curious, we struck forth again. At six, she tapped my shoulder and pointed at an exit sign. As far as I could tell, the helmet intercoms were working fine, though of course they'd had nothing to do since the Fort Defiance spat.

"You want to get off here?" I asked, more or less to illustrate how childish she was being by not talking. I was tired, too.

"Please."

I took the exit. Signs offered a choice of Hickman to the south and Gordonsville to the north. Hickman was hard against the whine of the interstate, so I opted for north. But Gordonsville seemed mean and scrawny ... or maybe it was just me. Carthage, next north, seemed like a promising little place sitting on the Cumberland River, and they were having Cumberland Heritage Days, with a parade and fireworks. Of one accord, we kept going. We were getting pretty far out of our way, but I was not the one with an agenda. At Pleasant Shade, Paula tapped my right shoulder, and pointed to an eastward-tending road. "Difficult, 2" it said.

"Ah."

There was not a wide choice of accommodations in Difficult, Tennessee. In fact, there was no choice at all but the Difficult Rest, and they had but one cabin available.

"Cumb'land Hurtage Days, don't ya know," the old man who checked us in apologized. "Got every room in three counties took up. Got one left with a double bed and a cot. I suppose you folks is married."

"No," Paula said, "we're not. Is that a problem for you? I will take the cot. I can assure you that there will be absolutely nothing untoward going on."

"I'll rig a curtain," the old man said, and by God, he did.

Like most towns of under 200, Difficult was not a blaze of light at night. I don't think you could pick it out from low Earth orbit, for example. That cabin was as dark as the grave, and as quiet, except for the low hum of an air conditioner. I lay in the back of the cabin, on the double bed, listening for sounds from beyond the silly curtain, and hearing none. Reviewing the bidding, letting myself work from weary self-righteous pissed-offedness through grudging fair-mindedness toward sorrow, regret, arriving at a determination to mend this if at all possible. A start, I decided after a long sleepless time, would be to offer to switch beds. It would be enough short of a grovel to salvage some dignity. Not that I was unready to grovel, if that's what it would take.

I didn't want to call out to her, and either wake her or give her an opportunity to compound matters by refusing at a distance. I rose and crept around the curtain, navigating by memory, rehearsing reasoned, friendly lines, stepping slowly to keep from barking my shin and looking even dumber than I felt. Paula's side of the curtain had the windows, and there was just enough light to see the cot. It was empty.

I sagged onto it in the dark, trying to comprehend that she had skipped out on me. Maybe I had slept during my mental journey from righteousness toward rightness. I groaned with hurt and anger. How do you get to North Carolina from Difficult, Tennessee, with no car and no money? How do you get to old age and death from the moral wilderness of a jilted middle-aged fool? I sagged onto her pillow and the smell of her shampoo mocked me. The next scent would be the ammoniacal tang of Assisted Living.

Paula's voice came from the darkness. "Hap?"

"Paula?!"

We rushed together in the dark and collided, harmlessly but on opposite sides of the damn fool curtain. It took fumbling, fragmented, whimpering seconds to get to the end that she had groped around, as ready to grovel as I'd been, exactly at the same time that I had groped around the other end. We laughed at ourselves and cried at ourselves for fifteen minutes, and tangled ourselves into a grateful ball of legs and bellies, to get some sleep.

*

In the mist and birdsong of the morning, we fell over each other to hog blame for the spat, each to cast ourselves as priggish snots and the other as a fine, fine person we were lucky to share an Interstate with, let alone a bed. All that humility was rewarded by a string of great little towns up there on the grey roads. I have photos of us in Hanging Limb, Lancing, Wartburg, Stainville, and Goad, all of which we hit in one morning's giddy ramble up the eastward rise of Tennessee. We didn't hurry, or look at maps; we had covered so much ground the day before that we just navigated by the wind (always in our faces) and by the little directional signs on peeling white two-by-fours, pointed always uphill. The picture from Goad, Tennessee, is before me now. Paula, the Harley, and the sign, "Goad / Pop 208," are alone in it, since there was no cheerful native to do the double portrait. Paula looks cheerful enough for two. Even so, her lips are a little puckered, which makes you just want to grab her and pucker back. They are that way because she was saying "problem" when the shutter went.

"Of course, we still have a problem."

I stuffed the camera in my pocket. "I'm afraid so."

"I am professionally fanatic about hygiene."

"I know you are, Paula. That isn't it, really. At least not much of it."

She hoisted the Harley onto its stand and led the way across the road to Goad Variety, which advertised Nehi Beverages. I have always loved stores that stock Nehi, and say so on little rusty signs.

"No, I think I understand what it is," she said, while I picked sodas out of the old-fashioned horizontal drink box. "But behind it is the contemptuous horror of venereal disease that arises directly out of notions of 'defilement' and so forth."

The leggy girl behind the counter gave me a curious look as she counted out my change. Wondering, I expect, whether I would be content with the obvious retort. I was, for the moment.

"So you're claiming there's no medical basis - " I stopped. The very last thing I wanted to do was win this argument.

Maybe Paula felt the same way. She put an arm around me. "No, of course not. I'm talking about the extra load of shame that perfectly ordinary diseases carry, if they're associated with sex. Look at the difference between genital herpes and cold sores. It's the very same virus, but in different places. Thank you, Miss. You have a nice day, too."

She strolled into the sunshine, chugging her cream soda. "Of course I'm not claiming that STD's are not a deadly serious matter, or that it would be acceptable for me to infect you with one. God forbid. I will always be the safest sex you ever heard of. However, sex is my special area of scholarship. I would be very, very reluctant to give it up."

"I wasn't asking that. In fact, I'm really not asking anything."

"I have thought quite a bit in the last 24 hours about what it seemed to me that you were asking. If I peel away the sting from what you said yesterday, I get two things. First, you find it inappropriate for me to be curious about your sexual life with Lee.

Very well, I was out of line. You were perfectly right, I am jealous of your life with Lee, all of it, and I didn't want to admit that. I apologize for walking on ground that must be both sacred and painful to you. It was very foolish. I could be a perfect fool, if I practice hard."

She sighed. "The second part is tougher. You characterize my scholarship as 'playing around on the side' for a living."

"Paula, please. Let's not get back into that. I didn't mean to insult you as a thinker and a scholar. You explore wherever your mind leads you. Just, some parts of it are hard to imagine, for me."

She was quiet after that. We put on the helmets and mounted the Harley. It was my turn to drive. She wrapped herself around my waist and just crooned odd little songs, mostly 70's pop stuff like "96 Tears" or "Delta Dawn," or "Puff, the Magic Dragon." It was nice to have a voice in the helmet again. When we got to forks in the road, I took easterly choices when I could, otherwise southerly ones, to keep us from ricocheting into Kentucky or Virginia.

"You like driving the Harley, don't you?"

"Yes," I said. "Once you showed me how, it's a lot of fun."

"You do it well. I always know which way to lean."

"You lean very nicely."

She was quiet for a while longer, setting the hook. "Sex is like that."

"Um?"

"It's knowing when to lean at the same time. Like dancing, which is a form of sex that is OK to do in public. I expect you're a good dancer. But at a more basic level, it is what makes us go. People say, love makes the world go around. What they mean, but it's not polite to say it, is that sex is the reason we're here on Earth. Like the Harley is the reason we're in Tennessee."

"Well," I said. "It's what got us here, OK."

"It's more than that, Hap. I defy you to name anything more essential, more varied, more soul-searching than sex."

"Music," I said, promptly. "Art, in general. Language. For some people, making money."

"Of course, most of music and art and language is about sex. Making money is definitely about sex. But OK, for some people, any one of those. For other people, another one. Two, they call you a Renaissance man. But intellectual pleasure is learned from physical pleasure. Humans - maybe all creatures, I can't speak for them, but I do know something about humans - we have evolved to be copulation artists."

She patted my tummy. "I'm in a really good mood about ... about stuff, Hap, so don't think I'm saying any of this with some kind of agenda. But some people love Picasso, some people love Ravel, some people love baseball or John Updike or the stock market. Everybody loves sex. Why else do we make such a big deal about it? Why is 'fuck' the third rail of polite speech? Why is there such a huge range of erotic response from different places on our bodies? You give me some time alone with you, and I guarantee, I will produce an erotic response from any square inch of skin you name. Try that with Shakespeare."

I thought about that. "Too late. He's dead."

She bonked my helmet, and told me she needed a pit stop.

"Already? We just had one."

"Partly given over to guzzling pop."

While she was off behind a sunny little copse on her business, I watched the view and mentally reviewed my skin to see if I could think of a square inch of it that I'd be willing to bet she couldn't use to turn me on. I couldn't. I tried to think when I'd had as good a conversation partner since Lee died. Well, Suellen, sometimes. But Paula was also about sex.

"Anyway," she said when she was back from the woods. "The point is, sex is a huge, very important subject, and there's almost no serious scholarship on the human transaction. It's the motor that gives us this lovely ride through life, and it's off limits to discuss it seriously. As if Harleys worked so well, it was forbidden to be a motorcycle mechanic."

"Is this about your particular approach to scholarship?"

"Yes, it is. You think it defiles me. It spoils me for you."

"I wouldn't put it that way. Do I act as if you're spoiled for me?"

"Sometimes, you do."

I thought about that. "I'm not used to somebody who's as enthusiastic as you. I certainly have never regretted making love with you. But the idea of the woman I ... " I fussed with the rearview mirror. Did I want to say this?

Of course I did. There is no fool like an old fool. "The idea of the woman I love, 'interviewing' a dozen johns a week. That is just very hard for me to get around."

"Oh," she said. And, after five minutes of radio silence, "Well, it's a bigger problem than I thought."

Some time later, as the Harley was boosting us up a heck of a grade on US 70, the intercom crackled with Paula clearing her throat.

"You might want to downshift. I think it's overheating on this hill. Did you intend to say that?"

I downshifted, awkwardly but with some sense of accomplishment. "Um. Help me out. Say what?"

"You know, what you said back there."

"About interviewing johns?" I sighed. I wished it were not so, but how could it not be? Why couldn't she see that?

"No, before that. 'The idea of the woman', da da ..."

"Oh," I said. "Well, sure. Yes, I did. The woman I love. I'm afraid I am very close to it, Paula. If we go on, it will certainly come to that, which I understand makes everything ten times worse. This is not something I was particularly planning on for the Golden Years."

The Harley got us to the top of this particular rise.

"Stop here, OK?"

I coasted onto a shoulder with a hell of a view of a lot of slanted ground. Paula dismounted and went to sit at the edge of the drop-off. When I got the Harley settled, I went to sit beside her. She was looking over about forty miles of Smoky Mountains, holding her head, crying softly. I didn't say anything. What was to say? We had another mess to deal with.

After a while, she pulled a wad of Difficult Rest toilet paper out of her hip pocket and blew her nose. "Wanta know who's the last person told me he loved me?"

"No. Well. OK, who?"

But please don't say it was some truck driver.

"Steve."

"Aw, Paula. I'm sorry. The guy with the hang glider? That's just, just ... "

"That's Aw Jeez." She laughed, tearily. "That's what you said last time, you glib so-and-so. No, as a matter of fact, Steve was the guy from St. Olaf. The pink-slip guy. The hang-gliding guy never got around to saying it."

I was a little shocked. "Really? No, but, still, he ..." *Shut up, Hap.*

"Really. He said This was It, and shouldn't we make it official. Not exactly the same thing, you'll have to admit."

"Well, isn't that the modern equivalent?"

"No. The modern equivalent would have been 'I love you, Paula,' and that's what you said was about to happen. I'm going to have to think about this very, very carefully."

"OK," I said. A woman says that, you don't try and help her think, or say helpful things. You stay out of the way.

23.

We got to Gabbro late that afternoon. Paula started loading her stuff into her car, which had been out by our garage since she left with Suellen, all that time ago. I brought her in for a glass of wine, because I was very reluctant to see her go, and she seemed ready not to go. There was a pile of mail and newspapers inside the door, left by Bethany on occasional visits. Messages from Suellen on the answering machine checking in from Burlington, Iowa, and Hannibal, Missouri.

"It's changed," Suellen said. "There's no more of the revivalists, the ones that we used to know. Nobody seems to need saving. Nobody does Land Hard. Not even dippy Tai Chi. Everybody's - I don't know. *On line*, for crap's sake. I'm still checking in with Rainwater, and he's not telling me much. I'll call again in a day or two."

I made a bundle of the newspapers while Paula rummaged the fridge and can cupboard and opened a bottle of wine. We settled ourselves on the screen porch with a plate of cheese and crackers, and toasted ourselves on safe arrival and a good trip with only one potentially lethal fight. I sipped my wine, leaned forward, opened my mouth, and froze there. I didn't see how I could say what I had to say, except stuffily. When things are crucial, I get stuffy; it seems to help.

"Doctor Vanek. I have had an opportunity, since we last

spoke of it here, to review my earlier decision in regard to your tenure case. I believe I spoke hastily. If you still want me to assist, I will be glad to do what I can. We can discuss my fee later, when we see whether I can help at all."

Paula put down her glass and looked hard at me. "Are you just saying that because I saved your life and gave you a screwing you'll never forget?" Her lip trembled, and she sniffled. "You grateful bastard?"

"On the contrary, though both of those things are true. I'm saying it because I also saved your life, and I figure there must be some purpose to that beyond mere survival." I toyed with my wine glass, lining up words until I was more or less satisfied with them; anyway, I don't really like wine all that much.

"I'm saying it," I said, "because whether you were shaking with fear of Amos Verry or boxing his ears, or driving a Harley, or screwing, or talking about screwing, or telling me what a jerk I am, or saving my life, you remained exactly the same size, shape, and consistency. You don't swell with indignation, and you don't shrink down all little and mean. You didn't get vaporous or mushy, and you didn't get tough."

I scratched my head. "Well, sometimes you got a little plucky. You can pose as an anthropologist, or a whore, a bureaucrat or a traffic cop or a big sister. I've seen you be a dozen people, but every one of them is exactly Paula Vanek, no more and no less. That is what I understand when people use the word "integrity" about somebody. People with your kind of integrity are rare, and should be helped when they need help."

"Hap..."

I held up a hand. Here was the hard part. "I'm also saying it because I had an opportunity to review some aspects of myself during this crazy, almost pointless trip with you. I had been slipping into a cramped, surly, self-indulgent, and narrow life, brooding on my cuckolded status and cultivating victimhood. I became somewhat less so as a result of things you did, or said, or are. If I ever amount to anything again, it will be because of you. That's all."

She blushed, and rubbed the outside of an eye. "That's all?"

"Well. The thought that there would be a reason for us to continue meeting certainly doesn't hurt. But even if that were not so, I would still want to help."

She reached out and took my hand. Even as the gesture was breaking my heart, I thought, Christ, she knows how to break your heart. Remember that, and watch it.

"I was hoping we would continue meeting, as you boyishly put it, in any case. To say that I am flattered and pleased - hell, I'm overjoyed - does it no justice at all. Thank you, Hap." She squeezed my hand and, alarmingly, kissed it. "If this goes much farther, I may be brought to the point that was bothering you so this morning. I'm close to talking about love. Let's change the subject."

Well, we changed the language, but not the subject. Some time in the middle of the night, when ordinary hunger had a chance to make itself heard, we went downstairs and dumped whatever food I had that was still edible into a frying pan, and took plates and a couple of Urquells out in the back yard.

This is something I used to do a lot with Lee. Our house is far enough out of town that it is quiet, private, and very dark at night. We were into September now, when Gabbro weather tends toward dew and chill after midnight; our bare feet sent little shocks of reality from the wet grass. We settled into the lawn furniture and chowed contentedly on mushrooms, scrambled eggs and Spam, admiring the silence and the darkness. Venus was gone from the eastern sky, her work done. This far into the night, the sky was blazing with fall and winter constellations. Paula's education had been short on natural history, except for the reproductive side, and she'd never lived in the country. I showed her Cassiopeia, and the Andromeda nebula, and Orion, rising in the East to hunt for the Pleiades.

"Won't catch 'em, though," she said, sleepily. "Like dumb old Amos, chasing skirts his whole life." She shivered and put her empty plate on the grass. "I don't know if he killed Trudi, but I know he could have. I wish to heck he was in jail. Want to go in now? It's cold out here."

I peered at her in the starlight. "You could put something on; you're actually steaming."

"I intend to, and it's you. C'mon."

I woke at dawn when hair tickled my nose, introducing a slapstick element into a dream of Darlene Feely, little Pea-Patch, and a dusty, sticky puddle of blood that I kept stepping in and tracking around, while Verlyn Rainwater flashed his glasses at me and took notes. Every time I tried to get away from it, I tripped over something and ended up with my hands and feet stuck to the floor.

My left arm was asleep from the weight of Paula's head. Everything below my collarbones was an undistinguished zone of tangled warmth and smells rolled into an itchy blanket and sticky with the night's exercise.

I extracted myself as smoothly as I could, leaving a couple of pillows that Paula wrapped herself around, slumbering on. I meandered downstairs to make coffee, wondering whose blood that had been, wondering how I proposed to defend Paula from the folks who didn't want to give her a lifetime contract to do prostitution research at Tri-Cities Tech.

I made no progress on either of those questions by the time I heard the shower running upstairs. I played around with the chimeric notion that there might be one brilliant thing I could do to solve both problems at once. I couldn't see what that might be, other than running off to Mexico with her. Not long after I gave up, Paula came down, transformed back to an assistant professor of transactional copulation.

"Goodbye, Hap," she said. "I'm going to hate this whenever it happens, so we might as well get it over with. I'll call you when I get back to Greensboro. I should have some kind of message from Summerton or Barry about my hearing. I think we might do a better job of planning for that - assuming you still want to help out - over the phone, or by e-mail. When I'm around you, I have trouble staying on message."

So I let her out the door she'd entered, with her Candleglo wig and her hooker's getup, all that time ago. When she'd disappeared down the road to the bypass, I noodled moodily into the kitchen and looked at the calendar; and astounded myself. Not three weeks ago. The whole thing had taken 20 days, from the rump session of whores to right now.

Thinking of that session reminded me of something else, and I found Suellen's childhood diary where, flustered by the influx of floozies, I had picked it up instead of The Dreadful Lemon Sky. Discovering my mistake, I had then dropped it off in the little powder room that nobody used any more, since Bethany moved out and left two real bathrooms for me to share with Suellen. And then forgot the whole thing, back when my mind was fogged by self-pity. Another perfectly good clue, meaningless as all the rest.

I settled at the kitchen table with the pile of mail and a cup of coffee, sorting and slurping. In the category of nonjunk, there was a medium-big check from Gabbro College that I'd forgotten about, and a feeler about consultation from the richest, stuffiest, most un-modern college in the Carolinas, in response to my ad in the Chronicle. I bundled the chaff with the newspapers and put them out for recycling, feeling that there was a chance I might not have to declare Chapter Eight just yet. Paula's call came while I was in town converting my windfall into a bank account, groceries, and a haircut.

"Hap, it's me," the tape said. "Guess what, my hearing's

tomorrow morning. The rat bastard must've set it while we were gone. I bet he figured I'd either miss it entirely, or not have time to prepare for it. I called and asked if they could postpone it, and it's a long story, but the answer is No. Please give me a call."

She sounded ragged and scared; I called her and spoke soothingly. The hearing was scheduled for 11 in the morning, with her department head, a representative from the student government, and of course good old Tim Summerton presiding. Apparently Academic Vice-Provost Barry would participate, if at all, by speakerphone.

"And that is so like him, Hap. He's a fastidious killer, he doesn't get his hands dirty. He looks like Calvin Coolidge."

"Silent But Deadly Cal? How many did he knock off?"

But Paula was not being jollied. "We're sunk, Hap. It's just the worst setup you can imagine. I know the student rep, she's this airy-fairy girl from High Point. Her father's a Pentecostal."

"I'll be working on it, Paula. Don't worry, we have Pentecostals in our family. I'll meet you at ten. Where?"

She gave me directions. I thought about what I could do that might help, and I could only think of one thing. A month ago, I'd have died rather than do it, but now I decided I kind of liked what living had turned into. Dignity is over-rated anyhow. I put on an old pair of swimming trunks and flip-flops, and spent half an hour burrowing through the trash before I came up with what I was after. Luckily, the trash guys in Gabbro don't do house calls, and if it's not out at the edge of the road, they don't take it. The load in question had spent the last half of August simmering and sweltering in a big can next to the house, and I smelled like a dead skunk when I was done. But I found the goddamn thing. I showered off the garbage extract, hoping to hell the heat hadn't deteriorated it too much. I left a little early the next morning so I could swing by the chemistry lab at the College for a final touch, and then I tucked the damn thing in my floppy, old-fashioned briefcase and lit out for Greensboro.

Tim Summerton was a little taken aback when he saw who Paula's consultant was. I had allowed myself, when I discovered his liaison with Lee, one confrontation with him. It was mostly words, but I did close it out by slamming him pretty good. He'd spent a little time considering pressing charges for assault, but really, only his dignity was damaged, and I think he decided that having the whole business aired in court would have resulted in more of the same. Still, I wasn't counting on his guilty conscience to help us out much. As far as I could see, he was pretty much like Trudi Ransom in matters of conscience. After a little huffery-puffery about whether I was a qualified consultant, he retreated behind his desk and started the proceedings by punching a little tape recorder.

"This is the tenure appeal hearing," he intoned, "of Dr. Paula Vanek, of the Department of Social Sciences. As a result of a divided recommendation of her department last spring, Dr. Vanek's application for a tenured appointment at this institution was denied. She is, as is her prerogative, appealing that denial. Also present are Ms. Julie Sue Waycross, a nursing major from High Point, who chairs the Faculty Affairs Committee of the Tech

Students' Association; and Dr. Arvo Bentsen, chair of the Social Sciences Department. Dr. Hap Maryland, an educational consultant, formerly Acting President of Gabbro College, will assist Dr. Vanek in her appeal. Dr. Stanley Barry, Vice Provost, will be joining us by conference - "

"It wasn't divided," Paula said.

Tim gave her a patient flutter of his eyelids. "Please. The first order of business here will be your opportunity to speak in behalf of your candidacy for tenure, Dr. Vanek. However, if you are referring to the Department recommendation in your case - "

"Damn right I am," Paula said, making Julie Sue Waycross flinch. I put a hand over hers, and she quieted down.

"I expect Dr. Vanek is referring to your calling the Department recommendation 'divided', Dr. Summerton." I tried to get as much sneer into "divided" as he'd managed to pack into "educational consultant, formerly Acting President," the little snot. "It was my understanding that the Department recommendation was unanimous for tenure."

"Dr. Bentsen, on closer examination of Dr. Vanek's credentials, changed his vote. And as Chair, his voice carries a certain amount of weight."

Bentsen had the goodness to look uncomfortable, but he nodded grimly at the air in front of him. "That's right, Paula. I tried to contact you, but you were not available. I admire the energy of your scholarship, but I must say that it amounts to little more than a practicing trade in fornication. I have to wonder - "

Paula gasped and turned white. "Objection," I yelled,

before she could say anything. "I object most strenuously to that characterization of Dr. Vanek's research." Boy, did I; though I still wouldn't have known how else to characterize it that wouldn't be saying the same thing. Luckily, I was saved by the phone.

Tim picked it up with a cheerful smirk. I think he liked the way things were going. Bentsen was in a huff, little Ms. Waycross was pink with embarrassment, and Paula was rattled.

"Yes, Miss Adams," Tim purred to his secretary. "I expect you mean Doctor Barry, don't you? Please put him through."

Tim smiled indulgently and cradled the handset on a speakerphone. "Hello, Dr. Barry," he said, in a carrying voice. "And welcome. I think you have a list of the folks who are gathered here. We are glad you could join us this morning."

There was a moment of humming nothing from the speaker, and then a voice that seemed unexpectedly familiar. "Summerton?"

"Yes, Dr. Barry. We can hear you just fine. We have just begun to discuss Dr. Vanek's appeal."

"Vanek? What, her sex appeal? You get into bed with her, you're finished with me. That business with Peggy Lou was one thing - heh, I remember you now, you were the guy that kep' calling her Leggy Pooh, ain't that right? An' she loved it. You were a slick one for getting a woman into bed, I will say. But God damn it, get focused, man, and get your mind off the cunts. Screw Vanek, is my advice. You told me to call, you promised me support and I need it bad now. I need anyways a hundred K, and I mean quicker'n shit in a Ex-Lax factory. How much can you come up with?"

There was a moment of shock so profound that it felt like the air in the room had crystallized, and shattered like glass. Tim stared at the speakerphone, squeaking and panting. Nobody else said a word.

"Summerton," the thing roared. "Listen to me. It's time to shit, or get off - " Tim's hand darted out and broke the connection. He looked around the room. Bentsen was peering glassily at Tim, looking like something in a taxidermist's window. Julie Sue Waycross, now deep red, was beginning to cry. Paula looked as if some hilarious but inexplicable truth was beginning to dawn. I did my very best - which is quite good, as I've said - to keep a straight face. Amos, I thought. It is so good to hear from you. Tim looked from the phone, to me, to Paula, wondering how we'd rigged this evil miracle.

"Folks," I said to Bentsen and Ms. Waycross. "Obviously, there has been some mistake. I find it difficult to believe that the administration of this institution takes that tone with each other, unless they believe that they are speaking confidentially."

Tim glared at me. "That was obviously some kind of prankster. Dr. Vanek, I very sincerely hope we will not find that this was instigated by you, or - "

The phone rang again. Tim looked menacingly at Paula, and picked up the phone again. "Oh," he crooned. "Dr. Barry again, is it? Well, Miss Adams, you can tell 'Doctor Barry' from me to go straight to hell. That's right. Thank you, Miss Adams. If the real Dr. Barry should call, you may put him through."

But there was no further traffic from Stanley Barry, or from Amos Verry. I never did learn whether the second call was the real Dr. Barry; I surely hope so. We went on with the hearing, though I have to say, after the speakerphone debacle, neither Bentsen nor Miss Waycross seemed to have their hearts in it.

But Paula did. Amos Verry's call reminded her that she'd slain that dragon, and gave her nerve to take on another. She pointed out in clinically neutral terms the pervasiveness of prostitution in time and geography, its heavy impact on law and public health, and the scarcity of careful scholarship on it. She remarked that in every scientific field, first-hand experience is the only source of knowledge that is respected. And she left us to rub those ideas together. Once in a while, she would throw in a "get focused," or talk about how much a john could come up with, that served a very real purpose of keeping us from focusing on anything but that wonderful phone call. She also didn't neglect to give impressive sales figures on "Johns, Jades, and Johnsons," and I had to reconsider what she'd said once about having a second income. Before she was finished, I was pleased to see that Miss Waycross was nodding sympathetically, particularly on points related to public health. Even Bentsen was doing little lip-tightenings of the sort people do when they are about to agree with you, against their will.

"And that," Paula concluded, "has been my scholarly contribution to this institution. I think there has been no exception taken to the uniformly high praise I have drawn for my classroom teaching, community service, and student advising. I therefore request that this institution reconsider its denial of tenure."

Tim sat for a moment, staring at the middle distance. He pulled himself together and asked if either Ms. Waycross or Dr. Bentsen wanted to ask questions, or to make further remarks. Both of them came through very nicely, I must say. Ms. Waycross in particular talked of having come in prepared to uphold the denial of tenure, but now having seen the value of Paula's brand of research. Bentsen made similar noises, in a slightly lower key.

Tim nodded. "Unfortunately, this is not a matter to be decided by a majority vote of the hearing. We may, if you wish, make a recommendation, which I will carry to higher levels. However - "

I cleared my throat. Tim glared at me. "Yes?"

"You didn't ask me what I thought."

"You are here as an advocate for Dr. Vanek. I thought it would be evident what you think."

I smiled. "True. Still, perhaps I might be allowed to focus the issues involved here by way of summing up. Tenure decisions at this institution are based on scholarship, teaching, advising, and service to the community. As I understand it, there are no issues except on the first of those, and that not because of the quality or amount of Dr. Vanek's scholarship, but its nature. She does field work in the role of a prostitute, in order to gather data about the relationships between prostitutes and their clients."

I smiled at Paula. "Leaving aside whether one might gather that information in some other way, the fact is that the institution - or perhaps one of its political allies - is put off by this research. It casts Dr. Vanek in a compromising light. I suppose some might say that it defiles her."

"It casts her as a prostitute," Tim said. "No more or less. Heaven knows, we are not a puritanical institution. We are capable of overlooking loose behavior, infatuations, minor sins of omission and commission of all kinds. But paid promiscuity - "

"Ah. It's the fact that she takes money? Outside employment is forbidden?" I knew otherwise, having researched this point. Consultants have to do something to earn their bucks.

"Well," Tim said. "No, of course not. Prostitution is illegal."

"It is, I agree, a misdemeanor. But so is adultery and ordinary fornication. Yet the University makes no attempt to remove fornicators from its student body, or even from its faculty and administration. Board of Trustees, for all I know."

That was a shaky assertion, and certainly beside the point of this hearing; but here I knew I could count on Tim's guilty conscience to distract him, and make him glad I had said nothing about his own adulterous past.

He glared at me. "Simple promiscuity, paid or unpaid, is in itself a very bad example to set for our students."

"Oh," I said. I beamed at Tim, and he knew I had him. "Isn't it just. I just could not agree with you more, Dr. Summerton. Please allow me to introduce a single artifact that will underscore how much I am on your side in that."

"Listen," Tim said. "I can imagine what scurrilous filth you're going to bring up here, and - "

"No you can't, you hypocritical little snot," I chuckled. Indulging myself, but I hoped the artifact would take people's minds off that.

I opened my ratty old briefcase, hoping to God the thing had held up through all this. And it had. Out of the floppy leather mouth there rose a helium-filled condom, as cheerful as the ones in the Whores' March for Justice. Almost any condom might have done, since I never used them, having been vasectomized since I married Lee. But this one was special.

For one thing, it had a crude but recognizable transfer of Tim Summerton's face on the end, copied by some high-tech means from the Gabbro College faculty handbook. That alone would have made worthwhile the ordeal of recovering it from the stinking garbage where it had lain since I cleaned it out of the Saturn's glove compartment. But there was the message, too.

"Happy Birthday, Lee," it said, as it rose. "And many happy turns from Timmy."

24.

It was a stiff, off-white envelope, and it said Evans and McLean PLLC, Attorneys.

Woe, shit, I thought. This'll be a subpoena from Verlyn Rainwater's folks. But the postmark was Fayetteville, and by the time I read ten words, I wished a Missouri subpoena was all that it was.

Dr. Harper F. Maryland
RR 1 Gabbro, NC

Dear Dr. Maryland:

The last will and testament of Mr. Wetmore Parsonage, late of this city, names you executor of his estate. Please contact our office for an early appointment, so that I may acquaint you with the extent of Mr. Parsonage's holdings, and discuss with you some rather sensitive provisions in regard to his ward, Ms. Suellen Ransom.

With condolences on the passing of your friend, I am
Yours sincerely,

It was signed with a squiggle that started with something like an "E" so I guessed it was Evans. I wondered for a moment if Evans had a first name, but that was only so I wouldn't have to face the real content of the letter. Wet didn't make it.

Wet was gone. Damn, damn, damn. He was getting better, damn it. Every time I talked to him after that frightening visit in the hospital, he sounded more like his old self.

It was unfair. Why did Amos Verry live on, apparently immortal, and Wet Parsonage not? Or Tim Summerton? Couldn't we just one time get a vote in these things? Trudi - well, never mind; Trudi Ransom didn't make it either. I groaned and sat on the grass next to my mailbox. I guess I was there for a while, thinking about all I'd been through with Wet Parsonage, because the dampness of the grass finally made my butt itch, and I hoisted myself erect. I felt old again. Creaky and old, as I had not felt since the New Branson tornado blew Paula Vanek into my life.

Paula had called just this morning with the expected news that the powers of Tri-Cities Tech had re-reversed themselves, and granted her a promotion to Associate Professor, with tenure and a handsome raise.

"Half that raise is your fee, and I will not hear a word otherwise. It should be half the whole thing, which I offered you in the first place."

"That was just silliness, Paula, and so is half your raise."

"It is not silliness. Name a figure then, damn you."

"Oh, shoot. Let's see. I worked on it a half a day, plus mileage. A hundred bucks."

"Ach! A hundred bucks, you stubborn old coot. Sure you don't want a hundred paper clips? How about a wad of gum? Honest to God, Hap. I should - well, wait, then. How's this?

Would you like me to come down this weekend? We can bargain it out then."

"Are you kidding? Of course I want you to come. As for bargaining, we'll see. You'll find I drive a hard bargain."

She laughed. "They all do, the first time. We'll see how hard you bargain by the time Orion clears the barn. You better get some sleep, boy."

I dragged myself over to Bethany's to borrow her Internet access, and after a little advice about search engines, I typed "Wetmore Parsonage" into a query window. There were two hits, both from the Fayetteville Observer. The first was something about an airplane, and the second was the obituary I was looking for.

Wet Parsonage had exited this world around mid-day on Saturday, August 28, more or less as we sat around Granny's Parlour being interrogated by Detective Verlyn Rainwater. The cause of death was given as a perforated ulcer, which had caused Wet to collapse at the Charlotte Airport. He'd been rushed to Mecklenburg General, but had been dead on arrival.

I found that damn near unbearable. Wet had seen too many victims and perps hauled off in the meat wagon not to find it depressing and humiliating as a death scene for himself. The poor bastard. Why couldn't he have had one friend there with him? The obit went on to recount what it called Wet's long and distinguished career with the Cumberland County sheriff's office. Distinguished chiefly by being underpaid, underappreciated, and overworked, it seemed to me. They closed with a quote from a source who asked not to be named, surely a remarkable thing in an obituary. "Wet was the best cop in the Carolinas," this source said. "There wasn't nothing he didn't know about crime and detection, and he passed it on to hundreds of good cops all up and down the coast."

Well, I thought, good. Let the sheriff of Cumberland County read that, and repent.

And then I thought, the Charlotte airport?

I clicked the Back button, and tried the other hit the browser had come up with. The obit had it wrong. Wet hadn't collapsed at the airport. He'd collapsed on a Fayetteville-bound airplane, causing the flight to be diverted to Charlotte in a failed attempt to save his life. I think I probably knew right then why Wet died, and more. My heart started to pound, and my breath shortened. I knew it, and I didn't. He's on a flight headed for Fayetteville, and they divert it to Charlotte to get him on the ground faster. A flight from where? Why, from somewhere beyond Charlotte, from the point of view of Fayetteville. Such as, from the Midwest. Memphis, say, or St. Louis.

What was the airline? Why, the article said, it was Northwest. Still, no way, right? It's not in the cards for Wet to hear from Suellen that Trudi is alive at - I strained to remember - say, ten o'clock in the morning, and to get himself onto an *east*bound plane the same morning, having already - I pounded the address of a travel agency into the browser. Oh, yes, I found. Yes, it is easily possible to get a phone call in Fayetteville, North Carolina at ten o'clock in the morning, and to be in Springfield, Missouri by late that same afternoon. To rent a car, maybe from the same agency

I'd used, since there were not all that many. To find out what you needed to know, or perhaps had already been told by Suellen, and do what you had to do before your strength played out. Before you retched your life's blood onto Granny's clean parlour floor. And still to catch an early flight the next morning on the cramped little feeder to Memphis. I could see Wet, sweaty and pale in his raincoat and his fedora, trundling out of the Hertz return lot at the Springfield-Branson airport, across the service road to the terminal. Tim the car jockey telling him, in case he asked, what a tough cookie Amos Verry was. Wet not caring, because it wasn't Amos Verry he'd gone there to kill.

*

"Oh," Paula said. "I didn't even know him and it still ... What are we going to do about Suellen?"

"God," I groaned. "I hadn't got that far. This will kill her. We just can't tell her what we know."

"Suellen is very sharp. Everything you found out is right there in the public record. She'll figure it out at least as fast."

"Faster. Damn."

"If I could suggest?"

"Please."

"I didn't know Wet, but I know how Suellen felt about him. She talked about him all the way out to Missouri. She must have told me a dozen times, she wouldn't have gone if she didn't think he was getting over this ulcer. So ... "

"I'm not sure that's necessarily true, or if it matters. She was in a very emotional state about Trudi when she left."

"In any case, she's too smart and too old to be sheltered. I suggest that we tell her. Maybe as soon as the next time she calls. Wouldn't it be better for her to hear it from us than to figure it out painfully for herself?"

"Ya," I sighed. "Probably. I dread it, though. Can I ask you something on a different subject?"

"Yes," Paula said. "The answer is, yes."

"Oh. What was the question?"

"The one you asked me in Summerton's office. Whether there is some other way to gather the data I have been gathering by posing as a prostitute. And there better be. I started one interview this week, and I had to break it off."

"Because of me? Oh, gosh, Paula - "

"No. At least, not at first. Half way through the interview, I got a terrible feeling that he was looking for a woman to beat up. He was just an ordinary truck driver. I think that might happen a lot now, since... since that business back there."

She shook her head. "I went back to my apartment and took off the hooker getup and made myself a cup of tea, so I could think that over. For years, people have been telling me I can't do that kind of research. So, of course, I grit my teeth and say, Yes I can. Now I was telling myself, I couldn't do it. And you. You never said, 'You can't do that,' or 'If that's what you're going to do, we're through.' You just said, 'It would be hard for me.' "

She sighed, and ran a hand through her hair. "I told you, if

I practiced hard, I could be a perfect fool. It takes me so long to get it, sometimes. But I finally thought, Duh, why am I doing something that makes life that hard for a guy I care about? Really, how dumb can you get? I sat down and devised a whole different line of research that, as a matter of fact, I am very excited about. So the answer is, Yes. There is."

"Well," I said. "That's a good answer. Really, a very good answer. Can I keep it, and use it on the question I was going to ask?"

She got quiet, and nodded. "OK."

When I didn't say anything, she looked up at me, and I saw what I had seen in her eyes before. The thing that is not Nothing. I suppose it is possible that she saw something like it in me, because she started nodding again.

"Oh, yeah. " she said. "Sure. Uh huh. You damn bet."

I grinned. "Is there a Yes somewhere in that?"

She grinned back, and clamped her skinny self around me. "Yes, there is. Yes, yes, yes!"

The phone pulled us unwilling out of a contented postcoital doze, during which night had fallen.

"Hi, Hap. You made it home, great. It's Suellen."

"Suellen, hi. Yeah, we're here. Where are you?"

"Independence, Missouri. What's wrong?"

"Wrong?"

Paula held out her hand for the phone.

"Hi, Suellen, it's Paula. Yeah, great, you too.... oh, shut up.

Honey, listen. We have some real bad news."

She paused long enough for a very short question from Suellen.

"Yes. Yes, it is. He passed away last week, while we were in Branson... Uh huh... No, he didn't, Suellen. He was on a plane headed for Fayetteville when... Uh huh. Uh huh. Really? Why don't you tell me about it? ... No, I don't think so." She pivoted the phone away from her mouth. "Hap, is your phone tapped? Or a party line, or anything?"

I snorted. "Nobody taps phones in Gabbro." It was true; nobody needs to. Everybody knows everything that happens within a half hour, whether it's done on a phone line or in a dark corner of your attic.

"Hap thinks it's a clear line, Suellen... Uh huh... Oh, honey, I know... Uh huh."

It took probably ten minutes of Uh huh's and Oh, Honey's. I don't know why I didn't pick up the other phone, but - well, yes I do. It would have been bad manners. And besides, I knew Paula would give me a complete and orderly account of it, and she did. But when she told Suellen that she was a completely good person and her righteous lambie-pie, and mine too, and got a number where she could call back, Paula looked shaken.

"Could we get some of that excellent beer and go out in the back? This is going to be a little surprising."

When we were settled, Paula said, "Well, just to break into this gradually, she knew it was about Wet right away."

"I gathered that. She knew before you told her."

"She didn't know he had died. But, Hap, here it is. She knew that he killed Trudi."

It felt like falling through the ice. "What? I just figured that out this morning. How did she?"

"She didn't figure it out. She was there."

Another chill. "She was there? She saw it?"

"No. She was asleep in the back room. Apparently, those video monitors also get regular cable TV, and Trudi was watching some show, probably to annoy Suellen. Suellen closed herself off and went to sleep. The shot woke her up."

Paula sighed, and put a shaky hand on my arm. "She crept into the front room under cover of the noise from the TV, and she saw Wet putting the gun into Trudi's hand to make it look like suicide. Apparently, Wet had no idea that Suellen was anywhere near Granny's. She'd called him from the Residence Inn, remember, and I guess he thought that's where she would be."

Paula shook her head. "And if I had to guess, I'd say Wet wasn't operating at full cunning. He was dying, hoping he could get finished with it and get clear before he collapsed. Anyway, Suellen knew right away that her mother was dead, there was no help for that. And - I think this is remarkable - she knew it would only make things much worse for Wet if he knew that she'd seen him. She must have nerves of absolute stainless steel. She deliberately let him go, knowing she might never see him again. And then she went in and took the gun out of Trudi's hand."

"Why?"

"I asked her that. She didn't think anybody would buy the

suicide setup. And, I guess she wanted Trudi to have at least the dignity of a murder victim and not a suicide. She figured that, with no gun, there would be more doubt about who killed Trudi. And, I have to say, I don't think she was thinking all that clearly at this point, either. She says she felt the whole time like she was floating about an inch off the ground, telling herself, God, this is an awful dream."

"Jesus, that poor kid. She must have been wrecked. Why didn't she spill it all out for us?"

Paula drained her beer and looked at the stars for a while. "She apologized for that. She particularly wanted you to know she was sorry she lied to us. She was afraid we'd give it away to Rainwater somehow. She figured the fewer people knew about it the better."

I hung my head for a few minutes, grieving for Suellen until something else forced itself into my mind. "She ditched the gun?"

"That's what the midnight ramble was about. It was to take that gun, which she was afraid would be linked to Wet, out in the country and lose it. She says she chucked it in the back of a truck full of scrap iron. But it's moot. Now that it doesn't matter to Wet, she's going to lay it all out for Rainwater."

"Hm. How is it sitting with Suellen, that her beloved guardian killed her mother? How can she sound so carefree now?"

"She wasn't so carefree when she was telling me all this. But I think we already know all we're going to know about that. You saw her the morning after Trudi was killed. You said she looked orphaned. Well, you were right. But it wasn't Trudi she was in shock from, I think."

"I was half right. Oh, God. Wet hated Trudi. He never forgave her for dumping Suellen like that. He did everything he could to keep her the hell out of Suellen's life."

We sat in silence for a while, listening to our hearts. Finally, Paula said, "Literally. It cost him his life. I hope this doesn't sound too awfully immoral, but I think Wet did Suellen a huge favor. I think she's not so much carefree as grateful."

*

Wet Parsonage's estate came to something over a million and a quarter dollars, not counting a couple of hundred acres of unvalued farmland in the butt end of Robeson County.

"What?!"

Lawyer Evans smiled remotely. "It is surprising, isn't it, considering the very modest style of Mr. Parsonage's life. Of course, that was one of the contributing factors. He never spent lavishly on himself, even when he came into a respectable sum a few years ago - "

"I remember that. A quarter of a million dollars, reward money he got from the business with EarthShine. That was just a few years ago, Mr. Evans. He parlayed that by a factor of five in that time?"

"That, and a few other sums that he'd accumulated over the years. I believe the quarter-million brought his net worth above a half-million, and from then on, it was just extremely astute use of this sustained bull market."

"Well. My hat's way off to him, but I have to say, I have no business managing an estate that size on behalf of Suellen. Can I hand this over to somebody else?"

Mr. Evans lifted a corner of his mouth, and dug an envelope out of the folder on his desk. "He thought you might be reluctant. If so, I was to give you this. It arrived, with a covering memo explaining that, a day before Mr. Parsonage's death."

I could see right away it was from Wet; it bore the green-and-yellow logo of a low-end motel chain. And anyway, it was addressed to "Mister Hotshot Maryland, c/o Evans and McLean". The letter itself was on Campbell's Soup stationary he'd picked up from the factory store outside Laurinburg.

Hotshot:

By this time even you may of figured out what I'm getting ready to do. I don't know that I can pull it off, but even if I do, I won't be around all that long. Guys like you, that kind of save themselfs, tend to live longer. So I'm making you executor, because I know you'll keep Suellen from pissing it away on kung fu and tattoos.

1. She is to take that fellowship at Chapel Hill, and turn herself into something. Get a Phd. Tho God knows when I look at you I don't see why I think that's such a big deal. But make her do it.

2. Far as I'm concerned, I never went to college, so now's my chance. See to it that my body goes to a medical school. East Carolina, not Wake Forest, and for God's sake, not Chapel Hill.

3. Do not dream of saying No to any of this or I will come back every night and haunt you between the hours of 2 and 5 AM. Don't think I can't either.

4. For a hotshot college president, you were not that bad of a guy. Thanks for taking care of things for me.

Wet

I folded the letter and put it back into its envelope. "Very well, Mr. Evans," I said. "I am prepared to do what I can to help."

"Good," Evans said. "Mr. Parsonage was confident that you would be. The management of a substantial estate is not, of course, something that can be undertaken lightly. Mr. Parsonage had every confidence in you, and therefore so do we, Dr. Maryland. He authorized a service fee, payable to you quarterly in advance, of one half of one percent of the total value of the estate, during the time it is your responsibility."

"Oh, for God's sake. No way, Mr. Evans, and I'm not kidding here. I will do it without fee, or I won't do it at all, and he can come around and haunt me all he likes."

Evans sighed. "I'm afraid this, too, is something about which Mr. Parsonage envisioned the need for persuasion. He instructed us be certain that you accepted a reasonable fee. The half percent per quarter is our opinion of a reasonable fee. If you fail to accept it, we will not be carrying out his wishes. That in turn would open us to a number of unpleasant difficulties which Mr. Parsonage built into his will. You simply must accept."

Evans beamed and showed me a palm. "You are, of course, free to do what you wish with it, once you accept it. Give it to charity, for example. Mr. Parsonage has set aside a small sum to be donated to the Cumberland County Police Benevolent Association."

"He has a lot of notions, for a corpse. Have you made the arrangements with the medical school?"

"Yes, we have."

Oh, Wet, Wet. Carved up by a bunch of snickering, fainting kids, because he cared about kids. I waved a hand. "All right."

"Excellent. We will require quarterly reports of all disbursements and an annual audit, the cost of which, of course, may come from the, mm, the corpus. I have drawn a check for the first quarter's fee, which would be, allowing a reasonable estimate of the value of the land, $6,750. Sign here."

I signed. I scrammed, before Wet Parsonage could reach from the grave and make me do some other thing I'd rather not.

About six o'clock on a Friday two or three weeks after that, I was opening a bottle of chardonnay - of which I am no fan - and polishing a pair of wineglasses, when tires crunched on the gravel out back, and grated to a stop. There was a longish silence, and a car door opened and, again after a longish wait, slammed, and another one clunked open. I went to the kitchen window.

Paula's car was in the drive, and Paula herself was jacknifed awkwardly beside it, rump a mile in the air, groping around under the back seat, bringing into the light one, three, a dozen raggedy pieces of paper. She hauled out a folder then, itself slithering with unruly paperwork, and stuffed it into a bulging portfolio.

Wonderful, I thought. You live without her all week, and she shows up on Friday night with a raft of papers to grade. It was a way of cohabiting I had become all too used to, married to Lee. I sighed, and got ready for a weekend of absent pecks on the cheek and nice views of the top of her head. I went to the door.

She had the exploding portfolio clutched to her bosom, and a pencil stuck in her hair. Her half-glasses were smeared, and ...

Wait a second. Paula doesn't wear glasses.

"Mr. Hardacre," she quavered. "It's all here for you." Her voice deepened, and she reached for the top button of her frilly librarian blouse. "I just need a place to spread it out."

She held out the mass of paper. It was rumpled, dusty, and grass-stained, with raggy-edged notepad sheets, yellow credit-card receipts, envelopes from department stores, an accordion of ancient green-and-white computer printout, construction paper, a dozen five-inch "B Drive" floppies and several sheets of Number 800 Extra Fine carborundum.

"Miss Christian," I said. I gave it as much longsuffering as I could, around the bubble of laughter. "Are you late with your summaries again?"

"Not my monthlies!" she said quickly. "It's the quarterly. I'm never late with my monthlies."

"Ha, I should hope not, Miss Christian. We should have to envision a nunnery in that dreadful event. I daresay, your monthly is as punctual as ever, is it not?"

She chewed her lip. "I knew you would understand, Mr. Hardacre. I'm so terribly sorry about the quarterly. I don't know how you put up with me."

I placed a carefully lascivious hand on her arm. "My dear Miss Christian, that is perfectly all right. Your most recent weekly was a gem, and a pleasure to contemplate for days afterward. May I take your wrap? I have another bottle of that wine that I know you enjoy. And please. I think of you as far more than a valuable employee. I think of you as my very special protégée. Do you think you could call me Harvey?"

"Oh! If only you knew how I value your regard. Only if you call me Laura ... Harvey."

Well, I will spare you more of this, because in fact the phone rang at that point. Laura and Harvey did their damnedest to ignore it until Suellen's voice sang out of the answering machine, buoyant and at ease.

"Hey, Hap, Paula, it's Suellen. Sorry I haven't called you lately, but things have been so completely crazy. Listen, I got a great idea but I need you guys here ... "

We peeled apart and slithered on scattered paper to pick up the phone.

*

Eight days later, I lifted a hand to twirl Paula while she winked and swung her fanny in its bib overall shorts, and twirled me in return. I pivoted into Suellen, who swapped her waitress for a decorous three-cornered spin with Paula and me. Think of it, sex in public with two women at once. We were all sweating like sailors, we all smelled glorious and human and giddily mortal. Around us, the tables of the Roselight were packed with dancers and partners, ashtrays and bottles. Our own special bottle sat on our table, surrounded by Gansetts and flintily guarded by Detective Sergeant Verlyn Rainwater. We had picked up a copy of the Springfield-Branson Beacon to wrap it in, folded to Len Saffel's politics column, *Greene County Grazings*. This one had a picture of a lumpy-faced Amos Verry, withdrawing his candidacy for the state Senate, citing a need to spend more time with his family.

Len's commentary expanded on that by noting that Verry's campaign, so far from amassing even the modest sum it took to run for the Missouri Senate, was substantially in debt. It had been tough for Verry to raise much money, Len noted, after being arrested and released in connection with the murder of his business partner, the madam Granny Ransom. Suellen's regular 9:30 call to Verlyn a week ago, laying out Wet's deed, came just too late to spare him a Beacon photo of the fingerprinting.

Of course, with one of its corners removed, the shaky three-way blackmail go-around collapsed. Darlene Feely had been the first to realize it, and to strike. Cleanly, self-effacingly, and entirely in the best interest of the practice, she saw to it that her dear René canned Amos Verry before Trudi's bones were cool. All in all, Len ruminated, Amos Verry was in a good position to spend quite a bit of time with his family.

And what a time that is surely being for Amos and Florrie. I expect their social life is more constrained now, what with their roster of helpers, Arthur to Zuckerman, depleted and no income at hand to recruit anew. Perhaps they are reduced to victimizing each other, pending investigation and indictment on allegations of sex trafficking by some of the staff of the Parlour.

Once Verlyn had interviewed me and Paula, tracked down the gun in the scrap dealer's truck, and shipped a sample of Wet's blood off to East Carolina for DNA matching, he was ready to call the case closed. Still, when Suellen - after a very stiff session with Verlyn about obstruction of justice - invited him for the ceremony at the Roselight, he had been pleased. "There is nothing you can do to make that place dirtier than it already is," is how he put it.

The wedding photo of Gerard and his little Pea-Patch appeared in the same copy of the Beacon, and I must say both look very pleased with simply getting him to the altar. I decline to speculate how he survives the marriage bed. Nor will you hear the least murmur from me in regard to alliances between older men and younger women. I am dancing as fast as I can.

The cowboy band got to the end of an instrumental bridge and broke into the chorus:

> *Last I saw her, she was bloomin'*
> *She was twice as big as life.*
> *She resembled nothing human;*
> *Trouble was, she was my wife.*

The Saturday crowd of truckers and realtors, dam builders and whores and tourists sweated and stomped and yipped, and we all sang along on the last line. Clouds of sawdust and grit rose from the floor and got in everybody's eyes and noses and teeth, and nobody much cared, because there was plenty of air outside, and plenty of beer in here, borne on swift white boots, to wash it away. I kind of did my best not to breathe too much of the dust. Not that I am trying to save myself. No, I have heard the voice of Wet Parsonage on that. *As I am now, so you must be.* But what kind of dust?

Well, the first of it was scattered very circumspectly, under the table (giggle, snort) and some in dark corners, and in the Ladies' behind the bandstand (hee hee) from our special bottle. I took a gingerly held handful into the Gents. And - as we got bolder, during the rowdier dances - no apologies, straight out of the urn, down to slide and grate under the stomping feet of the dancers. It is sobering how little Trudi came down to, in the end. When I spied a gleaming crumb down there with the native dirt and the sawdust, I did my best to dance it, respectfully, deeper into the cracks between the floor boards. I have said that the Roselight was Trudi's kind of place, in her better days. It is pleasing to think that some of her mortal part will spend time here, in her element.

While the beer flows and the band plays and the hookers hook, and the tourists wheeze and stomp and laugh, get screwed and get laid, and don't give a damn for the clouds of dust that mount in the neon roselight: vague forms that gather, persist, and are gone; and while those who still can, dance on.

www.ingramcontent.com/pod-product-compliance
Lightning Source LLC
Chambersburg PA
CBHW030020180626
46810CB00001B/130